SHERRI SHACKELFORD

Special Delivery Baby

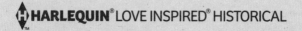

HARLEQUIN® LOVE INSPIRED® HISTORICAL

Special thanks and acknowledgment to Sherri Shackelford for her contribution to the Cowboy Creek miniseries.

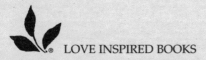

LOVE INSPIRED BOOKS

Recycling programs
for this product may
not exist in your area.

ISBN-13: 978-0-373-28359-0

Special Delivery Baby

Copyright © 2016 by Harlequin Books S.A.

www.Harlequin.com

Printed in U.S.A.

"Well, if it isn't Daddy Canfield. Taking your baby for a walk again, I see."

There was something awfully endearing about a man strolling through the stockyards with a babe in his arms. She'd seen little softness from the men in her life. She'd always had to work harder, ride longer and take more licks than the men. A woman in a man's job always had something to prove.

He jabbed her poster with the tip of his cane. "This Texas Tom person cannot stage a rodeo show in town," he declared. "Those posters will have to be removed immediately."

"I don't know who put a burr under your saddle, Daddy Canfield, but you sure are a cranky fellow. Maybe fatherhood doesn't suit you."

"Fatherhood suits me fine." He shook his head. "I told you before, I'm not a father. This isn't my baby."

"Whatever you say, Mr. Canfield. But you sure are getting comfortable with that babe in your arms."

"I'll speak with Texas Tom myself. When you see your boss, tell him I'm looking for him."

"I might be able to save you some time," Tomasina declared with a wink. "I'm Texas Tom."

* * *

Cowboy Creek: Bringing mail-order brides, and new beginnings, to a Kansas boomtown.

Want Ad Wedding—Cheryl St.John, April 2016
Special Delivery Baby—Sherri Shackelford, May 2016
Bride by Arrangement—Karen Kirst, June 2016

Sherri Shackelford is an award-winning author of inspirational books featuring ordinary people discovering extraordinary love. A reformed pessimist, Sherri has a passion for storytelling. Her books are fast-paced and heartfelt with a generous dose of humor. She loves to hear from readers at sherri@sherrishackelford.com. Visit her website at sherrishackelford.com.

Books by Sherri Shackelford

Love Inspired Historical

Cowboy Creek
Special Delivery Baby

Winning the Widow's Heart
The Marshal's Ready-Made Family
The Cattleman Meets His Match
The Engagement Bargain
The Rancher's Christmas Proposal

Visit the Author Profile page at Harlequin.com.

He hath inclosed my ways with hewn stone,
He hath made my paths crooked.
—*Lamentations* 3:9

To my fellow authors in the series,
Cheryl St.John and Karen Kirst, for making this
continuity series such a wonderful experience.
I hope we can revisit Cowboy Creek in the future!

Chapter One

Kansas, May 1868

Four thousand head of longhorn cattle parading through the center of town kicked up quite a ruckus. Three stories below, countless hooves rumbled over Eden Street, shaking the foundation of the Cattleman Hotel. Above Will Canfield's desk the chandelier swayed, the dangling crystals striking a discordant rhythm. The quaking sent a rippling bull's-eye over his coffee.

A knot settled in the pit of Will's stomach. The cattle drive filled him with a mixture of jubilation and dread. Jubilation because tomorrow the town would reap the financial benefits of thriving stockyards. Dread because cowboys fresh off the trail were known for their carousing and brawling. After four years serving in the Union Army, Will's instincts had propelled him to the rank of captain. The war might be over, but he'd learned to trust his gut. Trouble was coming with this bunch. The drovers were two weeks late, which meant those boys would be chomping at the bit.

The sheriff would have his hands full keeping the peace tonight.

A thin keening sound filtered through the commotion; a mournful squalling like the bleating of a baby goat. Will cocked his head toward the door, hearing only the muted roar of the funeral-slow procession below. His ledger vibrated, and the sharp steel nib of his fountain pen jumped. With a sound of frustration he capped his inkwell. He'd finish the accounts later.

By now most of the town had lined the streets for the astounding spectacle. A new band of drovers meant an infusion of cash, and merchants treated their arrival as a celebration. Earlier, Will had caught the fading refrain of a cowboy band playing "Sweet Nightingale" on dulcimer and fiddle.

As one of the town founders and owner of half the buildings in Cowboy Creek, he should join them. Kicking back in his chair, he threaded his hands behind his head and grinned. Instead of worrying about a bunch of drunken cowboys and the trouble they were bound to cause later, he might as well enjoy his success. All of his plans were falling into place. Along with his friends Noah Burgess and Daniel Gardner, he'd set out to make Cowboy Creek a thriving boomtown, and the steady stream of cattle drives into their stockyards proved their achievement.

The faint keening noise caught his attention once more, and he swiveled in his chair. Movement stirred outside the door. Probably the porter, Simon, with his noon meal. When another moment passed but no knock sounded, a twinge of apprehension skimmed along his spine.

Will absently rubbed his aching leg. A piece of shrapnel, a souvenir from the Battle of Little Round Top, remained lodged deep in his thigh. Fearful of sepsis, the doctors had advised cutting off the limb above the wound. Will had forcefully declined, taking his chances with an infection instead. His risk had paid off. Though saddled with a painful limp, he'd kept his leg and finished out his service in the Union Army.

With his cane propped near the door, Will limped the distance. His temporary rooms took up most of the third floor of the hotel. In the luxuriously appointed suite the furniture was covered in plush burgundy velvet. Forest green damask curtains lined with gold fringe draped the windows and filtered out the afternoon sunlight. The space had been designed to impress, and he'd spared no expense. Putting Cowboy Creek on the map meant courting politicians. And if there was one thing statesmen enjoyed, it was being impressed.

Prosperity had the unfortunate side effect of attracting thieves, as well. Upon reaching the door, Will nudged the kick plate with his foot. His senses on alert, he angled his body and peered into the empty corridor.

Nothing.

He glanced down. A lumpy basket of laundry had been abandoned on his threshold. Scratching the back of his neck, he searched for the person who'd left the hamper. Most likely a new maid had made the mistake. The regular staff knew he sent his washing to Chan Lin, who ran the Chinese Laundry on First Street.

The blankets twitched, and Will nearly leaped out of his skin. Heart pounding, he watched with a mixture of horror and wonder as a tiny infant fist attached to a reed-thin arm poked out from beneath the smothering mound. Though the explanation was obvious, his mind refused to believe his eyes. Keeping his body distanced, he stretched out his arm, flicked back the edge of the blanket and recoiled.

Two drowsy blue-black eyes peered up at him.

There was a baby in that basket, all right. The child's face was red and wrinkled and capped with a shock of dark hair.

Bracing one hand against the door frame, Will extended his bad leg and crouched then studied the odd sight. "Where did you come from, little...uh, person?"

Was it a boy or a girl? He gingerly lifted the opposite edge of the blanket, revealing a minuscule pair of feet encased in soft pink booties. "Girl."

Abandoning any further exploration, he let the blanket fall back into place. He hadn't survived the War Between the States without learning when a calculated retreat was in order. He was taking those pink booties at their word.

Sitting back, he dragged one hand through his dark hair. Clearly the baby had been deliberately abandoned in front of his door. Since there weren't too many women in town, he considered the handful of suspects. Opal Godwin was pregnant, but there was no way this baby was hers. She and her husband were good people with a thriving business. They'd never abandon their child.

Of the four mail-order brides who'd arrived on last month's train, the widow, Leah, had been four months pregnant with her late husband's child. There was no missing her condition, which ruled out the other three women. If Leah was obvious in her fifth month, how did a woman hide a full-term pregnancy?

As Will considered other possibilities, the infant's face screwed up like an apple left too long in the sun. The sound started off innocuous enough. A quiet mewling that barely registered. All too soon the quaint noise intensified into a boisterous wail. Will's eyes widened at the sheer volume the infant produced. Miniature fists pummeled the air and diminutive pink-swathed feet kicked in frustration.

Growing alarmed, he tentatively reached for the bundle, scooping up several layers along with the infant. The child was impossibly light and small. Even with the enveloping blankets, her entire body nestled into the crook of his elbow.

A flash of movement at the end of the corridor snagged his attention. Not wanting to spook whoever might be hiding in the shadows, Will cautiously searched for the cause of the disturbance. From the corner of his eye he spotted a flicker of blue calico. His discovery was quickly followed by the sound of footsteps hastily pattering down the stairs.

He hesitated only an instant before snatching his cane with his free hand and giving chase. The woman had taken the back way. Planning to block her escape, Will took off in the opposite direction, toward the guest staircase.

As he clumsily navigated his descent, his feet sank into the Oriental carpet overlaying the treads. Mindful of the babe in his arms, he traversed the distance in short order, his bad leg screaming at the sudden exertion. He burst into the lobby and caught a glimpse of familiar blue calico pushing through the crowds. Ignoring his shout, the woman slammed through the brass-lined double doors.

His young porter, Simon, shot him a curious glance as he raced past and followed her outside.

The smell hit him first. A wall of dust polluted with the stench of four thousand animals. Bodies jostled. Men discreetly elbowed each other. Heads bobbed, eyes searching for a better look at the spectacular procession.

In front of the horrified onlookers, the mysterious woman charged straight into the parading line of cattle. Someone shrieked.

In a fraction of a second, the scene descended into chaos. People pushed and shoved. The cattle lowed. The crowd parted. Will's heart lodged in his throat as an enormous steer with a great spread of pointed horns lunged toward them. He ducked behind a boardwalk support beam, shielding the infant with his body, then braced for a devastating blow.

A whoosh of air skimmed past their scanty shelter. He glanced up.

A cowboy riding a brown-and-white paint horse galloped into the pandemonium. In a blur of hooves, the rider dodged lethal horns and redirected the steer. Spooked animals set off in a trot. Displaying singular precision, the talented horse and rider feinted and parried, urging the steers back into line and slowing their frantic pace. When one particularly stubborn bull refused direction, the cowboy wheeled his horse around, nearly sitting the animal on its haunches, and forced the steer into line.

In a matter of seconds the drive was under control. Expelling sighs of relief, the crowd surged forward once more, people tittering nervously about the close call.

Will glanced at the infant in his arms and heaved his own sigh of relief. His mad dash had distracted the baby girl from whatever had set her crying earlier.

As the nimble cowboy moved toward him, upstream among the cattle, a smattering of applause followed his progress. Meaning to thank the man for his timely rescue, Will tipped back his head.

The words died on his lips.

A stunning redheaded woman with brilliant green eyes gazed down at him from atop the paint horse. He stared, transfixed. Those big, expressive eyes weren't just green; they were the purest shade of emerald he'd ever seen. Her hair wasn't just red, either; it was a copper fire, curling in abandon around her shoulders, quelled into submission beneath a drover's hat fastened with a string of leather beneath her chin.

Her amused gaze washed over him like a cool breeze off a mountain spring.

Realizing she expected him to speak, he cleared his throat. "Thank you for your assistance, Miss...?"

Tomasina Stone extended her arm, presenting the handsome stranger with a hand encased in a fringed leather glove. "Miss Stone, if you're looking for a cap to that question."

She'd seen some peculiar sights in her time. She'd seen a cowboy so lonesome he'd howled at the moon. She'd seen a dog raise an abandoned skunk baby alongside her own pups. Once she'd even seen a river in the Colorado Territory run uphill atop the continental divide. However, never in her twenty-two years had she ever seen a sight this odd.

The man standing on the boardwalk in front of her was holding a baby in one arm and an expensive-looking, silver-handled cane in the other. Despite his peculiar circumstances, the man appeared strangely calm and in charge. As though he'd just finished adding a column of numbers instead of dodging a near mauling beneath the deadly hooves of a longhorn steer.

"Was anyone hurt?" he demanded.

"No one was hurt," Tomasina assured the man. "No thanks to that fool woman who tried to cut across the street. She turned back soon enough. Disappeared into the crowd, so I expect she's fine."

The man anchored his cane beneath his arm and clasped her hand in greeting. His touch was firm without being crushing.

"The name is Will Canfield," he said. "Thank you for your assistance, Miss Stone."

"You sure picked a dangerous place to take your baby for a walk, Daddy Canfield. Might want to reconsider your route next time."

The measured expression on his face faltered a notch. "Oh, this isn't my baby."

Having been raised around men her whole life, Tomasina had never given their looks too much thought. This fellow stood out. He wasn't overly bulky, like some of the cowboys she rode with, or reed-thin, like the bankers in town, but something in between. His beard was trimmed in a precise goatee and his head was bare, revealing his neatly clipped brown hair. He was polite, but there was a clever edge in his dark eyes. This wasn't a man easily crossed.

He reminded Tomasina of her first impression of Cowboy Creek; a mixture of the wild, untamed West with the appearance of cultivation brought by the easterners after the war. There was something more about him, though; an inherent air of authority. She'd give her eyeteeth if he hadn't once been a soldier, and an officer, by the way he carried himself.

She hoisted an eyebrow. "Reckon who that baby belongs to is none of my business one way or the other." She gestured toward the child. "Judging by how that little fellow's mouth is working, you'd best find his mama soon. Looks like he's getting ready for feeding time"

"It's a girl," Will corrected. "She's wearing pink booties. I checked earlier."

"Is that a fact?" Their exchange was turning into a real doozy. Tomasina tucked away the conversation for the next time the boys were telling tall tales around the campfire. "I think your girl is getting hungry. Better get mama."

"That's the whole problem." The man spoke more to the infant in his arms than to her. "Someone abandoned her. I found her on my doorstep just now."

Yep, Tomasina had seen a lot of strange things in her life, but this spectacle topped them all. "I can't help you there. Any reason the baby's mama picked you in particular? Maybe you should start with all the ladies of your acquaintance."

His face flushed. "I can assure you this child's origins are a mystery."

Oddly enough, she believed him. He had the sharp look of a man who didn't miss a detail. Probably someone had left the baby with him because of his wealth. He definitely appeared well-off. Even Tomasina recognized the expensive cut of his charcoal gray suit and the fine workmanship of his crisp, white shirt.

He glanced over his shoulder and then back at her. "The woman—the one who spooked the cattle. Did you see which way she ran? I think this child belongs to her. If not, then she might have seen something. She was hiding in the shadows when I discovered this little bundle."

"Sorry. I wasn't paying attention."

"Did you get a good look at her?" he persisted. "Would you recognize her if you saw her again?"

"Nope," Tomasina said with a slow shake of her head. Much as she'd enjoy assisting the gentleman, her attention had been directed elsewhere at the time. "Everything was a blur. Like I said before, I was focused on the cattle."

Clearly frustrated by her answers, Daddy Canfield muttered something unintelligible.

He grimaced and held the bundle away from him, revealing a dark, wet patch on his expensive suit coat.

Tomasina chuckled. Oh, yeah, the boys were going to love this one. They'd never believe her, but they'd love the telling. Her pa always liked a good yarn, as well. At the thought of her pa, her smile faded. He'd died on the trail a few weeks back, and they'd buried him in the Oklahoma Territory. The wound of his loss was still raw, and she shied away from her memories of him.

"Fellow…" Tomasina said. "As much fun as this has been, I'd best be getting on."

"Thanks for your help back there," Will replied, his tone grudging. "Your quick action averted a disaster."

The admission had obviously cost him. He struck her as a prideful man, and prideful men sometimes needed a reminder of their place in the grand scheme of things.

"Baby or not," she offered with a wide grin, "it wasn't your life I was saving. I was looking out for the bull. My job isn't protecting greenhorns who don't have the sense to stay out of harm's way. It's getting four thousand head of longhorn cattle safely to market."

"Point taken."

Tomasina smothered her disappointment. His easy capitulation had neatly dodged her goading. She'd best watch herself around Will Canfield. He didn't play by the rules.

His gaze settled on the holster strapped around her hips. "You can't carry your guns in town. There's a sign on the outskirts stating the policy of Cowboy Creek."

"I saw it."

"Then you know you need to check your guns with the sheriff during your stay."

"That's what the sign says, all right," she answered evasively. There was no way under the sun she was relinquishing her guns. She'd encountered this sort of policy before, though, and she had a few tricks up her sleeve. "Who's the sheriff?"

"Quincy Davis."

"You pay him by the arrest?" she asked.

"That's how it's done around here."

"Excellent." A sheriff paid by the arrest was a sheriff willing to make a deal. "We'll see what Quincy Davis and I can work out."

As a lone woman in a man's profession, she was constantly on guard. Her guns ensured her safety. Especially now that Pa was gone. He'd warned her it was time to hang up her drover's boots and settle into a regular job fit for a female. She wasn't having any of it—then or now. Driving cattle was all she knew. She'd never worn a skirt in her life, and she had no intention of starting now. Her pa's reputation hadn't been the only thing protecting her all these years. She'd built up her own name. Once this herd was safely delivered to market, she'd carry on as usual.

Her heartbeat stuttered and her eyes burned. Not exactly the same. Pa was gone. She fisted her hand on her knee and straightened. Swallowing hard a few times, she corralled her emotions. The first rule of being a lone female in a man's domain was to stay tough.

Will Canfield frowned. "You all right, Miss?"

"Right as rain."

She hadn't planned on staying in Cowboy Creek long, but the man standing in front of her piqued her interest. If he didn't like guns in town, he'd probably balk at the idea of a rodeo show. For reasons she couldn't explain, the thought of provoking him cheered her.

The baby fussed, and Daddy Canfield awkwardly bounced the bundle in his arms.

Tomasina had to give the man credit. He was clearly out of his element but doing his best all the same. A sentiment she understood all too well. Her pa's death had left her in charge of the cattle drive, but the position was as hollow as it was temporary. The boys had only stayed on this long because of loyalty to her father. Although they'd finish the job, they'd made it clear they weren't taking orders from a woman. That meant she'd have to join up with another outfit.

She was a drover by trade and a drover by blood. She'd stay a spell and then hire on with another outfit. Same as always. First she'd stage the rodeo show she and her pa had performed dozens of times before. Let the boys blow off some steam after the long, demanding ride. Same as always.

"Daddy Canfield," she declared. "Since you don't like guns, how do you feel about rodeo shows? You know, trick riding and fancy target shooting?"

"Not in my town. Too dangerous."

"Excellent," Tomasina replied with a hearty grin.

Yep. She felt better already.

Chapter Two

"Can you at least tell how old she is?" Will asked beseechingly then caught himself.

This was a baby, not a catastrophe, and there was no reason for panic.

While Leah Gardner examined the child, he stood in the archway of the dining room of her well-appointed house. A lifetime ago in Pennsylvania, he and Leah had been engaged. Their lives had changed drastically since then. A month back she'd married his closest friend and fellow soldier, Daniel.

Will couldn't be happier for the pair.

Five months pregnant with her late, first husband's child, Leah was the perfect candidate for caretaker of the baby. Surely she'd see the practicality of his plan once he explained his problem.

Daniel's wife tilted her head and smiled at him with the warmth of a timeworn friendship. "Relax, Will. You'll wear a hole in my carpet if you keep pacing."

He caught sight of the depressions his cane tip had left and mumbled an apology.

"I was only teasing." Leah sobered. "How is your leg these days?"

"Same as always. But at least it's there. Opal Godwin said the cane makes me look dashing."

"Opal Godwin thinks the man on the cigar box is dashing." Leah's dimpled smile returned. "Sometimes I wonder if you even need that walking stick or if it's a convenient excuse to keep people at a distance. Half of Cowboy Creek is intimidated by you and the other half is afraid. Most of the townsfolk think you have a sword or a gun hidden in that cane of yours."

"I've certainly never encouraged the rumors. Although a little healthy respect never hurt a fellow. I won't be seen as weak." The walking stick was more than an affectation. His balance suffered without assistance. "At least I can hide my affliction. Not everyone is as lucky."

"Many men were injured in the war. Their wounds don't make them lesser men."

Though neither of them had voiced a name, they were both thinking of the same person. Will pictured Noah and the disfiguring burns that covered his lower left jaw, under his ear and disappeared beneath his shirt collar. "The wounds heal but the scars remain."

"You couldn't save them all. Noah's injuries were not your fault. He lived. As did you and Daniel. Many more did not. I know you worry about Noah, but he's strong. He'll find his own way by and by."

Noah Burgess, a friend and fellow soldier, had brought Will to Cowboy Creek. Noah had staked a claim first and his letters had lured Will and Daniel West. Born a Southerner, Noah had fought harder than any Northerner to prove himself worthy. During the Battle of Little Round Top, while taking the place of a brigadier general felled by a sniper, his gun had backfired. Wounded himself, Will had not been able to reach his friend before the flames had engulfed him. The army had discharged Noah due to his injuries, and he'd made his home in Kansas.

"He keeps to himself more and more these days," Will said with a frown. "He'll turn into an irascible old hermit soon."

"Is that why you decided to order a bride for him without his consent? He'll have both you and my husband tarred and feathered for interfering. Leave him be from now on," Leah admonished. "He'll mend in his own time."

Her words pricked his conscience. Will was having his own doubts about sending for a bride without informing Noah. At the time, the idea had seemed inspired. They were all celebrating the success of the first bride train and the subsequent marriage between Leah and Daniel. He'd been uncharacteristically optimistic. After posting the letter, his enthusiasm had waned almost immediately. Leah was correct. Noah was bound to have their hides once he discovered the interference. At least there were plenty of other eligible bachelors if Noah balked. That thought let Will sleep at night.

"I interfered with you and Daniel," Will said. "And look how well that turned out."

"Twisted Daniel's arm, did you?" She aimed a playful swat in his direction. "I'll forgive you this once."

"There was no arm twisting, I can assure you," Will retorted. "Noah and I only nudged Daniel in the direction he was already heading."

At the mention of her new husband, Leah's blue eyes took on a soft, misty look. Will rubbed his knuckles against the recent ache in his chest. Daniel and Leah had found an extraordinary love together. He was happy for them and a little jealous, as well. Their abiding affection was a rare and brilliant thing. If Noah let someone into his heart, he might find something equally lasting.

His buddy's injuries had taken more than a physical toll. He needed a nudge in the right direction, as Daniel had. Either way, there was no going back now. The letter had been posted. When Constance Miller arrived, Will and Daniel would explain the situation. They'd smooth over any awkwardness.

"I'll forgive you because I adore Daniel with every fiber of my being." Leah touched her cheek. "I wasted so much time when the perfect man was right there waiting for me all along."

Her head bent, and Will admired the pale gold hair caught in a neat bun at the nape of her neck. "We were all young and foolish."

"Perhaps children are supposed to be foolish," she remarked lightly. "We've all changed."

Growing up in their hometown in Pennsylvania, he and Daniel and Leah had been inseparable. When Will and Leah had gotten engaged, they'd been little more than children making the awkward transition from playing with slingshots and splashing through streams into adulthood. The war had changed everything.

The war had changed everyone.

He and Leah had gradually drifted apart during the years of his enlistment. The fragile threads of their romantic connection had not survived the physical distance between them. Deep down, both had known they were best suited as friends and nothing more.

During their years serving together in the army, Will had realized Daniel's feelings for Leah had been far deeper than his own had ever been. With death constantly looming near, Daniel had never given voice to his yearnings, and Leah had eventually married another man.

Will had not expected to see Leah ever again, so her arrival in town had been a shock. With the original collection of dilapidated shanties growing into a thriving community, the three friends soon realized Cowboy Creek needed women to flourish. Only four women had arrived on that first train and, much to Will's amazement, Leah had been one of the prospective brides. Her ill-fated marriage had abruptly ended when her husband had been shot by a jealous spouse. Pregnant with her late husband's child, she'd needed to remarry quickly.

Will's lips quirked. He recalled how he, along with Noah, had urged Daniel and Leah to wed. Their intervention had been inspired. After a rocky start, Leah and Daniel had admitted their feelings, both past and present, and were now more in love than ever. Their success gave him hope that Noah would find the same.

Leah cooed at the baby propped on her rounded belly. "This sweet little thing can't be more than a few days old. She appears healthy enough. Her mother must have nursed her."

"What now?" Will spread his hands. "How do we feed her? *What* do we feed her?"

"I have some glass bottles. As you well know, I'd planned on serving as the local midwife, and I brought along a few supplies when I came to town." She patted her stomach. "Of course, any work will have to wait until after this baby is born."

Normally a whirling dervish of activity, Leah instead called for the maid and dispatched her instructions. The telling gesture left Will uneasy. Though married to her first husband for several years, Leah had been unable to carry a child successfully to term. In deference to her health, Daniel treated her with kid gloves. He'd hired the undertaker's spinster sister to help out, and his friend kept a close and loving eye on Leah. He'd probably pitch a fit if he knew Will was here pestering her about the abandoned baby instead of letting her rest.

Narrowing his gaze on the infant, Will considered his options. "The hotel restaurant has fresh milk delivered each day."

"That's probably best. With the general lack of women in this town, I don't suppose Booker & Son carries pap. Might be something you should look into before long."

"I haven't checked, but you're probably right. We haven't had much call for infant supplies."

When he and the other two men had invested in the town, they'd anticipated most everything. They'd built a church and a school. They'd even hired a doctor trained in one of the finest schools back east. Too late, they'd discovered the doctor hadn't been as interested in delivering babies as he was in other forms of medicine. Leah's arrival was fortuitous in more ways than one.

They'd thought of a lot of things but, being men, they hadn't thought of everything.

Leah lifted the baby and grimaced at the damp spot on her skirt. "You'll need more nappies, as well."

She rested the infant on the dining room table and peeled back the layer of blanket.

The basket had been stuffed with a supply of miniature outfits. Tiny dressing gowns of yellow calico had been carefully pressed and folded then nestled beside crocheted booties and knit caps. The loving craftsmanship of the work and the expense of the materials were obvious.

"It doesn't make any sense," he said. "Someone planned for this baby. Someone sewed that clothing. Someone carried this child for nine months. Why abandon her on my doorstep?"

"Because you're wealthy." Leah shrugged one shoulder. "Because you're one of the town founders. Because you're known for your compassion. You'd seem a logical choice to me."

"I'm not compassionate," he grumbled. "And none of that explains why a mother would abandon her baby."

Leah tucked a stray lock of blond hair behind her ear. "There are all sorts of reasons. You know that full well. Maybe the woman's husband passed away. Maybe she didn't have a husband. Maybe she fell on hard times."

Will stared in rapt fascination as Leah rapidly divested the squirming infant of her wet nappy and deftly exchanged it for another. The maid returned with the washed and filled bottle.

"It's Miss Ewing's day off." Leah motioned toward a rocking chair set at an angle in the corner of the dining room. "You'll have to feed the child while I check on supper."

Will limped back a pace. "I should be going..."

"Oh, no, you don't."

She moved around him, crowding him toward the chair until he had no other choice but to sit.

Reluctantly accepting the wiggling bundle, he appealed to Leah's better nature. "Can you watch her for a few days? Just until I decide what to do?"

"I'd help you, Will. You know I'd do anything for you." She protectively cupped her growing stomach. "But I can't right now."

Tears pooled in her eyes, sending a kick of guilt straight to his gut.

"I'm sorry. I shouldn't have asked."

He knew full well how much she wanted her baby born healthy. How frightened she was that something might happen.

"I'm a watering pot these days." Leah wiped at the moisture on her cheeks. "I don't mind the asking as long as you respect my answer. You have more money than you know what to do with and enough space in your suite of rooms to house an orphanage. Hire someone. Then wait. There's a good chance the mother will come back for her child. Sometimes...sometimes people make decisions they regret."

Her words were an obvious reference to her past. As she handed him the bottle, he touched her hand. "We're all praying for you, Leah."

"I know. This time is different. Everything feels different. Everything feels...right."

She did look beautiful. Joyful. Yet despite their past connection, the only thing he felt for her was a deep, abiding friendship. "You and Daniel will have a whole passel of children before you know it."

"That's what we're hoping for." Her expression turned sympathetic. "I'm sorry about what happened with Dora."

"You did me a favor. There's no need for an apology."

Until a few weeks ago he'd been engaged to Dora Edison. Leah had overheard Dora bragging about how she was marrying Will for his money. When he'd confronted his fiancée, Dora had eventually admitted her true motivation. The breakup had been more humiliating than heartbreaking. While he'd enjoyed Dora's company before he'd discovered her deception, he'd never looked at her the way Daniel looked at Leah. Perhaps he simply lacked the capacity for an abiding love.

His thoughts drifted toward a certain stunning redhead dressed in leather chaps, and he quickly marshaled them. That particular female was a thorn in his side, and he'd already had enough aggravation to last a lifetime.

He'd vowed to do everything in his power to keep the country from sinking into war once more. To that end, he'd dedicated his life to politics. The peace between the northern and southern states was uneasy at best. The country was torn apart, and only men who understood war were fit to put it back together again. He'd devoted himself to the cause of former soldiers as well as the widows and orphans they'd left behind. Miss Stone with her six-shooters strapped to her hips was nothing but an example of disorder and chaos. She was a distraction he'd rather avoid.

Will wanted peace and quiet and children to dandle on his knee. He did not want to get mixed up with a beautiful vagabond who possessed magnificent horsemanship skills. Her clear and quick thinking had averted a disaster, and for that he would always be grateful. But she was too clever by half and would make his life miserable. Gorgeous, intelligent, quick-witted and capable, Miss Stone had already occupied too much of his time.

The infant in his arms howled, yanking him back to the present. "She's hungry, all right." Will chuckled. "And letting us all know it."

"Babies have a way of getting what they want. You'll find that out soon enough."

Will accepted the bottle of warmed milk from Leah. The infant puckered her lips then stuck out her tongue, pushing it away. He retracted his hand, and her tiny mouth worked. Smiling at her confusion, he replaced the tip against her lips again. With only a little more coaxing, the child ceased her fussing. Having finally accepted the bottle, the baby suckled greedily.

Once she'd settled, Leah quietly left the room. Will braced his boot heel against the floor, gently rocking his chair. He couldn't recall the last time he'd been around an infant. There were plenty of camp followers during the war, but he'd discouraged the practice around his own regiment. The battlefield was no place for women and children.

Sometime during the war, death had gotten its teeth

into him and hadn't let go. He'd seen so many boys die, he'd lost track of the count. The realization kept him up at night and haunted his dreams when exhaustion finally overtook him. He'd been responsible for those lads, and they'd fought and died beneath his command. He'd penned letters to their families when there was time and signed the letters his secretary had prepared when there wasn't. There'd been far too many letters; their sentiment weak and inadequate next to the tragedy they represented.

Cowboy Creek was a fresh start. Too many soldiers couldn't go home again, their farms and livelihoods destroyed. Some of them, like Noah, had needed a fresh start. They'd traveled west instead, building new lives and putting the past behind them. He'd give those men a chance at least. Despite all the work he'd done and the money he'd made, the voices of all the soldiers he'd lost whispered in his dreams. Was it hundreds? Was it thousands? He'd never know, and that was his penance. Cowboy Creek was his atonement.

His hold on the bottle grew lax, and the babe in his arms turned toward him, her rose-petal lips working.

Will adjusted his grip. "All right, little lady, I'm paying attention."

The boundary between life and death was incredibly fragile. This child represented everything he'd fought for... what he was rebuilding. She represented a better future. If he kept her safe, cared for her and saw that she found a loving home, then the deaths of all those boys would not have been in vain. This little girl, born in a time of peace, represented their sacrifice. He'd settle up whatever debts he had left when his own time came.

His chest tightened with emotion. "What shall we call you?"

His first officer had been killed during the Battle of the

Wilderness. Collecting the soldier's belongings, he'd discovered a picture of an infant swathed in her christening finery. The name "Ava" had been scrawled across the back. The memory of that photo had stuck with him.

"How about Ava? Someone told me the name means 'bird.' One day you'll fly away from here. Won't you, little bird?"

The infant's eyes blinked slower and slower. The frantic suckling grew lax. She was utterly defenseless, utterly dependent. A fresh sense of purpose filled him. If he could protect her innocence, maybe then he'd be whole again.

Leah tiptoed into the room and peered at the sleeping baby. "She looks all tuckered out. How about you?" she whispered. "How was the cattle drive this morning? I heard the excitement all the way from Eden Street."

"Much as you'd expect," he grumbled. "We'll be cleaning up the mess and repairing the street for days. Sheriff Davis already has three of the cowboys in jail drying out."

"Cattle built this town, Will." She straightened and crossed her arms. "You can't run the drovers out."

"The railroad will put an end to the cattle drives, mark my words. We'll have to find another way to survive eventually."

"The railroad?" she scoffed. "I don't see thousands of head of cattle riding the rails."

"Change is coming whether we like it or not. The railroads are already experimenting with icebox cars."

"I hope the change doesn't come too soon. The stockyards account for a large portion of our income." Leah's expression remained skeptical. "Whatever the future holds, those drovers are here now. And you'd best make them feel welcome. The merchants in town need their business."

Will recalled the talk he'd heard on the way over about a rodeo show the cowboys were planning. "They can spend all the money they want here, but I'm putting a stop to any rodeos they're planning. All the boys can talk about is this sharpshooter called Texas Tom. There's liable to be other events, as well, and bull riding is too dangerous." He tucked the blanket more snugly around the baby. "The last time the drovers held a show, the doc fixed up two broken legs and administered more stitches than I can count. If one of those bulls breaks free, Miss Stone won't be around to save the day."

"Miss Stone? Who is Miss Stone?"

"No one. Never mind," he mumbled. That woman was trouble, and he always avoided trouble. Especially beautiful trouble with dazzling green eyes. "I'll shut down Texas Tom before the week is out. I don't want the new brides trampled before they find husbands. We promised them a nice, safe town. A good place to raise a family. I can't risk a stray bullet."

"I see there's no changing your mind," she said with a plaintive sigh. "What about the baby? Have you decided what to do about her?"

"Yes," Will replied resolutely.

He'd never been one to shy away from a difficult decision, and he wasn't about to start now.

A week after her arrival in town, Tomasina dipped her push broom into the bucket of glue and shook off the excess. The printer had done a fine job with the posters, even though she'd rushed him. Normally, James Johnson, a fellow drover who usually rode with their outfit, traveled ahead and arranged for the printing.

James had been like a son to her pa, and Tomasina treated him like a brother. Her brush stilled midair. Something had been troubling James since their trip to Harper, Kansas, last September. He'd been so distracted, he'd nearly been gored. Worried about his safety, they'd argued and James had ridden with another outfit this time out. She'd discovered James was in Cowboy Creek, as well, but he'd been avoiding her. She sure hoped the kid had finally gotten his head on straight or he'd be no use to anyone.

Tamping down her annoyance, she spread the thick adhesive on the outside wall of the stockyards' office then reached for another poster and smoothed it over the glue.

Yep. A shoot 'em rodeo show was a prime diversion. Judging by that handsome, uptight fellow she'd met that first day, the whole town was crying out for a little entertainment. A place called Cowboy Creek deserved some excitement. A rodeo and a sharpshooter contest were just the thing.

A sound caught her attention, and she whirled. Her jaw nearly dropped before she caught herself. "Well, if it isn't Daddy Canfield. Taking your baby for a walk again, I see."

There was something awfully endearing about a man strolling through the stockyards with a babe in his arms. An unexpected rush of tenderness washed through her. She'd seen little softness from the men in her life. She'd always had to work harder, ride longer and take more licks than the men. A woman in a man's job always had something to prove. These past few weeks without her pa had taken a toll on her endurance. She didn't want to be better than everyone else. She simply wanted to be good enough.

Will didn't look as though he cared a whit what anyone thought of him. He looked...well, he looked rather appealing, all things considered.

Tall and commanding, he wore his charcoal suit with dapper charm.

Her goodwill lasted until he jabbed her freshly glued poster with the tip of his cane, ripping the damp paper.

"This Texas Tom person cannot stage a rodeo show in town," he declared. "And a sharpshooter contest is out of the question."

"You're not much for small talk, are you?"

"No guns. I believe I mentioned that before."

"I believe you did. You even posted your own signs, if I recall." She ran her hands over the jagged tear, mending the edges. "Have a little care. These posters don't come cheap."

"Those posters will have to be removed immediately."

"You don't have the authority to give me orders." She planted her hands on the gun belt strapped around her hips. "The sheriff enforces the law around here."

Quincy Davis, the sheriff of Cowboy Creek, had already proved himself rather cooperative. He'd even accepted a week's worth of fines levied against her for wearing her guns in town, saving her several trips to his office.

Will Canfield shook his head. "I understand your reasoning for hosting the show, but we've had problems in the past. Serious injuries. Last time we had a sharpshooting contest, Walker Frye dug two bullets out of the side of the livery wall. What if someone had been standing where those bullets struck? We've got more settlers with children living in town."

"I don't miss what I aim for."

"No one is perfect. Eventually, you'll miss."

"No one will get hurt." She rolled her eyes. "I've seen this show staged a hundred times before. Never had a problem yet."

"You need permission to put up those posters, as well."

"You got a rule for everything, don't you, fellow?" The glue on her palms had adhered to her gun belt. She pried her hands loose and rubbed them together, pilling the adhesive. "You must keep mighty busy caring for that baby of yours and making up all those ridiculous rules."

"If we don't limit the number of posters people hang, they wind up three and four deep. The fence behind the Drover's Place collapsed beneath the weight last spring."

"Then build a stronger fence."

The frown line between his brown eyes deepened. "I don't know what you're used to, but this is a *civilized* town."

He was probably one of those foolish men who considered a woman in trousers a disgrace. "A civilized town, huh? Where the ladies wear the skirts and the men wear the pants? I wouldn't be too picky if I was you, seems like this town is short on ladies already."

"This has nothing to do with your attire," he snapped. "It's about following town law. If everyone thought they were the exception to the rule, there wouldn't be much point, would there?"

She lifted her chin a notch. "I have permission to hang these posters. Just ask the fellow who manages the stockyards." A couple of silver dollars in his outstretched palm hadn't hurt her case. "He'll tell you."

"Daniel Gardner, the owner of these stockyards, might have something different to say than his foreman." Will flashed her a stern look. "You've wasted your time and Texas Tom's money. He's not putting on a rodeo show in this town. All they do is incite the cowboys to shoot guns and carouse. Like I said before, I won't have someone shot by a stray bullet."

"I don't know who put a burr under your saddle, Daddy Canfield, but you sure are a cranky fellow. Maybe fatherhood doesn't suit you."

"Fatherhood suits me fine." He shook his head, uttering something that sounded suspiciously like a growl. "I told you, I'm not a father. This isn't my baby."

The wind shifted, and she caught his distinct scent—a

mixture of starch and bay rum. For once she didn't find the odor nauseating. The boys sometimes doused themselves with the stuff before going into town, but Will showed more restraint. He actually smelled quite nice.

She'd had the chance to study plenty of men in her life, and they all fell into certain categories. There were the bullies and the heartbreakers, the men who stuck to themselves and the men who always seemed to have a crowd around them. Will was unlike any of them. He kept her off balance, and she wasn't used to being off balance.

Her pulse fluttered. "Whatever you say, Mr. Canfield. But you sure are getting comfortable with that babe in your arms."

His caring for the child set him apart, as well. None of the men of her acquaintance would have ever been caught dead holding a baby.

Her father had been a good man, and he'd loved her, but he was a hard man. There'd been no time for coddling in the Stone family. He'd treated her like one of the boys. Come to think of it, everyone treated her like one of the boys. Maybe that's what was different about Will. Even though he was clearly annoyed with her, he regarded her with a deference she was unaccustomed to receiving.

"I'll speak with Texas Tom myself." Will tucked the sleeping infant into the crook of his elbow. "When you see your boss, tell him I'm looking for him."

Tomasina grinned up at him. If having a baby dropped on his doorstep wasn't shocking enough, he was about to receive another surprise. "I might be able to save you some time."

"Do enlighten me."

He'd fight her tooth and nail on the rodeo, and she was going to enjoy every minute of their sparring. He'd lose eventually. She had the sheriff in her pocket, after all.

Daddy Canfield had finally met his match.

"I'm the one you're looking for," Tomasina declared with a wink. "I'm Texas Tom."

Chapter Three

Tomasina marched down the boardwalk, her spurs jingling with each step. Quincy Davis had refused her appeal. The rodeo show was off unless she convinced Will otherwise. Daddy Canfield had obviously gotten to the sheriff first. With no other choice, she was bearding the lion in his den.

Once inside the Cattleman Hotel, she flipped off her hat. The strings caught on her neck and she adjusted the knot. If Will Canfield thought she was canceling her rodeo show on account of a silly town ordinance, he was about to be sorely disappointed.

She paused in front of an enormous oval mirror framed with gold filigree. Turning this way and that, she studied her reflection. She wasn't a bad-looking woman, but she was definitely rough around the edges. Since she'd never seen Will with a hair out of place or stains on his crisp white shirt, she'd better put her best foot forward.

As she pondered how to improve on her appearance, a porter hustled by holding a tray topped with several glasses and a pitcher of water.

Tomasina snagged the young man's coat sleeve. "Hold up there a minute."

She grasped the pitcher, leaving the porter struggling with his unbalanced tray, then poured a measure of water into her palm and replaced the pitcher.

"That'll be all, fellow."

Ignoring the porter's glaring reflection, she rubbed the water between her palms then smoothed her hands over her hair. For one brief, shining moment her curls remained plastered against her head. The next instant they sprang free, leaving her hair damp and more disordered than before.

Tomasina shrugged. Her hair was a lost cause. At least the rest of her looked presentable enough. She'd worn her newest chaps today instead of the pair with half the fringe missing. Her clothing was freshly laundered and her face was clean. Brushing her hands down her best chambray shirt, she searched for any remnants of her breakfast. She wasn't giving Mr. Canfield any reason to find fault with her.

Feeling almost respectable, she approached the desk.

The young porter scowled. "Can I get you any more water, Miss?"

"Nope. I'm here for Mr. Will Canfield."

"He's busy. Everyone's always busy since that baby arrived."

The porter was young, maybe fifteen or sixteen, and handsome in the sort of way that probably sent the young girls swooning. He kept his dark hair slicked back neatly beneath his round cap, and his bottle-green uniform was crisply pressed, his collar starched and white. He had the appearance of someone who liked to keep things orderly. From what Tomasina had heard, newborns had a way of creating all sorts of chaos and disorder.

"You don't say." She leaned forward and pitched her

voice low. "What if I told you I had information about a certain abandoned baby?"

The young man's eyes lit up like a kid let loose on penny candy. "Third floor. Room 311. Up the stairs and take a left. The sooner that infant is out of the hotel, the better. That child has thrown the whole place into an uproar. We've lost our best housekeeper to babysitting duties, and now the maids are running amok."

Tomasina grinned. This was even easier than she'd expected. "I'll see what I can do."

The porter proudly straightened his cap. "The name is Simon if you need anything else."

She touched her forehead in thanks and pivoted on her heel. She hadn't lied. Not exactly. She'd asked the young man a what-if question, and he'd replied. No harm in that.

Her conscious clear, she took the stairs two at a time. Huffing by the third floor, she braced one hand against the wall and pressed the other against the stitch in her side. They must have high ceilings on all the floors, because it sure was a long way up those stairs. As she caught her breath, a distinctive racket filled the corridor.

Even if she hadn't known the room number, there was no mistaking Will's suite. She followed the sounds of the squalling baby and rapped on the solid wood panel.

The door swung open, revealing Will with a familiar, red-faced bundle in his arms. "It's about time." He caught sight of her, and his hopeful expression fell. "Oh…it's you. Never mind."

"Were you expecting someone else?"

"Clearly." He elbowed shut the door.

"Not so fast." Tomasina stuck her booted foot over the threshold. "You and I have business."

"I believe we concluded our business yesterday, Miss Stone. Or shall I call you Texas Tom? I should have realized it was you immediately." He grimaced as he clutched the squirming, angry baby tighter in the crook of his arm. "Except I've been distracted lately."

"Tomasina will do just fine." She scowled. "You have no right to interfere with my rodeo show."

"The town ordinance is clear, as I'm sure Sheriff Davis informed you."

"I'm guessing you spoke with him first."

The sheriff's previous conciliatory mood had taken a sudden turn for the worse. It hadn't taken a genius to figure out who had changed his mind.

Will moved deeper into the room, and she followed close on his heels.

Blowing out a low whistle, she gaped. His suite was positively dandified. Fancy fringed curtains the shade of pine needles hung from the windows, and the furniture was covered in wine-colored velvet fabric. She'd never seen the White House, but she imagined this room was fit for a president. Well, except for the nappies strung out to dry across the archway and the blankets and tiny clothing littering the furniture and the floor. She didn't suppose those were the usual accoutrements of the White House. Despite the mess, peeking out from beneath all that clutter were some fine pieces of furniture. Having lived most of her life out of a tent, she savored the feel of the cushy rug beneath her feet.

"You sure live fancy," she declared.

"This is only a temporary residence."

Tomasina collapsed onto a tufted chair and draped her arms over the sides. "I could get used to some temporary quarters like this."

Closing her eyes, she let her body sink into the cozy stuffing. Rarely had she enjoyed such luxury. Chairs of any kind were scarce on the trail; she preferred traveling light. Most times she sat on the hard ground. Occasionally she rustled up a stump or a rock. This chair was pure bliss. Not even the wailing baby could put an immediate damper on her enjoyment.

"Looks like you have your hands full." She opened one eye and squinted. "Where's your housekeeper? The porter said she was helping out."

"Not that it's any of your business, but Mrs. Foster is on her lunch break."

"You ought to hire someone else. I hear the maids are running amok."

"Simon talks too much." Will leaned heavily on his cane. "If you must know, the reverend's daughter has offered to assist, as well. She's coming by this evening."

The infant's wailing continued unchecked, and a sharp pain throbbed behind Tomasina's temple. "Word of that baby sure spread fast." She drummed her fingers on the arm of the chair. "You think her mother will ever come back? Most mamas are protective of their young'uns."

"That's what I'm hoping for."

"Then again, maybe she won't. I once saw a heifer reject her calf. Almost killed the poor thing before we separated them."

Clenching his jaw, he glowered down at her. "Your optimism is comforting. Truly. If you've finished cheering me up, you may go."

"I'm not leaving that easy," Tomasina retorted. "About the rodeo…" She leaned forward and raised her voice over the squalling baby. "Look, we've been on the trail for more than three months. The boys just need to blow off a little steam."

"You're a tenacious little thing, aren't you? When cowboys blow off steam, property is damaged."

"I'm not little. And nothing will be damaged. The boys

can be a might rowdy, but they're good men. All of 'em. I can vouch for that."

Will quirked a brow. "You can vouch for all of them?"

Okay, he had her there. Tomasina wrapped a curl around one finger. Drovers were a nomadic bunch by nature. While she knew most of the men on her crew, there were always new faces coming and going. "Most of them."

Will barely spared her a glance, his attention now fully focused on the fussy baby. The infant's arms stretched out wide, and her face screwed up. Silent for a breath, she seemed to be struggling for air. Her arms and legs flailed. The next instant she let out an earsplitting wail, her lower lip trembling with the effort.

Will held the baby away from his body and juggled her lightly. "There, there, Ava," he crooned. "There's no need to fuss."

"I didn't know she had a name." Tomasina paused. Giving the baby a name made her more real somehow. Not that the baby wasn't real before. She was just easier to dismiss. "It's a nice name."

"I had to call her something until her mother returns."

"Have you fed Miss Ava lately?" The baby's distress was getting to her, and Tomasina temporarily abandoned her argument. "Maybe she's hungry."

"She has been fed. She has been burped. She has been changed. There is absolutely no reason for this behavior."

Tomasina stood and peered at the infant's scrunched-up face. "Did you hear that, li'l missy? Daddy Canfield doesn't think you're being reasonable." Tomasina sighed and reached for the bundle. "Here, let me have her. You're doing it all wrong."

Will hesitated for several long seconds before handing over Ava.

He pressed the heels of his hands against his eyes and

heaved a breath. "I don't know how such a tiny creature can make such a racket."

"Maybe she misses her mama." Tomasina tucked the baby snugly against her body. "I bet your mama misses you, too, Ava."

Tomasina had only meant to quiet Ava, but a curious warmth enveloped her. Pacing back and forth, something unfurled inside her; a gentle awakening. She'd been around lots of baby animals in her life, and they were all plenty cute. Ava was different. Once she quit her squalling and Tomasina got a good look at her, she marveled at the change. As those beautiful eyes blinked, long, dark lashes swept over plump cheeks. Her chubby hands fisted restlessly against the blanket. Tomasina had never seen such tiny, perfectly shaped fingernails. Ava even smelled good. The infant's sweet scent teased her senses.

Nuzzling her forehead, Tomasina whispered comforting words. The tune of an old camp song tugged at her memory. Unheeding of Will's curious stare, she sang softly.

"O bury me not on the lone prairie
Where coyotes howl and the wind blows free
In a narrow grave just six by three—
O bury me not on the lone prairie

It matters not, I've been told,
Where the body lies when the heart grows cold
Yet grant, o grant, this wish to me
O bury me not on the lone prairie.

I've always wished to be laid when I died
In a little churchyard on the green hillside
By my father's grave, there let me be,
O bury me not on the lone prairie."

With each verse, the infant gradually calmed. Ava's eyes drifted shut, and her breathing grew deep and even.

Will sighed. "I don't know how you did it, but I thank you all the same."

"Babies are no different than any of God's creatures. Everyone wants to know that someone loves them." Caring for Ava had eased the tension between them a notch. "What will you do if you can't find her mama?"

His face softened. She sensed that something had shifted in their relationship. They were shared victors of a sort—soothing the savage beast. The baby had given them something in common. Tomasina snorted softly. The baby was about all they were likely to find in common. She couldn't imagine two more opposite people.

"I always have a plan," Will said a touch wearily. "First I'll give her mama the chance to change her mind."

A grudging respect for the man sifted through Tomasina's annoyance. After holding the tiny new life, she sympathized with his dilemma. "Sometimes people make decisions they regret later."

"You're the second person who's told me that in the last week."

"I guess most folks have a regret or two. You better hire some good help." The baby squirmed, and Tomasina lowered her voice to a whisper. She'd already made herself a new personal rule to never wake a sleeping baby. "You have your hands full with this one. She's got a mind of her own."

"I trust your judgment on difficult females."

Tomasina relinquished the infant and stuck her hands in her back pockets. There was no need to get all soft and squishy over one little baby girl. "I know you're looking out for Cowboy Creek, but I'm looking out for my crew. They're gonna let loose one way or the other."

"The answer is still no." Will took the seat she'd vacated earlier. "I don't suppose we'll be seeing each other again. Best of luck, Miss Stone."

"Oh, I don't know…" Tomasina replaced her hat and tightened the strings beneath her chin. "I have a feeling we'll be seeing a lot more of each other real soon."

He'd thought he'd won, but she wasn't giving up the fight just yet.

Will's cane kicked up dust with each thudding stride. Texas Tom had defied his orders.

His anger growing with each step, he followed the festive crowds swarming toward the stockyards. Chatter and laughter swirled around him, and a sense of excitement filled the air. Enterprising merchants had set up booths for food and drink along Eden Street, and knots of people clustered around the offerings. The scent of fresh-roasted nuts teased his nose. Carriages and wagons clogged the way, but no one seemed to mind the wait. The unofficial town band played near the temporary fairgrounds, and the chords of a toe-tapping melody drifted above the chatter.

Will caught sight of his friend Daniel Gardner and picked up his pace.

Daniel loped over then slapped him on the back. "Looks like the whole town turned out for Texas Tom's Rodeo Show. I hope she's a crowd pleaser."

"Then you know Texas Tom is a girl?"

Daniel lifted his hat and raked one hand through his chestnut hair. "Doesn't matter to me as long as she puts on a good show."

"I can't believe you encouraged this risky display." Will didn't bother hiding his annoyance. "The last time someone staged a show, two men suffered broken limbs. A fight broke out in the saloon, and someone knocked over a kerosene lamp. Nearly burned down half the town. Mr. Frye dug two bullets out of the livery."

"You're not the captain anymore." Daniel's jaw tightened. "You're not in charge."

"We agreed on the rules for the town."

"We did. Except the stockyards aren't part of the town proper."

Not only had Texas Tom gone around Will's back, she'd enlisted the support of his closest friend.

The betrayal smarted. "It's your choice."

"Look, if I'd known you were dead set against the show, I'd have acted differently. It's too late now." Daniel shrugged. "I'll help you keep an eye out for trouble. Sheriff Davis is here, as well."

"What about Leah?"

"She stayed home. She's resting."

"Probably for the best." Will's anger waned. They'd been through too much to let something like this alter their friendship. "I need you on lookout."

"You've had one of your hunches, haven't you?"

"Something like that." During his years in the war, Will had learned to trust his instincts. His men had learned to do the same. "Keep a sharp eye out."

"I own the stockyards, remember? I'm not letting anything happen." They'd nearly reached their destination, and Daniel slowed his pace. "I'm sorry about the rodeo. I didn't think you'd care as long as we kept it outside town. How long are you going to be sore?"

"I'm not sore."

His friend visibly relaxed. "Hey, Leah told me about the abandoned baby. What—?"

"Daniel!" someone shouted.

They turned and caught sight of Sheriff Davis jogging

in their direction. He halted in front of them and stated without preamble, "I've got some bad news."

The sheriff was a tall, broad-shouldered and lean-hipped man with a thick mustache that enveloped his upper lip. He was dressed in his usual uniform of a brown vest and jacket over a white shirt. A good man, he'd been a fine choice for keeping the law in Cowboy Creek.

Will smoothed his beard with a thumb and forefinger. "What is it this time?"

"We caught some fellows by the railroad cars."

"Not again." Will and Daniel exchanged a glance. "Did they take anything?"

"Not that I know of." The sheriff leaned closer. "They were sniffing around the supplies again."

Will made a sound of frustration. The saboteurs had caused plenty of problems already. They'd burned a shipment of wood, stolen supplies and poisoned several dozen head of cattle. The town council had hired extra guards for the railcars and the lumberyard. Instead of backing down, the vandals had grown more brazen.

"Do you think it's the Murdoch Gang again?" Will asked.

"Maybe, maybe not." The sheriff shrugged. "Those boys robbed a church in broad daylight. I don't see them keeping to the shadows."

"You're probably right." With most of the town gathered for the rodeo, this was the perfect time for another strike. "Why don't we—"

Raucous applause drowned out his words. Will and Daniel exchanged another glance before heading toward the corral. Since most of the townsfolk knew Daniel owned the stockyards, the crowds parted for them. People lined the entire circumference of the corral and crowded two and three deep in some places. Only a few feminine hats stood out against the mostly male crowd.

Upon reaching the fence, a distinctive paint horse carrying a redheaded rider galloped through an open gate. In a blur the pair sped around the corner and cut a diagonal across the center of the corral. Dirt clods kicked up by speeding hooves peppered the delighted audience. As Tomasina raced by, the men waved and shouted encouragement. With a flying lead change, the duo switched courses and curved across the opposite side, then galloped back toward the center once more.

The rider pulled up short. At the sudden stop the animal's hooves cut trenches in the soft earth. The horse sidestepped left and back again. Horse and rider wheeled in a tight circle then changed directions just as quickly before stilling once more. The boisterous spectators shouted and whistled.

Tomasina Stone, better known as Texas Tom, waved to the crowd from her perch. Only then did Will notice the horse wore no saddle or bridle. Tomasina had controlled the racing animal with nothing but her legs and heels. The dawning realization sent a collective gasp erupting from the audience.

Clearly feeding off the attention, she bent one knee and braced it on the horse's haunches then pushed off until she was standing. She wore her familiar leather-fringed chaps and blue chambray shirt with mother-of-pearl buttons on the flap pockets. Hatless in the afternoon sunlight, her flowing red curls glistened.

Save for the flicker of its tail, the horse remained motionless. The crowd grew hushed. Balancing on the paint's back, Tomasina swooped her arms higher, urging the men into a cheer. Her plea was met with thunderous whoops and hollers.

Even Will had to admit she was magnificent. Her smile was infectious, her confidence alluring. Every man in the audience was admiring her, as well. An unexpected surge of jealousy caught him by surprise. The urge to protect her was nearly overwhelming. Not even Dora had inspired this confusing flood of emotions. Yet this slip of a girl he'd only met a handful of times had him captivated.

In an instant the mood changed. Her balance faltered. The horse lunged forward. Tomasina vaulted into the air. Strangled cries sounded from several onlookers. Will instinctively pitched forward. She landed in a crouch then popped upright and swept one arm across her stomach in a shallow bow. Her trick drew deafening applause. A vein throbbed in Will's temple. The whole thing had been a stunt.

She whistled, and the horse veered straight at her. Though Will knew by now her act was all for show, the muscles in his shoulders tensed. At the last second Tomasina neatly sidestepped and caught the horse's mane in both hands. Using the forward motion, she swung one leg over the animal's haunches and resumed her seat once more.

Will's knuckles whitened around the top rail of the corral fence, his heart thundering in his chest as he watched the scene unfolding before him. Tomasina spun her mount and trotted toward him. Her vivid green eyes pinned him in place.

Halting in front of his spot on the fence, the horse's hooves kicked more dirt over his boots.

With her mischievous grin firmly in place, Tomasina winked at him. Apprehension snaked up his spine. His instincts were correct once again.

Texas Tom meant trouble.

She flourished one hand. "For my next trick, I need a volunteer from the audience." She sidled her horse nearer

Will's vigil and extended her arm, indicating him with a hand encased in a fringed leather glove. "How about you, kind sir? Are you man enough to take on Texas Tom?"

Chapter Four

Before Will could react to her unexpected challenge, a commotion at the far end of the corral distracted Tomasina. He followed her gaze. A saddled but riderless horse, almost identical to the one she rode, trotted toward them. Loose reins trailed in the dirt while empty stirrups flapped against the animal's sides.

Tomasina's stance instantly focused on the odd sight. Her fingers flexed on her horse's mane. Her attention sharpened. Though the proud lines of her profile remained inflexible, Will sensed something was wrong. Her curls fluttered in the soft breeze. This wasn't part of the show. Uncertain as well, the crowd remained hushed in anticipation.

Waiting.

Tomasina sat straighter. A crash sounded.

An enormous white bull galloped into the corral, thrashing and snorting. The nostrils on the riderless horse flared, and the animal lunged away from the steer's path. Tomasina spun her mount and charged toward the bull.

His heart racing, Will dropped his cane and vaulted over the fence. Upon his landing, pain shot up his leg and rattled his teeth.

Daniel grabbed for his coat. "What are you doing, Will?"

"Don't be a fool!" Quincy Davis called out.

The riderless horse bolted past, and Will caught the reins, yanking the animal to a halt. Using his good leg, he stuck one foot in the empty stirrup and hoisted himself into the saddle. The animal danced beneath him, frightened and confused. Grasping the pommel, he squeezed his legs, asserting his dominance over the skittish horse.

Quickly snagging the second rein and establishing control, he searched for Tomasina and the bull. Cornered at the far end of corral, the horned animal reared and snorted. Tomasina sidled her mount toward the fence. Nostrils flared and sharp hooves pawed the earth. The animal was set to charge, and she'd positioned herself directly in its path.

An icy chill pooled in the pit of his stomach.

Placing two fingers in his mouth, Will let out a sharp whistle. Distracted from its closest prey, the bull shook its enormous head. Will waved his hands above his head. The bull changed direction and charged toward him. Keeping his mount steady, Will held his position to the last second. Feinting left, he narrowly escaped the sharp horns.

A flash of red caught his attention. Blood darkened the animal's fur. The bull had been injured, though not badly enough to slow it down. In preparation for the bronc-busting contest, a rope had been fastened around the bull's middle along with a halter around the snout. If Will caught hold of that halter, he might be able to flip the bull. If Texas Tom was the marksman she claimed, he'd buy enough time for a shot. Will spun his mount and intercepted her.

She waved him toward the opposite end. "Help me herd him back to the gate."

"No." Will shook his head. "Too dangerous. That animal is hurt. He's better off in the corral, where he can thrash about." He followed the bull's frantic bucking. "Let the cowboys clear out the spectators, then I'll grab his head and flip him. You take the shot."

There was no other way.

Her expression revealed an embarrassing level of skepticism. "Have you ever flipped a bull before?"

"No time to argue." He'd seen the trick plenty of times, but he'd never actually performed the task. If the war had taught him one thing, it was that sometimes a man learned skills on the fly. "Grab your guns and prove you're a sharpshooter."

"It's too dangerous," she shouted. "I won't let you."

"You don't have a choice."

The more time they wasted, the more they risked. Wild with pain, the bull charged toward the corral fence. The crowd scrambled away. Startled cries rippled through the fleeing audience. The white bull kicked and bucked, its back legs smashing the fence, splintering the rails.

With the enclosure breached, the whole town was in peril. Will dug his heels into his mount's sides and galloped the distance. He maneuvered his horse between the bull and the broken fence. A horn caught his horse's flank, and the animal brayed. A second lunge narrowly missed Will's thigh.

People pushed and shoved, madly fleeing the area.

Tomasina frantically gestured toward the cowboy at the far end of the corral. "Grab my rope."

They had to keep the bull occupied until the majority of the crowd dispersed. The animal kicked at the fence once again, cracking the top railing in two. Time was quickly running short.

With the bull breathing down his neck, Will galloped toward the exit. "Open the gate for Tomasina!"

Several cowboys frantically unlatched the fastening. He gestured toward her. "Get out of here."

There was no reason for both of them to take the risk. His only chance at limiting injuries to onlookers was to keep the animal contained.

He glanced over his shoulder, and his heart skittered and stalled. Instead of galloping toward the gate, Tomasina approached the bull at a dead-on run. She worked a rope in her hands, winding her arm in a rhythmic motion. Like a furious Valkyrie, her focus remained fixed on her target, and her hair streamed behind her. Twirling the lasso high above her head, she launched the loop and neatly snared the animal's head then yanked her horse to a halt.

Shocked by the sudden obstruction, the bull's speed faltered. The animal shook its head, bucking and snorting. The steer sat back on its heels and spun in a taut circle. Tomasina held tight. Will whistled again, and the frightened steer paused only a moment before resuming its agonized pitching.

Tomasina's hold faltered. Time slowed. First one hand broke free then the other. The rope caught her legs and yanked her from her mount. Fear urged him forward. She'd be pulverized beneath the bull's hooves in an instant. Will slapped his horse's hindquarters with the extra length of reins and charged. The steer pawed the ground, and Tomasina scuttled away. The steer ducked its head and plunged forward. The tip of one horn grazed her head.

Tomasina dug in her heels and frantically scooted backward. Will galloped between the pair and leaped from the saddle. He grasped the bull's horn and concentrated all his weight into the collision. Twisting his body, he landed on his back, hauling the bull to its side in the process. The air whooshed from Will's lungs and stars shot like shrapnel behind his eyes.

A gunshot sounded.

The cowboys sprang into action. Bodies swarmed them. Will shook the fog from his vision and kept his grip, draping his leg over the bull's neck. Another shot sounded and the animal went still.

Will collapsed onto his back and stared at the cloudless sky. His breath came in harsh gasps. The enormous steer lay sprawled in the center of the corral. He touched the animal's side, felt a great heaving sigh and then nothing. Pushing off, he lurched away and gritted his teeth against the pain firing up his leg.

Thrown from her horse, Tomasina sat back on her heels and brushed at her pants.

The events of the past few moments played out in his memory with sickening detail. She'd nearly been killed.

Daniel appeared in front of him. His friend stuck out his hand and helped Will up, discreetly passing him his walking stick in the process.

Daniel shielded his eyes against the sun. "You all right? That was quite a show you put on."

"I'm fine." Will mumbled his thanks.

"Quincy and I will start assessing the damage."

"I'll join you in a minute."

Once his friend had walked out of earshot, Will advanced on Tomasina. "Have you taken leave of your senses?"

She staggered upright, a relieved grin on her expressive face. "That was a real humdinger. I didn't think you had it in you, Daddy Canfield."

"Do you have a death wish?" he thundered. "Did you actually think you could slow thousands of pounds of charging bull?"

He couldn't recall the last time he'd raised his voice to anyone, let alone a woman. Normally his rage was a cold thing. He'd discovered early in his military career that low tones were more lethally effective than shouts. Tomasina was singularly unaffected by his ire, which only increased his fury.

"Don't get riled at me." Her expression morphed into annoyance. "You jumped on him!"

"We're not talking about me."

She lifted her eyes heavenward. "And I suppose because you're a man you think you're the only one who can risk his life?"

"It's not about who can risk their life, it's about being sensible."

"You didn't look too sensible when you were diving toward those horns." She blew out a heavy breath. "I don't think men are as interested in protecting women as they are in taking all the glory."

"Glory? I can assure you, glory was the very last thing on my mind."

She scowled, circled the steer and then knelt near its haunches. "Look at that."

"If you'd listened to me, none of this would have happened." He realized she was no longer engaged in the conversation. "What's wrong?"

"Someone speared this animal." She wiped her forehead with the back of her hand, smearing red across her face. "This didn't happen by accident. We check all the animal pens for weaknesses and breaches. How did this bull get into the corral in the first place? Someone released him on purpose." Glaring at Will, she demanded, "Did you have anything to do with this? You wanted my show shut down from the beginning. It's as good as over now."

"My whole concern was the safety of the spectators." He looped the horse's reins in his hands. "Why would I endanger them this way?"

"All right, all right." Her shoulders slumped. "It's just that I promised no one would get hurt. Nothing like this has ever happened before. Ever."

"I'm not exactly thrilled that my premonition was accurate."

Will crouched beside her and unfurled his handkerchief.

He reached for her head and Tomasina flinched away. "What are you doing?"

"You've got a cut on your forehead." He dabbed at the flow of blood then pressed against the wound. "You'll need that stitched."

"I'm fine." She pressed her gloved hand over his. "I don't need stitches."

Despite her bravado, he felt the delicate trembling of her hand beneath his fingertips. Her face was pale, and her eyes were wide and glassy. The adrenaline gradually drained from his veins, leaving him oddly lethargic. His gaze dipped to where their hands touched. His mouth went dry. He shook his head, clearing his thoughts. He'd never lost his temper after a battle or crises. He'd always been known for his cool head, and yet he'd been raging like a lunatic only a moment before. What was *happening* to him?

"If you don't want stitches, that's your choice." His words were strained, his voice husky. Slipping his hand from beneath her fingers, he left the handkerchief in place. "You'll be left with a scar."

Free from her touch, his head cleared. Her expression remained mutinous.

"So what? I ain't looking to impress no one." She squinted into the distance, her brilliant green eyes flashing. "I don't mind killing when killing needs to be done, but someone deliberately wounded this animal. There's no call for this kind of cruelty."

"Which leaves the obvious. Someone deliberately riled

that animal during your performance." Will stood and surveyed the trampled grass and scattered debris. Most of the
crowd had dispersed. Only a few huddled knots of people
remained. He limped toward the fence for a better look at
the damage. "You have an enemy, Miss Stone."

"Me? You're the one with all the rules and regulations.
Maybe someone is tired of following 'em. Maybe your
loyal subjects aren't as happy with the leadership as you
think. Maybe somebody has it out for Cowboy Creek.
There's no reason to assume this is *my* enemy."

Her words struck too close to home. Was the Murdoch
Gang involved? They'd been having trouble with those
fellows since the snow melted. One of the gang had been
grazed by a bullet in their last encounter with the law of
Cowboy Creek. Rubbing his forehead, Will considered the
possibility. Something didn't quite fit. The Murdochs were
far bolder than this slipshod attempt at revenge. Men who
robbed churches in broad daylight didn't hide their actions.
No. The Murdochs weren't behind this particular event.

This message was for Tomasina. Will tightened his fists,
his heart still racing from the fear he'd experienced when
she'd fallen from her horse. Even in death the enormous
steer was intimidating, its carcass stretched across the dirt.

He stared at the flattened grass and the hats and other
items abandoned by the fleeing crowd. His vision swam,
and he was back at Little Round Top once again. His nostrils burned with gunpowder and a haze of smoke hung
low in the sky. Men writhed and screamed. They were
the lucky ones. Others were still. Horse carcasses littered
the field.

The stench of blood filled the air. Will's trousers were
damp with it. A pall of grief settled over him. He'd never
become accustomed to losing horses in such a grizzly fashion. At least the men understood what they were facing,

what they were fighting for, in those horrific battles. But the animals were innocent. As innocent as children. As innocent as the babe asleep in his rooms at the Cattleman Hotel.

Grasping the reins of his borrowed horse, he approached a cowboy loitering nearby.

"He's been injured," Will said. "Hindquarters."

The cowboy grasped the horse's lead.

Two men leaned over a prone figure, and Will leaned heavily on his cane.

Tomasina touched his sleeve. "Are you all right?"

He shook off her hold, forcing himself back to the present. He wasn't at Little Round Top. The war was over. He wasn't the captain anymore. But this was his community. He'd sworn to protect this town, and he was a man who kept his word.

"There's been an injury." He grit the words out. If the man hadn't risen by now, it must be serious. "Find Doc Fletcher."

Tomasina followed his gaze. "Do you think it's bad?"

Had she realized how close he'd come to slipping back into his memories? Had she sensed his agony? He couldn't let her see him like this. He couldn't let anyone see him this way. He wouldn't be seen as weak.

Channeling his shock at the unexpected reaction, he snapped, "Well it sure isn't good."

The flash of hurt in her eyes stabbed him with regret. He'd apologize later. And say…what? How did he explain the scars he carried from the war that remained out of view? He'd never let anyone see inside his pain.

Weak men made poor leaders.

Tomasina retrieved her hat and reached for her horse. She pressed her forehead against the animal's haunches and sucked in a deep breath. Her heart continued to pound painfully in her chest. She'd have laid down her life to prevent that bull from crashing through the fence. She'd taken precautions. Her pa had always stressed the importance of safety and common sense. She'd made a promise that no one would get hurt, and she'd believed in her own word. Nothing like this had ever happened before. She'd staged dozens of shows without incident.

Clenching her jaw, she straightened. This had nothing to do with her. She didn't have any enemies.

"Let me help," she called toward Will. "I'll send one of the boys to fetch the doc."

"You've done enough already," he barked over his shoulder. "Don't make this any worse than it already is."

Her whole chest ached. She could have weathered his anger, but his disappointment was her undoing.

Someone had sabotaged her show, and she wasn't resting until she discovered who had spooked that bull. The act was deliberate; it had to be. She'd seen plenty of animal wounds over the years, and she recognized full well when an injury was man-made.

Several of the cowboys clustered around the downed bull. She motioned for one of the younger men and bid him to fetch the doc. Eager to help, the cowboy sprinted off.

A man she recognized as Theo Pierce, a drover of her father's generation, rubbed the back of his neck. "That bull is going to cost you."

"You shot him." Tomasina crossed her arms. "Why do I have to pay?"

If Will had listened to her from the beginning instead of treating her as though she needed protection, she might have saved the animal. His interference rankled. Mostly because she hadn't expected his prowess. Though he always moved with an inherent grace, his horsemanship was faultless. Picturing him as a staid banker whose only skill rested with ledgers and numbers had insulated her against the bewildering feelings he stirred. Seeing this other side of him, the fierce warrior, had shattered the last vestige of her illusion. Will Canfield was a dangerous man.

"That animal was on loan to your show," Theo said. "That makes its death your responsibility. We already lost more than a dozen on the trail. I can't afford to lose any more." He leaned closer and touched the reddened flank. "This isn't from a gun. What happened?"

"I'd ask you the same thing. Someone speared this bull and sent it into the corral." She gauged the other men's reactions, searching for any sign of guilt. "Are you telling me that no one saw anything?"

"My outfit was watching the show," Theo replied easily. "Same as everyone else. We had plenty of time before the bronc busting, and that's the only event any of the boys entered."

The men appeared as confused as Tomasina. No one looked away or shuffled their feet.

"Which means someone opened the gate and speared that poor animal without anyone seeing anything. Seems far-fetched to me. Who was closest to that end of the corral?"

She'd find the person who had been standing near that gate and see if he had anything more to say outside the prying eyes of the other cowboys.

Theo rubbed the back of his neck. "James Johnson was the last fellow I noticed near the gate."

Tomasina took an involuntary step backward. *James.* He was right smack-dab in the middle of trouble yet again. She spun around lest someone see the tears welling in her eyes. Was Will correct? Did she have an enemy? Had the man she considered a brother done this deliberately?

They'd argued, but this action was malicious even for James. It was high time the two of them had a showdown. They'd gone through too much together. He'd been avoiding her for far too long.

Truth be told, she'd been avoiding him, as well. He was a reminder of her pa. A painful reminder of all she'd lost. Tears threatened once more, and she clenched her jaw. Pa was gone, and blubbering about it wasn't going to bring him back. There was work to be done.

"Theo," she said, turning back. "I'll pay you fair market price for the bull. Throw a picnic for the rest of the boys. Tell 'em it's from the Stone outfit." She might as well spread some good will. Who knew what the future held. "The rest of you fan out and help with the cleanup. We've got injured folks."

Another drover she recognized as a fellow named Dutch grumbled. "They've got their own folks who'll see to the injured. It ain't our responsibility."

"It was our cattle that caused the ruckus." Dutch wasn't known for going out of his way, but he was a good man at heart. "If someone had been keeping watch, this never woulda happened. I think we owe these townsfolk some decency."

Theo chucked the man on the shoulder. "Come on, Dutch."

"If you say so, boss."

Tomasina clenched her teeth. Dutch wasn't opposed to taking orders, as long as those orders didn't come from a woman.

"That's right Christian of you, Dutch," she grumbled. "I bet your momma would be real proud."

"Aw, don't get sore at me. I could use your help. You're the best tracker we got. Can you come around tonight?

The fellows on the last drive lost a few of their cattle along the creek bed."

"I'll help."

She'd always be the lowest ranking drover. The men had never been much for taking orders from her even when her pa was alive. They didn't treat her as a woman so much as an adolescent. They admired her skill and joked with her around the campfire, but she was never an equal. The distance had grown more pronounced following her pa's death. The cycle had begun anew, and once more she had to prove herself. Another reason she had to ride better, shoot better and take the jobs the other men didn't want.

Shoving those worries aside, she rounded up the remaining men and gathered bandages and supplies before setting off to assist with the injured. Most of the wounds were minor cuts and scrapes from getting pushed and shoved by the fleeing crowd, and most of those folks had dispersed already. If the doc was around, she didn't see him.

She passed by the two cowboys tending the injured horse.

"It's not bad," the taller one said. "Just a scratch."

Relieved, she marched on. Will knelt in front of a red-faced man clutching his ankle. She squared her shoulders and approached him. He didn't look up. She cleared her throat and held out a roll of bandages.

When he continued to ignore her, she planted her hands on her hips. "You gonna be mad at me or you gonna let me help?"

Without lifting his head, he waved her nearer. "Hand me those bandages."

Tomasina blew out a breath she hadn't realized she'd been holding and knelt beside him. His acknowledgment wasn't exactly a declaration of forgiveness, but at least it was a start.

After a quick examination they concluded the man's ankle wasn't broken, only badly sprained. During her ministrations, the man alternately cursed and gritted his teeth. She sat back and unfurled a length of bandage. Will supported the man's leg while she tightly wound the bandages around the man's ankle.

Will kept the man's attention diverted with a steady stream of questions. Nonsense mostly. He even had the man laughing at one point. Their banter shut her out, and a strange little ache settled in her chest. No matter where she traveled, she was always the outsider. Even surrounded by dozens of cowboys she was alone. She was alone because she was different. As she completed her task, Will helped secure the wrapped end.

She served as the unofficial doc in the outfit for minor injuries; another duty that had somehow fallen on her. Until now she hadn't realized how telling it was that the boys had assigned her that duty. They let a woman do the nursing.

"You're a good medic, Mr. Canfield," she said, wiping her forehead with the back of her hand. "You've done some doctoring before."

A shuttered look came over his face. "In the war."

A flush crept up her neck. Her own brush with the war had been brief but memorable. Mostly she and her pa had worked and stuck close to Texas. Her father had been too old to fight. Though he couldn't serve, he'd done his bit to support the war effort.

An army traveled on its belly, and there was no better supply for the southern states than Texas longhorns. Her pa had gone to work for an outfit that raised and sold cattle to the army at a fair price. While driving a small herd east, they'd come across the remnants of a previous skirmish. Men lay dying on the blood-soaked field. The heat of the day had been excruciating, and the bloating bodies had heaped on the misery. The stench was nauseating. They'd done what they could, but it wasn't enough. She'd never seen such a ghastly sight, and she prayed she never saw the like again.

The soldiers who survived that day had gone on to fight other battles. How did someone witness bloodshed over and over again without stitching the horror into their very souls? Did those stitches ever unravel?

Will wiped his palms on his trousers and stood. Hobbling, he kept his weight off his bad leg. Two men who'd been hovering nearby flanked the injured man Will had been assisting. They draped his arms over their shoulders, and the trio limped toward town.

She glanced around, noting the field had cleared. The cowboys had gathered most of the litter left behind and were attending the steer left in the corral.

"I think that's everyone," Tomasina said.

"I hope so." Will shrugged into his jacket once more. "We got off lucky."

The damage might have been worse, much worse.

She'd barely breathed a sigh of relief before another man approached, a child in his arms. "We need a doctor, Will."

Her throat tightened. The man held a boy of no more than nine or ten years old. *A child.* The bandage wrapping the boy's head oozed red.

Recognition flickered across Will's face. "I've sent for the doc, Mr. O'Neill. Bring him over here."

She caught sight of the doctor making his way toward them at a brisk clip, his leather bag clutched in his hand. She'd seen him checking the chalkboard outside his office on her walks through town. In his late fifties, the man was rail thin and small framed, and his kind gray eyes were bracketed by laugh lines. Waving her arms, she frantically motioned him over.

Together with Will, the man rested the boy's still form on the ground. Shucking his coat once more, Will balled the material into a pillow, and Doc Fletcher knelt beside him.

The doc pulled out his stethoscope. "Are you the boy's father?"

"Yes. The name is O'Neill. This here is Owen."

"Did you see what happened, Mr. O'Neill?"

"We were all here for the show. Owen and I were standing on the north side of the corral when the commotion started. People started running. Someone knocked me aside and Owen fell. I think—" The man fisted one hand over his mouth. "I think he was kicked in the head."

Looking grim, the doc nodded.

Will placed a hand on the father's shoulder and led him a short distance away. Tomasina hesitated another long moment before turning away. There was nothing more she could do here. She pressed her hand against the pang of longing in her chest. They'd shut her out. She was the outsider.

Feeling as though her cowboy boots were made of lead, she melted into the background. Will already blamed her. There was no use sticking around for more accusations. None of this had been her fault, and there was only one way to prove it.

Outsider or not, she vowed to find whoever had incited that bull and make him pay.

Turning away, she didn't see when Will reached for her then let his hand drop against his side.

Chapter Five

The following day Will had barely sat down, loosened his tie and closed his eyes before he was summoned once more. Between the cattle drives, the baby, the rodeo and the subsequent injuries and investigation, he hadn't had a moment's peace. His questions had yielded no answers about the incident at the rodeo. Neither had he located Tomasina for an apology. A task that required his immediate attention.

His behavior had been inexcusable.

After wearily rising, he winced with each step as he made his way to the sheriff's office and discovered Noah waiting for him.

"I didn't expect to see you," Will said.

Tall and broadly built, Noah was dressed in his working clothes, his lengthy blond hair visible beneath his hat, his scars shaded by his brim. Since Noah rarely came to town, his business must be important. Will put his confession about the letter on hold. Though he wasn't normally given to maudlin sentimentality, he owed his friend. As his commanding officer, he owed Noah the life he should have had before the war had ravaged more than just his body. The battles might be over, but loyalty among soldiers never faltered. There was a woman worthy of Noah; a woman who'd see past the scars. Was it so unlikely that the bride they'd sent for might be that woman?

Noah motioned Will inside. "You won't believe what I discovered on my way to the feed and grain this morning."

Whatever Noah had discovered must be exceedingly unusual for him to linger in town. Will followed his friend through the building, and they paused in front of the jail cell.

A feverish man writhed on the single cot, a dirty bandage wrapped around his head. His clothing was damp with sweat, his face ashen. Doc Fletcher had taken a seat beside the prone man, a deep crease between his eyes.

Will started. "Is that Zeb Murdoch?"

"I reckon so."

A few weeks back Zeb Murdoch had been winged in the ear by one of the Cowboy Creek deputies after he and his gang had robbed the church. The gang had subsequently made their way to Morgan's Creek, where they'd stolen horses and robbed a saloon. One of the witnesses had identified Zeb Murdoch and noted his injury.

The wound had obviously gone septic. The skin visible beneath Zeb's scraggly beard was pale and waxy. Dark blood matted his greasy blond hair, while his painfully thin frame bordered on gaunt.

The doc leaned over the outlaw and gingerly lifted the edge of the bandage, grimacing at the oozing wound. "He'll live, but he'll wake up with one less ear."

Though Will had seen plenty of lacerations in his lifetime, the angry infection had him wincing. He asked Noah once more. "Where did you find him?"

"He was propped up behind the laundry on Fourth Street. Wolf sniffed him out."

Noah's dog was part wolf and, though intimidating, the animal was an excellent tracker and fiercely loyal.

"How long was he there?" Will asked.

"Since yesterday, I'm guessing. He didn't have his horse, and there were two canteens of water set out. Like someone left him there." Noah doffed his hat and threaded his fingers through blond hair that nearly touched his collar. "I heard from the deputy that you had some trouble at the stockyards, as well. Anyone hurt?"

"Someone riled up a bull and set it loose. No serious injuries. Cuts and bruises from when the crowd panicked and ran. A sprained ankle. Owen O'Neill fell down and took a boot to the head, but he was only grazed. Last I saw him, he was having pie at the Cowboy Café." Will paced in front of the jail cell. "I don't believe in coincidences. The Murdoch Gang left Zeb behind the laundry about the same time that bull cut loose in the ring."

"The timing works out," Noah agreed, replacing his hat and running his thumb and forefinger over the brim. "He didn't get here by himself. Not in his condition."

The pieces fell into place with sickening clarity. "Which means the Murdoch Gang created a diversion and dumped him."

Remorse socked Will in the chest. He'd accused Tomasina of having an enemy, and she was innocent. He already owed her one apology. Now he owed her a couple of them.

"Why go to all that trouble?" Noah mused. "Why didn't they shoot him or leave him for dead?"

"Who knows? Family loyalty. Honor among thieves. Seems like Xavier wants his brother healed."

"But why travel forty miles south with a sick man? Why not leave him in Morgan's Creek?"

"The sawbones in Morgan's Creek died last fall. If they

were riding south anyway, and Zeb took a turn for the worse, Cowboy Creek is the logical choice."

"Good point." Noah braced his forearm on the bars and studied the outlaw. "Zeb gets shot during the holdup at the church. The gang robs Morgan's Creek, but Zeb's wound turns septic."

"There's no doctor in Morgan's Creek," Will said. "Xavier can't kill his own brother. Can't leave him for dead, either."

"Instead they create a diversion and dump him in Cowboy Creek. They've been here before. They know the town. They know we have a doctor."

Will crossed his arms. "What now? If Xavier risked his life saving his brother, he won't let us hang him."

"Which means he's sticking close."

"Bad news for Cowboy Creek. If the gang is in the area, they're bound to be a nuisance."

"Not necessarily." Noah pushed off from the bars. "They'd be fools to stir up trouble. Not with Zeb in our jail cell. I'm guessing they'll lay low for a while, let things cool off and wait for Zeb to heal. That's when we worry."

"We'd best double our guards anyway. The Murdoch Gang will need supplies. And they can't exactly waltz into Longhorn's and buy grain for their horses." Zeb groaned and Will studied the sick man. "Let's hold them off as long as we can. If anyone asks, Zeb is near dying. That's not far from the truth."

"What if we spread the rumor he's already dead?"

"Too risky. We can't chance pushing the Murdochs to retaliate."

"Too bad," Noah said. "One less Murdoch is one less problem. You're right about Xavier, though. He went to a lot of trouble to save his brother. He's not going to let him hang."

Will slanted a glance at the outlaw. "Which means they'll be back to bust him out."

"We better be ready when that happens."

"Don't worry." Will spoke with grim determination. "We'll be ready."

By the time he'd finished at the jail, Tomasina was nowhere to be found. According to Theo, one of the drovers, she was tracking strays along a creek bed. There'd be no apology today. He'd seek out Tomasina tomorrow. And that meant he'd be carrying another burden for a spell.

The day stretched out ahead of him, bleak and lonely. *Lonely.*

He was accustomed to solitude. An only child, he'd grown up without the constant patter of siblings. In the army, his rank had kept him isolated. He valued his privacy. He should be relieved the preacher's daughter had taken Ava for the afternoon. He could catch up on his work. Yet the thought of spending the day alone left him oddly empty. The feeling itched like wet wool beneath his collar.

Any chance at peace was a long time coming for him.

Tomasina's first step was to find James Johnson. A fellow named Butch directed her toward the saloon. Inside, she spotted James's distinctive fringed vest. He'd had the back beaded in the shape of Texas, and leather fringe dangled from the hem. She thought the vest atrocious, but James had bragged about the ladies admiring his style. She snorted softly. When it came to a handsome face, sometimes ladies didn't have the sense of a peahen.

Unheeding of the curious stares, she stomped across the saloon, planted a hand on James's shoulder and spun him around.

His scowl lasted an instant before he masked his temper with a cool grin. "I thought you didn't like saloons."

"I don't. But you and I need to talk."

He turned his back on her and lifted his drink. "I got nothing to say to you."

Tomasina planted her boot on the brass foot rail and leaned close. "Pa is dead and you've got nothing to say? I thought he meant something to you."

James's hand stilled midair, then his drink hit the bar with a thud, splashing his whiskey. "What happened?"

"He went to sleep and never woke up. Smitty thought it was probably his heart." Her throat tightened. "You didn't know, did you?"

"Nope."

The chill in his voice sparked her anger once more. "He never got over you leaving. You know that, don't you? We took you in when you had no one."

Not a flicker of emotion showed on his face. That was James, all right. Always stoic. Why did men figure that showing their feelings made them weak? There was nothing wrong with sorrow. Except with James, there was always something to prove.

James appeared to gather himself. "Your pa was a good man, but he was too old for the trail." Taking a long draw from his whiskey, he fixed his gaze on the mirror behind the bar. "He shoulda quit years ago. He only stayed on as point man 'cause of you."

"That's not fair and you know it. He stayed working because the trail was his life."

"Think about it, Tom." James cast her a sidelong glance. "Your pa was always working and saving for your future. You weren't getting married or anything. And he knew once he was gone, you'd never be able to protect yourself. So he worked and he saved. Worked himself right into the grave."

His words picked at her conscience like buzzards on a

carcass. She shook her head. *No*—James was lashing out to hide his grief. Her pa hadn't worked himself to death because of her. He'd always been a frugal man. They'd never needed much between the two of them.

"You're being hateful because of your guilt," she said. "Taking out your anger on me isn't going to bring him back. Near broke his heart when you left, and you know it."

James had all the charm in the world when a pretty face was nearby, but none for her. She wasn't a woman as far as he was concerned. She was one of the boys. She wasn't worthy of his fawning attention. That suited her fine. His fake charm was wasted on her. His words were as shallow as a creek bed in a drought.

"Too bad." James ducked his head. "Maybe your pa should have had a stronger heart."

"How can you say that?" She hitched in a breath. His indifference cut her to the quick. "After everything he did for you?"

She didn't know James anymore. He wasn't the boy she'd grown up with, the boy she'd considered family. This was a stranger. A hateful, bitter stranger.

"I'm not arguing with you anymore, Tom." He turned away. "I said all I got to say."

"This isn't who you are, James." She felt as though her whole world was tipping upside down. First she'd lost her pa, now she was losing James. "Why are you acting like this?"

He stumbled back from the bar and glared at her. "Why is everyone trying to tie me down? To change me? This is exactly who I am. I do what I want when I want. I'm not beholden to anyone. I stayed on with your pa's outfit because it suited me. Nothing more." Shrugging his shoulders, he mumbled, "Doesn't matter anyway, now. Without your pa, the Stone outfit is finished."

"At least he didn't live to see this." She fisted her hands against her sides. "I'm glad he's not here to see what you've become."

"Take my advice, Tom. Find a job in town. Your days on the trail are over. Without your pa, you'll never be safe."

"Fine talk coming from you." Though angry, she grasped for one last shred of hope. "There's no reason you and I can't carry on the Stone name. We can build on that name and create our own reputation."

"I'm not a Stone, Tom. And I'm sure not riding trail with a girl."

"Oh, so I'm a girl now?"

"Let it go, Tom."

She blinked rapidly before recalling the reason she'd come in the first place. "You were supposed to be watching the corral gate at the rodeo. Someone let a bull loose during my show. Speared the animal. Almost killed me. You know anything about that?"

Guilt flicked quickly over his face, replaced just as quickly with that same indifference. "That's not my fault. I had some, uh, someone I had to meet. Stop pestering me. I wasn't even there."

One of the men at the bar winked at her and let out a low whistle, then sidled closer. "Your fellow giving you trouble, pretty lady?" Her rotund admirer was unkempt with breath like kerosene. "Why don't you come on over here? I'll treat you real nice."

"I'd rather swim in a latrine."

James caught her around the arm and dragged her toward the batwing doors. "You shouldn't be in here."

"Neither should you."

Once outside, she shook off his hold. "Theo saw you near the gate before the accident. Were you trying to get revenge on me or something? Are you still mad about what happened back in Harper?"

Hot color suffused his face. "You don't really think I had anything to do with what happened at the show?"

Orphaned early in the war, James had joined the Confederate Army at fifteen seeking revenge. His commanding officer had quickly discovered his deception. By the time James was old enough to serve, peace had been declared. He was a man with something to prove and no way to prove it.

Tomasina's mouth twisted. "You were awful mad when you left."

"You tell me your pa died. Then you accuse me of sabotaging the show. You have no right, Tom. No right to accuse me of something like that."

His denial only fueled her outrage. "But you were there. Did you see anything?"

"I didn't see anything. I told you before. I left to meet someone." James narrowed his gaze. "Maybe someone else has it out for you. Did you ever think of that?"

Her stomach clenched. Will had come to the same conclusion. "I don't have any enemies. Why would someone come after me?"

"You tell me. You're not exactly the easiest person to get along with, you know. Your pa let you give orders, but no one else will. Now that your pa is gone, you'd best keep your pistol cocked and at the ready." His voice softened. "I'm telling you this as a friend."

"Oh, so you're my friend now? You sure weren't treating me like a friend a few minutes ago."

"That's because you never pay me any mind. Listen this once."

The sharp finality of his words settled around her. She pressed her hands against her chest, halting the flow of emotions. She'd never cared much one way or the other what people thought of her. Why did their opinions matter? She liked herself well enough.

Once or twice she'd tested James's flattering style during a negotiation, but the role had never sat well with her.

Will Canfield certainly found her difficult. How many others had thought the same? She'd goaded Will because she wanted her way. She'd dismissed his objections to the rodeo without considering his concerns, and his fears had come to pass. Theo had warned her that Will was looking for her. Unsure how to atone for her mistake, she'd been staying clear of him instead.

"You're like a brother to me, James." She spoke quietly. "I don't want bad blood between us."

Her future had always seemed vast and never ending, the possibilities infinite. Except her world wasn't the mountains and the prairies and herding thousands of cattle to market. Her future consisted of the people around her, and that reality was rapidly shrinking.

James scuffed at the ground. "There's no bad blood, but things have changed. We're not kids anymore, Tom. With your pa gone—" His voice broke. "With your pa gone, it's time for you to act like a girl for once."

Her throat constricted. He was angry. He was grieving. Even if he didn't show his pain, he was hurting. But so was she. Her heart was breaking, as well. When had anyone ever spared her feelings?

The events of the past weeks caught up with her, and pain throbbed behind her eyes. "Don't you dare start in on me. I can take care of myself."

"You'll have to, won't you?"

"Fine words coming from you. You take care of yourself, as well. It's what you're good at."

Everything she'd thought about herself crumbled. Had

she ever had the respect of the men she rode with, or had they only tolerated her in deference to her pa? Without him, where did she belong? Even James, the one person she'd thought was loyal to her, had turned his back on her.

Unable to face the pity in his resigned expression, she pivoted on her heel.

James reached for her. "Tom, wait."

Shoving him away, she glared. "You think of anything you may have seen at the rodeo, tell the sheriff. If you can tear yourself away from the saloon long enough, that is. You and I got nothing to say to each other." She poked his chest with a finger. "Being a jerk doesn't make you more of a man. Just makes you more of a jerk."

She stomped off without waiting for an answer. Once she rounded the corner, she searched for a darkened corner. Pressing one hand against the side of the building, she heaved a sob. She'd lost her pa already. Now she'd lost James.

There was no reason for her to take his hurtful words to her heart. Except that doubt had already wormed its way into her soul. Pa's death had peeled back the covering on her life, and she didn't like what she saw hidden beneath the surface.

How quickly her life had changed. Her pa was gone, James was gone, and she wasn't any closer to discovering who'd sabotaged her show. Her knees weakened, and she braced her back against the wall, sank down and hung her head.

She thought of how Will was caring for Ava, his unabashed affection for the baby, and her chest grew so tight it hurt. Now that her father was gone, she didn't suppose she'd ever feel that sort of love again.

She'd always considered herself a solitary person, and yet this was the first time she'd ever been truly alone.

She pushed off from the wall and stood. Feeling sorry for herself had never solved a problem.

When she arrived back at the drover's camp, she discovered Will had left a note for her with one of the fellows. He wanted to speak with her.

She crumpled the message and tossed it in an open fire. Until she figured out who had sabotaged her show, she was steering clear of Will Canfield.

Chapter Six

Two days later, with Ava under the care of the reverend's daughter, Will searched through the tents for Tomasina. She hadn't replied to any of his messages. Given the rag-tag assortment of cowboys, he wasn't even sure if she'd gotten them. The last two times he'd visited the drover's encampment, he'd been told he'd just missed her. This time he wasn't leaving until they'd spoken.

He'd been harsh with her because he'd been embarrassed by his own weakness. She'd been just as upset over the accident as everyone else. And what had he done? He'd shouted at her. He'd accused her of having enemies when the enemies were his own. She'd nearly been killed because of him.

Will sighed. He owed her an apology, but that wasn't the only the reason he'd sought her out. Their encounters had left him with an insatiable need to discover more about her. How had she managed this long as a female in a profession dominated by men? Who was watching out for her? The more he thought about her situation, the more he feared for her safety.

Never a demonstrative man, in the quiet of the evening he'd prayed for her safety.

The drovers had set up their own city of tents and open fires. After three months or more on the trail, the cowboys often took the opportunity to rest before hooking up with another outfit. Their seasons followed much the same pattern. They'd drive the cattle to winter pastures before the first snowfall and start all over the following spring.

For now, whiskey flowed freely and tobacco smoke fogged the air. Occasionally rival groups broke into fisticuffs. Following a grueling trail ride, the men played as hard as they worked. Will encouraged the impromptu tent city as long as the drovers kept their roughhousing away from town and spent their wages in the local stores.

The idea of Tomasina living this way sent his stomach lurching. She was tough, but she was no match for these men. She was only a slip of a thing. Despite her bluster, she was too young, too innocent, for this life.

He paused in front of a grizzled old-timer perched on a leather sling chair. The man was whittling a hunk of wood. The sun had already sunk low on the horizon, and Will squinted through the smoke from the man's campfire.

The old-timer glanced up. "What can I do you for, young man?"

"Looking for the Stone outfit."

According to Daniel, Tomasina rode with her father. Since marrying, Daniel hadn't been as involved in the stockyards operations, and he hadn't seen Mr. Stone this time around.

"Folks around here call me Domino." The old timer fisted one gnarled hand on his knee. "Ain't much left of the Stone outfit these days."

"What do you mean by that?" Will frowned at the gent's cryptic words. "They brought in a herd last week."

"Tom's pa died on the trail a month or two back. James Johnson used to ride with the Stones, but he took up with another outfit this last spring. Theo Pierce's, if I recall correctly."

"I know James. He's a good kid."

The young drover had volunteered for sentry duty after the trouble with the Murdoch Gang. He was a good sentry, for the most part. Will had seen him flirting with one of the women from the bride train. Pippa Neely. She'd appeared flattered but nothing more.

"The only one left is Tomasina." Domino resumed his whittling. "The rest of the boys finished the drive out of loyalty to Stone, but ain't none of those men gonna take direction from a pretty girl. All of the hands signed on with other outfits. Tom is on her own these days." The old-timer clicked his tongue. "Bad business, if you ask me. Change is coming. This country ain't fit for a woman alone."

Will's unease increased tenfold. The more he learned, the less he liked what he was hearing. "Then she has no other family now that her father is gone?"

"Nope. It was just the two of them. Buried her pa on the trail, they did. Paid my respects when we passed by. There wasn't anyone like Old Man Stone. You could have driven nails with that man's hard head. He was tough but fair. He'd earned his respect around here."

"What about Tom? Has she earned her respect?"

"With some folks, sure," Domino answered. "But nothing is ever the same from season to season. Men come and they go. Since the war ended, the soldiers have flooded West. Without a uniform, it's harder to tell which side folks are on these days."

"The country has been united. We're all on the same side."

"Not when it comes to land and money."

An edge in the man's voice gave Will pause. "How do you mean?"

"These days a guy will slit your throat for water rights. It ain't like before. Every war has winners and losers. Some men become heroes and some men are left desperate."

Though Will figured the old-timer could talk for hours, he was impatient to finish his business and return to the hotel. The problem of Tomasina had grown even more complicated.

"You know where Tomasina is camped?" he asked.

"Why are you looking for her, anyway?" Domino sat straighter, his watery blue eyes narrowed. "Don't go messing with Tom. Some of the other fellows and I, we keep a watch out for her as best we can. We don't want any trouble."

"I have business with her. That's all."

The man took his measure and nodded. "I'll be keeping an eye on you."

"Good."

At least one person around here had the sense to realize the danger. Will picked his way through the tents and campfires. Tomasina had recently lost her father. She was alone. She was in mourning.

He'd lost his own father near the beginning of the war. He'd buried his sorrow on the battlefield and forged ahead. Much to his shock, after the war his loss had come rushing back, as though his grief had simply remained dormant until he'd acknowledged the pain.

What had Tomasina been feeling these past few weeks? She'd given no indication that she'd suffered a loss, and yet the old-timer's words spoke of an affection between father and daughter. Sooner or later she'd have to let down her guard, as well.

A grief buried never stayed dormant. There was always a reckoning.

When he reached the edge of the tents, a commotion

snagged his attention. Two drovers wrestled in the dirt.
A small knot of men had formed around them, jeering
and shouting encouragement. Always up for a good brawl,
more tents emptied, and Will lost sight of the scrapping
men among the sea of onlookers. He shrugged and moved
on. The pair was evenly matched, and he rarely interfered
with the drovers when they settled their own disputes. It
didn't look like much of a fight anyway.

With most of the cowboys occupied, Will scrutinized
the tents, searching for any sign of Tomasina. The dwell-
ings were plain canvas, giving no clue as to the occupant.
A pair of men snagged his attention. Their movements
were quick and furtive. His instincts flared.

These men were clearly using the distraction of the fight
as camouflage for their actions. Ducking out of sight, Will
pursued the furtive men from a safe distance until the two
reached the edge of the tent city. Shouts and cheers covered
any noise they made. One of the men gestured to the other
and pointed at a tent. The second man nodded.

The first man produced a knife and sliced through the
canvas. Will lunged. A feminine voice screamed. The hairs
on the back of his neck stood on end. *Tomasina.*

Colliding with the first man, he drove the attacker to
the ground. A flash of blade glinted in the moonlight,
and he dodged left. Thwarted from his target, the man
flipped awkwardly. His blade plunged into the ground
near Will's side.

The attacker ducked back and sprang to his feet. Groping for his walking stick, Will swung, catching the man
around the ankles. The attacker yelped and stumbled backward. With the man caught off balance, Will regained his
footing.

Tomasina erupted from the tent and barreled headlong

into the arms of the second man. The outlaw's eyes widened in surprise, and he snatched her upper arm.

"I got 'er!" the man hollered. "Let's get out of here."

Tomasina cracked the man across the jaw with her fisted hand. He pitched sideways. Lowering her head, she rammed his chest, sending him flying. The outlaw collapsed on his backside, his face contorted in fury. A bolt of pure terror shot through Will. If the enraged man got in a solid blow, he'd kill her for certain.

A vicious wallop against Will's jaw caught him by surprise. His vision shattered in a haze of red. Squinting through the pain, he swung his fist, catching the attacker beneath the chin. The man's knees twitched then buckled beneath him. Unconscious, he flopped onto his back.

The second outlaw pushed off from his prone position. He clawed for Tomasina, and she scooted back, kicking at his reaching hands. Will crossed the distance in three pounding strides.

As he reached her side, she planted her booted foot in her attacker's chest and pointed her cocked pistol between his eyes.

The outlaw went still.

"You owe me a new tent, mister," she declared.

Flexing his aching knuckles, Will shook out his throbbing hand. Now that the immediate danger had passed, he caught his breath.

He glanced around and realized the drovers had abandoned their rowdy fight and were gathering around the new drama.

Will rubbed his tender jaw. "Two bits to the man who fetches the sheriff."

"I'll go," a young man eagerly volunteered. He touched two fingers to his hat and dashed off.

The outlaw staring down the barrel of Tomasina's gun

frantically shook his head. "This is all a mistake, Miss. You got this all wrong."

One of the cowboys sidled away from the crowd. Recognizing the man, Will elbowed his way through the drovers and blocked the man's exit. "Not so fast."

"Me?" The man rubbed at his rapidly swelling eye. "I didn't do nothin'. I had my own fight. Everyone here saw. They can tell you. I had nothing to do with this."

"I'll wager you started that fight as a diversion." Grabbing the cowboy who'd started the fight by the scruff of the neck, he yanked the third man toward his friends. "And I'm growing heartily sick of staged diversions."

The unconscious attacker groaned, and his eyes fluttered open. "What happened?"

Will shoved the third attacker forward.

Having barely regained consciousness, the first man blinked in confusion a few times. "What happened, John? Where's Frank?"

John groaned. "Shut up, fool. You're giving us away."

"I guessed as much." Will glanced between the two men. "I only had to see two licks of that fight to realize you weren't giving it your all. Then I saw these two skulking around the tents. Figured the three of you were up to no good."

The old-timer Will had spoken with earlier chortled and elbowed Tomasina in the side. "Good thing this fellow was around to save you."

"I can take care of myself." Tomasina holstered her pistol and glared at Will. "What were you doing here anyway?"

"Checking on you."

The men gathered around them snickered. One drover nudged his companion. "Looks like Tomasina has a fellow."

Whistles and hoots followed.

"He's not my fellow." Tomasina's glare could have melted iron. "He's…he's…he's the fool who owns the hotel in town."

Sheriff Davis chose that fortuitous moment to make an appearance. "Heard you had some trouble here, Will." He caught sight of Tomasina and jerked his head in a nod of greeting. "Miss Stone."

"Sheriff Davis."

Will straightened. "Quincy, these three men were attempting to abduct Miss Stone."

"It ain't like that at all," John insisted. "We were just having some fun. I heard from the fellows around here that Texas Tom is good for a laugh. She knows we didn't mean any harm."

Will flicked the cut edge of her tent with his cane and flashed the knife he held in his opposite hand. "You want to reconsider your story?"

The sheriff turned toward Tomasina. "Do you know any of these men?"

"Nope."

"Which outfit you fellows ride in with?" Quincy asked. "Anyone here want to lay claim to these guys?"

"They ain't from around here," one of the cowboys in the crowd shouted.

"They rode in this morning," another called. "Said they was looking for work."

Sensing a change in the mood of the crowd, Frank's gaze darted between Sheriff Davis and Will. "I'm tellin' the truth. This is just a misunderstanding. We're here to work. We were just playing around."

"Change of plans," Will declared. "You'll be spending time in jail before moving on."

"Wait just a second," John demanded. "What's the charge?"

"I think we all know what you fellows were planning," Will said through gritted teeth. "You want me to say the words?"

"Whoa, whoa, whoa." John held up his hands. "I ain't going to jail for her. She's riding with a bunch of men. She knows what that means."

Will clipped the man beneath chin, neatly leveling him.

Quincy raised an eyebrow in question.

Shrugging, Will said, "He talked too much."

"He was bugging me, too," the sheriff replied easily.

A bucket of water was fetched. The man came up sputtering and hollering. All three men's hands were tied and a rope strung between them before the sheriff marched them into town. Now that the excitement was over, the drovers gradually dispersed to their fires and tents.

Will turned to Tomasina. "Pack up your stuff. You're coming with me."

"No."

Her stubborn reply only hardened his resolve. "It's going to rain tonight, and your tent isn't fit for habitation."

She stuck out her chin. "I ain't afraid of a little rain."

"Please," Will said, feeling more tired than he had in ages. What if he hadn't come along when he had? Would anyone else have noticed? The others had been more interested in the fight than keeping an eye out for the lone woman in their midst. "After what happened tonight, I can't leave you here. Seeing to the welfare of the town is part of my job."

Tomasina scuffed at the dirt. "I'm not part of your town."

"As long as you're living in Cowboy Creek, you're a

part of this town." He pinched the bridge of his nose. "It's been a long day. I don't want to argue with you."

Her mutinous expression faltered. "I'm fine here."

"I'll tell you what." This situation called for diplomacy, and diplomacy was all about give-and-take. He had something she wanted; she simply didn't know it yet. "As long you stay at the hotel, I won't harass you about your guns."

Tomasina squinted. "What are you getting at?"

"What I said. Clearly you need to protect yourself. If you want to keep your guns, I'll see that no one questions you. But only if you're living at the hotel."

"I already have a deal with the sheriff."

"And the sheriff answers to me."

"Fine." The stubborn set of her jaw remained. "But don't go acting like you won or something. I'm staying in town because it's late, I'm tired and I don't feel like sewing up my tent in the dark."

"Understood."

"I'll pay my own way at the hotel," she said in a clipped tone. "I've got money. I won't be beholden to anyone."

"Of course."

A wary silence stretched between them. With the ruckus over, the small tent city had grown hushed once more. Only a hint of moonlight filtered through the gathering clouds.

A drover tossed a piece of kindling onto his fire, and embers shot into the sky. The mournful wailing of a harmonica sounded in the distance. Will didn't push her. He let her mull over her options.

Tomasina huffed. "Give me a minute to pack my stuff."

His sense of victory failed to materialize. There was something wrong. She'd given in awfully easily. He stepped closer, studying her face in the dim moonlight. The evening's events had transpired too quickly, and he hadn't taken the time to look at her—really look at her—since the attack. Was she injured? His pulse thudded.

"Wait." He caught her hand and tugged her closer. "Are you all right? Are you hurt?"

"They didn't hurt me."

She slowly closed her eyes, her shoulders drooping. For a moment he thought he caught a hint of tears glinting on her eyelashes. Her chin wobbled. Without giving himself time to regret his actions, he folded her close. She sagged into his embrace and wrapped her arms around his middle. A fierce need to protect and cherish this woman overwhelmed him. She trembled, and he tightened his hold.

"It's over," he said, his voice gravelly with emotion. "They're gone. They can't hurt you anymore."

"I know. It's not that."

"What, then?" He put some space between them and wiped at the tear glistening on the apple of her cheek. "What is this for?"

Without meeting his gaze, she slumped against him once more. "No one has ever asked me that question before," she said, her words muffled against his shirt. "You know, asked me if I was all right."

His breath seized. "They should have."

"This has been a really, really long week."

"Yes."

A person could only be strong for so long, and she'd reached her limit. He rubbed her back in soothing, rhythmic circles. Her hair tickled his nose, smelling of warm sunlight and lazy spring days. Because of her fiery personality, he sometimes forgot how petite she was, how delicate. Standing amid the sea of tents, he sensed her loneliness. Her sorrow stretched between them like a thread. They'd all lost people. He understood better than most the heavy burden of unshed tears.

She sniffled loudly. "If you go blabbering about this, the deal is off."

"A gentleman never blabbers."

She'd had a fright this evening, and now wasn't the time for asking about her father. He sensed a certain restraint in her; a wariness he didn't always understand. He was hesitant to push her further. Though open and forthright in most matters, she kept a part of herself hidden. He had a gut feeling if he pressed her too quickly, she'd withdraw and shut him out completely. The past few days had sapped them both. He'd approach her later, when she was rested, when some of her strength had returned.

Their gazes met and locked. Her lower lip quivered, and he rubbed the pad of his thumb against the trembling. "You have quite a left hook."

A little of the spark returned to her eyes. "He never saw it coming."

Only a complete blackguard would kiss someone in her vulnerable condition. Too bad he was feeling more and more like a blackguard these days.

Sensing the shift in mood between them, her gaze grew watchful. She was a delightful mix of contradictions. One moment she was drawing her six-shooters, the next she was trembling in his arms because he'd asked a simple question. How could she embody tough and innocent at the same time?

She sniffled quietly and gently shoved him away. "I can't have anyone thinking I've gone soft."

Suddenly bereft, his arms hung in the air another moment, keeping the memory of her shape. There was no easing her pain. Only time healed those wounds. He'd keep her safe instead. With added security at the hotel, he'd ensure her well-being. At least for now. She was too independent to stay in one place for long.

Oblivious to the effect she had on him, Tomasina quickly gathered her belongings, and they collapsed her tent.

With her pack slung over one shoulder, he accompanied her to the hotel. "I want to apologize for my behavior the other day. Little Owen is no worse for wear from his ordeal."

Her skepticism was obvious. "Are you admitting that you were wrong about something?"

"You've earned the right to gloat." He paused. "Don't overdo it. There's substantial evidence to prove the diversion was created by the Murdoch Gang. You've heard by now we've captured Zeb."

"I heard. How's he doing?"

"Not well. I don't know if he'll pull through."

"If he lives, will the Murdoch Gang come for him?" Tomasina asked.

"I reckon so."

She paused and caught his gaze. "The cowboys should have been watching the gate. The Murdochs never should have gotten that close."

"What happened was my fault," he said grimly. "I shouldn't have blamed you."

"I accept your apology."

"Good."

"And part of the blame."

He quirked a brow. "Tomasina Stone. I thought you'd embrace gloating with more enthusiasm. Must you always have the last word?"

"Yep." She grinned, her white teeth flashing in the moonlight.

She'd gotten him again. At least she'd let him apologize. Sort of. She was staying at the hotel, too, which eased some of his worries. Will heaved a sigh at this small victory, although he didn't linger over his short-lived relief. He'd sort out the rest when the time came.

They reached the hotel, and Simon arranged for a room and fetched a key.

Will followed their progress up the carpeted stairs. "Try to stay out of trouble for the next few hours, would ya? Simon needs his beauty sleep."

His porter shot him a blistering glower.

"Hey, Will," Tomasina called.

He paused. "Yes?"

"Word."

Grinning, he allowed her the last word. He'd been in enough battles to realize this war was far from over.

Chapter Seven

Tomasina woke early the next morning and stared at the ceiling. Sleeping on the soft mattress had proved difficult, and she'd finally moved her bedroll onto the floor. After years of sleeping on the trail, the solid wood was more comfortable than soft tick.

Crossing her ankles, she threaded her hands behind her head. She'd only be here a day or two, just until she found work. She had a little money stashed, sure, but there was no sense in wasting her savings on a fancy room when she had a perfectly good tent that only needed a little mending.

After last night she'd reconsidered returning to droving. Her pa and James had both warned her, but she'd been too stubborn to listen. She'd let down her guard because she hadn't expected an attack quite that soon. She'd been naive, assuming she'd be safe among the men she'd ridden beside for years. At least she'd discovered her mistake sooner than later. Though it galled her that Will had witnessed her troubles, she had to face the truth.

Alone among the men, she was a target.

Despite her embarrassment, she recalled feeling safe, almost cherished. The instant he'd held her in his arms, the loneliness she'd felt since her father's death had abated.

Either way, what she needed was a new profession.

With that thought in mind, she dressed and set off to search for a new job. Considering her odd list of skills, she was expecting a long search. As she crossed the lobby, she caught her reflection in the oval mirror once more. Pausing, she examined herself. This morning she'd dressed in her usual drover's uniform of dungarees, chaps and a chambray shirt. She'd never considered altering what she wore because her clothing suited her job as a drover. However, now she had a bad feeling her current mode of dress would be an impediment to her future employment.

Her brow furrowed, and she searched the people milling around the lobby. The maids and the housekeeper wore black dresses with starched white aprons. Simon had donned his familiar bottle-green uniform, and the hotel manager was crisply dressed in a dark suit. While she'd never heard anyone admit as such, people tended to dress in a uniform that indicated their position in society. Since she was temporarily giving up her role as a drover, she'd best pick a new uniform.

Only two ladies were present in the restaurant. One of them was dressed in a simple calico print; the other wore a fancy, bright blue dress. Of the two women, the one in blue had obviously spent more time on her appearance. She was young, too; about the same age as Tomasina. Petite, she wore her strawberry-blond hair braided and tucked beneath a pert blue hat decorated with a peacock feather.

Tomasina rubbed her hands together. This was definitely the woman she needed to see. If you wanted something done right, you picked someone who knew what they were doing.

Tugging on her sleeves, Tomasina approached the lady in blue. "Where can I get a dress like that?"

The woman blinked rapidly, and she touched her chest

with one gloved hand. "Well, uh, I'm afraid I purchased this dress before I arrived in Cowboy Creek."

"Never mind." Tomasina shrugged then squinted. "How'd you get your hair like that? Can you show me?"

Her own hair was definitely a problem. She'd never had much luck taming her curls. She'd cut it short some years back, but that had only made matters worse. Her sheared curls had given her a wild, red halo. After that she'd settled for ripping a length of fringe from her chaps every so often and tying the heavy mass in a queue at her neck.

"First things first." With a smile, the woman held out her hand, palm down. "Perhaps we should begin with an introduction. I'm Pippa Neely."

Tomasina awkwardly pinched her fingertips. "Tomasina Stone."

Pippa was petite and willowy with bright hazel eyes and lustrous hair that lay smooth against her head. Tomasina touched her own unruly curls. What she wouldn't give for locks that could be wrangled into place.

The elegant woman inclined her head with a smile. "Why don't you have a seat, Miss Stone, and tell me why you need a dress."

Tomasina flopped onto the opposite chair. "I need a new uniform. I need to look like a girl."

Leaning forward, Pippa rested her elbows on the table and balanced her chin on her threaded fingers. "And why is that?"

"I'm not sure I can be a drover anymore now that my pa died." Saying the words out loud took away some of their sting. "Pa warned me things were going to change. It used to be him and me and James Johnson. Now Pa is dead and James has turned into a real jerk."

A sage nod sent the feather on Pippa's hat fluttering. "The end of a romance is always difficult."

Screwing up her face, Tomasina reared back. "Ew. It wasn't anything like that. Me and James are like brother and sister." She snapped her fingers. "Why didn't I think of that before? James must be in love. I bet that's why he was so cranky in Harper last fall. That old dog. Falling in love and being tied to one person would sure make him ornery. Mostly because he has a girl in every town from here to Galveston."

"Some men balk at the idea of settling down."

"James Johnson is that sort of fellow."

"Hmm." Pippa tapped her index finger against her chin. "Is James handsome in a swarthy sort of way with a fringed jacket?"

"That's him."

"He is rather charming, although not my sort. He tried to flirt with me at the county fair."

"That'd be James." For some reason Tomasina was relieved Pippa hadn't fallen under his spell. She liked a woman with common sense. "Anyway, after James left, Pa died. All the other cowboys took off after we reached Cowboy Creek. Wasn't a one of them willing to take orders from a woman. That isn't even the worst thing that happened, though. The worst came last night. A couple of the boys cut my tent and tried to drag me out."

With a gasp Pippa rested her fingers over Tomasina's hand. "Oh, my. You poor thing. Are you all right?"

"I'm fine. I had my guns with me. And that other fellow, Will Canfield, helped out."

"Will Canfield came to your rescue?" The petite woman leaned back in her seat and tilted her head. "My, my, my. What was Will doing in the drover's camp?"

"Looking for me." Tomasina scowled. "It wasn't a rescue. I was doing just fine on my own before he helped out."

There was no need for folks to go reading things into

something when there was nothing there. Whether she'd needed his help or not, he'd been handy with his fists. She'd especially enjoyed the part when he'd knocked out that fellow who'd been insulting her.

Pippa tapped her chin once more. "Mr. Canfield doesn't strike me as the sort of man who engages in fisticuffs."

"He should. He was real tough." The man had all sorts of hidden talents. Tomasina absently rubbed her lower lip, recalling his gentle touch. She didn't know how she'd ever face him again after blubbering in his arms.

"And now I need a different job."

"What is the situation with your funds?" Pippa asked. "How long can you survive without a job?"

"Come to think of it, I don't rightly know." Tomasina pumped her shoulders once in a shrug. "Pa and I just kept what money we needed to live on and put the rest in the bank. I never paid much attention to the balance. I never needed anything I didn't already have before now."

"My days have been rather dull of late. This new challenge suits me." Pippa stood and reached for her reticule—a ridiculous little beaded bag with a dangling gold tassel. "First things first. You and I will visit the bank. We need to figure out the extent of the crisis before we form a plan."

Tomasina rose to her feet with a grin. She liked a person who didn't dillydally. "Lead the way."

The two walked the distance, and Tomasina gave her request to the teller. He dispatched a telegram runner. Taking a seat on a bench opposite the teller booth, the women waited. Each man who entered and exited the building tipped their hat and offered Pippa a polite smile. She answered each of them with a dignified nod in return. One of the men even made a show of dropping his handkerchief at her feet. The "accident" gave him a convenient excuse to compliment Pippa on her hat while completely ignoring Tomasina.

About the time she figured she'd lose her breakfast if she had to witness any more of the nauseating flirting, the runner returned with a folded piece of paper. The teller glanced at the number, cleared his throat and slid the folded square beneath the grate of the teller cage.

Tomasina unfolded the paper and gasped.

Pippa gazed over her shoulder and gasped, as well. "Oh, my! You don't need a job, Miss Stone. You need an accountant."

"I guess it added up over time," Tomasina said, a touch of awe in her voice. She'd never considered having that much money. Not all at once. The amount was downright obscene. "How did that happen?"

The reed-thin teller behind the counter adjusted his glasses. "Don't forget compound interest."

She couldn't imagine spending that much money in a lifetime. Then again, her needs had always been simple. Living in town probably came with a lot more expenses. Dressing as a girl didn't come cheap, either. That little beaded bag Pippa carried must have cost a fortune.

Pippa straightened her jaunty blue hat. "I think you should hold off on the job search and do a little shopping instead."

"I have to work." Tomasina stared at the enormous sum. "What do people do if they don't have a job?"

"Well, um, there's all the usual things a lady does. You can embroider."

"No way. No how."

"Many wealthy women volunteer for a charity. I believe Cowboy Creek has a thriving widows and orphans fund."

"I'm not suited for work with orphans." Coddling was

not her strong suit, and orphans probably needed a lot of coddling. "Or widows."

"What about the church?"

"What about it?"

"You could start a prayer group."

"I don't like spending too much time with God indoors. We're more comfortable with each other out in the open."

"If that's the case, you can grow a garden." Pippa hooked her arm through Tomasina's elbow. "You could always spend your time courting. A lady with an income is quite a catch. Especially for some of the fellows around here."

"Where would I grow a garden?" Tomasina scoffed. "And I sure don't want a fellow. I'd rather get a job."

Unbidden, an image of Will Canfield sprang into her head. She blinked him away. A fellow like that would marry someone like Pippa. Someone who didn't gag when men flirted with her. Someone who knew the purpose of all the fancy silverware at supper. She doubted Pippa had ever discovered a snake in her bedroll and eaten it for supper. Tomasina had once heard there was a special fork just for pickles. She doubted there was such a thing as a snake fork.

"You do realize," Pippa continued, "that you could purchase a house with this sum?"

"A house?"

"Yes, silly. There are oodles of houses for sale in Cowboy Creek. You could buy one with a large lot and take up gardening between your charity works."

A sudden panic seized Tomasina. A house was permanent. If she changed her clothes and found a job, she could always go back to droving if things didn't work out. Buying a house meant her life had changed forever. Growing a garden meant she was staying put for at least a season. She'd never once stayed in one place that long.

Tomasina vigorously shook her head. "No. I don't want a house. I'd rather have a job."

"Suit yourself." Pippa exhaled loudly. "Still, you'd best withdraw some money if you want new clothes. Trust me, being a girl doesn't come cheap."

"I kinda figured that."

With what seemed like an enormous sum of money stuffed safely in her pocket, she and Pippa set off for Booker & Son. Once inside, Pippa took charge. She grabbed several ready-made dresses from a display and plucked half a dozen hats from their perches.

Twenty agonizing minutes later Tomasina emerged from the dressing room. "I don't think this is going to work."

Pippa held her gloved hand in front of her mouth. "It's on backward, my dear." She giggled.

Tomasina glanced at the hooks she'd spent ten minutes wrestling closed. "Backward? But how are you supposed to wear something if it fastens in the back?"

"A woman's life is fraught with difficulties."

Tomasina stared at the scattering of fashion plates. "A cowboy would never design a shirt that buttoned up the back."

This was hopeless. *She* was hopeless. All the buttons and bows in the world couldn't cover who she was on the inside. She wasn't a lady, and she wasn't a drover anymore. Not in practice, at least. But she'd always be a drover in her heart.

Maybe that was the difficulty. A body couldn't move in two directions at once. Part of her found the idea of a fresh start intriguing while the other part of her wanted to turn back time. She wanted her pa back. She wanted her old life—her previously assured future.

"Trust me, Miss Stone." Pippa stood in front of her

and grasped the hat she'd balanced on her head. She set the feathered cap at a spirited angle and secured the brim with a hatpin. "Men have plenty of other problems. They simply hide them better."

Tomasina would rather face a rattlesnake than the dressing room once more.

Heaving a sigh, she reached for the buttons with a groan. "I'll try on another dress."

She'd spent her whole life proving people wrong. Becoming a girl was simply another endeavor. She'd never backed down from a challenge, and she wasn't starting now.

She couldn't wait to see Will's face the next time he saw her.

Chapter Eight

Will stared at the infant slumbering in his arms. He had a problem he could no longer ignore: Ava's mother had yet to make an appearance. He'd been certain she'd return by now.

The little thing was starting to grow on him. Once they'd established a proper eating and sleeping schedule, things had improved immeasurably. The addition of Hannah, the preacher's daughter, as a caretaker had removed much of the pressure from Mrs. Foster. The maids were no longer running amok, which meant Simon and the rest of the staff were content, as well.

Despite the success of their newfound routine, a nagging sense of worry remained. The more time passed without a single lead, the more his unease increased. The longer someone remained missing, the less likely they were to be found.

A soft rap interrupted his troubled thoughts, and he called entrance.

Mrs. Foster appeared with a basket of laundry.

Will smiled. "Just in time. I was running out of shirts."

"As to that." Mrs. Foster tsked. "You better take a look at these."

She tipped the basket, revealing a stack of soft pink shirts.

His smile disappeared. "Those can't be mine."

"They can and they are. Two days late and they're pink, as well." Mrs. Foster shook her head with another tsk. "I'd best talk with Mr. Lin. I can't believe he'd let this happen."

Holding the babe in his arms, Will struggled to his feet. "Don't bother. I'll take care of it. I want to stop by the boardinghouse and deliver Hannah's pay. I can take these shirts by the laundry on my way. I'll bring Simon along. He'll be overseeing more of the hotel accounts once my house is finished and I move out of the hotel."

Mrs. Foster set down the basket and propped one hand on her rounded hip. "And here I thought you'd be a permanent guest. I sure won't miss you pacing and working at all hours of the night."

"You'll miss me, don't lie."

"Maybe a touch." She held her thumb and forefinger a hairbreadth apart. "How much longer will we be enjoying your company?"

"Won't be long now. All the framing and the interior walls are finished. It's only a matter of weeks before I can move in."

"Surely that great monstrosity won't be finished in a few weeks' time?"

"Not finished, no. But livable." He adjusted Ava to his opposite arm. "I'd rather oversee the finish work in person."

She blew out a low whistle. "Seems a shame, one man living all alone in that great beast of a home. A house like that needs a wife to look out for the kitchens. Children running underfoot." She set about clearing the plates stacked on his side table. "Just because you had a bit of difficulty with that snooty Miss Dora don't mean you can't still find true love."

Her back turned, she tossed a speaking look over one shoulder.

"Enough, Mrs. Foster. I've already sent for twelve more mail-order brides. What more do you want of me?"

Holding the tray with two hands, the housekeeper backed out the door. "Marry one of them."

The door swung shut behind her.

Crossing to the window, he stared down at Eden Street. Of course he wanted a wife and children. The entire house had been designed for a large family. Having survived the war, he viewed each subsequent day he had on this earth as a gift sent straight from God. He'd been letting that gratitude slip of late.

Ava gurgled and cooed. Adjusting her blankets, he bounced her lightly in his arms. "Would you like some fresh air, Miss Ava? You and I have a mystery to solve. The mystery of the pink shirts." He stilled. "Actually we have two mysteries to solve, don't we? I'll find your mama. And if I don't, then I'll find you a good family."

In an astonishingly short amount of time, her future had become of paramount importance to him. "But first things first," he said solemnly. "I cannot be seen about town wearing this particular shade of rose."

Twenty minutes later Will approached the Chinese Laundry on First Street with Simon trailing a safe distance behind him.

"It's unnatural," the porter grumbled. "A man walking down the street with a baby. What will people say?"

Will rolled his eyes and let the space between them stretch. "Show some backbone, Simon."

He'd never realized what an oddity a man carrying a baby was in Cowboy Creek. Some people were charmed, others were incredulous and some were downright scandalized. Simon was simply mortified.

Pippa Neely approached him on the boardwalk from the opposite direction.

She glanced at the bundle in his arms and clapped. "Oh, my. Is this little Ava? I've heard so much about the mysterious abandoned baby of Cowboy Creek."

Extending one gloved hand, she caressed Ava's forehead and fussed over her smocked sleeping dress. "Why, she is just precious."

Simon elbowed closer. "Do you need any help, Mr. Canfield? Would you like me to carry the baby for a moment?"

"I can manage, young man." Will quirked an eyebrow. "Have you two been introduced?"

Pippa was the darling of the new intended brides. Of the four, she'd been the most popular. Leah had married right off, and Hannah and Prudence had showed little interest in any of the men in town. He'd never understand those two. Why travel all this way as a potential bride only to shun the chance at marriage?

After making the proper introductions, Will exchanged a few more pleasantries with Miss Neely.

Once she'd taken a few paces down the boardwalk, he turned toward Simon. "I thought a man carrying a baby was unnatural?"

"That was before I saw how much Miss Neely liked her. She's a right looker."

The petite woman was indeed striking. Lovely and effervescent, she attracted men like a lemonade stand on a hot summer's day. Will had caught more than one bachelor slicking back his hair and purchasing a posy of flowers from the corner vendor. However, despite her many suitors, Pippa hadn't settled on one fellow yet.

Trained as an actress, she was a touch too dramatic for

Will's tastes. He felt as though she was always on stage, always playing a part. He preferred someone more authentic, someone with brilliant red curls and expressive green eyes...

Once again the little firebrand held his thoughts hostage.

He'd missed her two days in a row. He'd wanted to check on her to ensure there were no bruises or raw nerves from her ordeal. If he didn't know better, he'd think she was avoiding him. Unlike the other women of his acquaintance, she monopolized his thoughts. He'd even caught himself lingering on the stairs, hoping to catch a glimpse of her. She'd probably sock him in the jaw if she knew. He grinned at the image.

Once outside the doors of the laundry, voices raised in anger grabbed his attention. He'd been using the laundry for years, and he'd never once heard the soft-spoken proprietor raise his voice. Concerned, he pushed his way inside.

Complete chaos reigned. The normally scrupulous laundry was littered with clothing in every hue of the rainbow. Steam billowed from the back room. An Oriental gentleman in a flowing black tunic he recognized as Mr. Lin shuffled through the door, gesturing with his hands.

A very familiar redhead followed close on his heels. For the first time since he'd met her, she was wearing a simple blue-calico dress. The unadorned style showed off her figure and highlighted her delicate stature. His heartbeat picked up rhythm. Her red curls had been piled atop her head. Several strands had escaped and clung damply to her forehead.

Chan Lin gestured toward the clothes and spoke rapidly in Mandarin.

Tomasina knotted her arms over her chest. "It's no use yelling at me. I don't know what you're saying."

The man heaved a sigh and pointed toward the door. "Out."

Will glanced between the two. That seemed clear enough.

Tomasina gasped. "Are you firing me? I haven't even worked two whole days yet."

The man pointed more forcefully. "Out!"

Mr. Lin pivoted and caught sight of Will. His expression instantly transformed. "Mr. Canfield. How nice to see you. What can I do for you today?"

Though heavily accented, his words were easily distinguishable.

"You *do* speak English!" Tomasina shouted. "All this time you've been muttering at me."

"I had nothing to say to you, Miss Stone." The older man hushed her. "So sorry, Mr. Canfield. It is very difficult to find good help these days."

"Don't I know it." Will admired Tomasina's trim figure. "New dress?"

She scowled and blew the hair from her forehead. "What's it to you?"

"Nothing." He gestured Simon forward. "Just making an observation."

She'd been appealing in dungarees, but seeing her in a dress left him speechless. Though simply designed, Tomasina's garment nipped in at her waist and accentuated the gentle swell of her figure. With her hair pulled back, the enticing nape of her neck drew him forward. He cast a wary glance in Simon's direction. If the boy sensed his infatuation, he'd never let Will live it down.

The young man tipped the basket forward.

"There is a reason for my visit." Will indicated his pink shirts. "I'm assuming I have you to thank for these."

"Yes." Sighing, Tomasina dropped her arms to her sides.

"Working as a laundress is much more difficult than it looks."

"I don't think washerwoman is your calling." It was for the best. This was no place for her. The work was too hot and too heavy. She'd be stooped and wrinkled in a fortnight. "You've been sacked."

"Thank you for pointing that out once more."

Her hair was glorious. At least the steam suited her curls. Mr. Lin reached for her arm, and she jerked away. Will growled deep in his throat. His thoughts took on a fierce possessiveness. He didn't like Mr. Lin touching her. He certainly didn't like the idea of her eking out a miserable existence in the stuffy back room of the laundry.

Sensing his distress without understanding the cause, Mr. Lin yanked the basket from Simon and grimaced. "I will fix for you."

"Excellent."

Will forcefully unclenched his teeth. The stress from the recent attacks on Cowboy Creek, not to mention the added danger of an outlaw recuperating in the jailhouse, had shortened his temper. Except none of that excused his sudden overprotectiveness. Tomasina evoked his tenderness and incited his ardor. His urge to safeguard her had become irrevocably linked to his need to care for her. He wanted to possess her thoughts as she'd possessed his.

Gathering his wayward feelings, he cleared his throat. "You've always done fine work, Mr. Lin. You won't lose my patronage." He faced the laundry's former employee. "Since you appear to be at a crossroads, why don't you accompany me? I'm delivering a check to the boardinghouse. The reverend's daughter has been looking out for Ava."

Rocking back and forth on her heels, Tomasina cast him a wary glance. "I suppose I've got nothing better to do."

"That's the spirit. Chin up."

"You're starting to annoy me."

He bit back a grin. "Only starting? I'll try harder."

"Please. No. I have an awful headache. I've been up since well before dawn."

The dark smudges beneath her eyes and the weary tone of her voice tugged at him.

"Return to the hotel and have a nap. Simon will bring you lunch in an hour."

"I'm fine. I can sleep in tomorrow. There's no reason for me to wake up early anymore, is there?" They stepped outside, and she reached for Ava. "Let me hold her. The past two days have been an absolute misery. I've got steam burns on both my arms, and I think my fingertips are permanently puckered. I could use a little sweetness in my life."

The porter touched the brim of his hat. "If you don't need me anymore, sir, I'll meet you back at the hotel."

"Actually, Simon, why don't you speak with Mr. Lin about the hotel's laundry needs for the next few weeks? We'll be full up for the town-founding celebration. Mr. Lin may need temporary help."

Tomasina rolled her eyes. "Good luck to those who apply."

Tugging on his lapels, Simon grinned. "Right away, sir."

She rested Ava on her shoulder and cupped the back of her tiny head. "I never knew there were so many rules to fabrics and colors and all that other whatnot. I've never had to separate my laundry before. I always just washed everything in one big pile."

"Yes." Will didn't bother hiding his amusement. "Pitfalls are hidden all around us."

He followed the boy's progress as he strutted into the laundry once more. "It's time Simon took on more responsibility."

"I'd say he has plenty." Her glance held a hint of accusation. "He's always at the hotel. Doesn't the boy ever go home?"

"He doesn't have a home." She stumbled over an uneven spot in the boardwalk, and he steadied her with a hand beneath her elbow. "The lad came around looking for work when the hotel opened. He's been my right-hand man ever since."

"What happened to his family? To his parents?"

They'd reached the corner, and she paused, staring up at him.

My, but she was beautiful in the sunlight. Holding the baby, she was a wild, untamed Madonna. He was gripped with an emotion so strong it was suffocating. Her eyes were questioning, and he grappled with his powerful reaction to her.

Since she carried the baby, it seemed the most natural thing in the world to let his hold linger on her elbow. "I don't know what happened to Simon's parents. He never offered an explanation, and I never asked."

"Aren't you even a little curious?"

"If Simon wants to confide in me, he's had plenty of opportunity. Beyond that, I don't pry."

Another skill he'd gleaned during the war. Oftentimes men chose silence for a reason.

Tomasina shook her head. "I suppose. Still, I'd have been curious."

Should he have pried? He wasn't the boy's father, after all. Simon appeared content with his lot. And yet he sometimes caught the lad staring at him with something akin to hero worship. He'd been uncomfortable with the attention, but perhaps he'd kept too much of a distance. Trying to keep Simon from working was like trying to hold back the Smokey Hill River with a slotted spoon. If speaking with the boy erased the gentle censure in Tomasina's eyes, he'd gladly try.

"For you," Will said with a wry twist of his lips, "I'll interrogate him until he begs for mercy."

"Simon is going to murder me in my sleep."

"He's not the murdering sort. He's more likely to salt your tea or burn your toast."

She rolled her eyes. "I'll keep that in mind."

They walked the next block in companionable silence, and he paused at the corner of Second and Eden Streets. The sun glistened off Tomasina's red hair and highlighted the smattering of freckles across her nose. The sounds of progress filled the air. He caught the crack of the blacksmith's hammer, the clip-clop of hooves as a carriage passed by, the click of heels on the boardwalk. Five years ago he had never laid eyes on this place, and now this was his home.

Tomasina tipped back her head. "What are you thinking about?"

"The past."

"On such a beautiful day as this, you should only think of the future. Remember what Thomas Jefferson once said. 'I like the dreams of the future better than the history of the past.'"

"Maybe you're right."

She shrugged. "Of course I'm right."

"And modest, too."

Not for the first time he noticed her smile was tinged with sadness. With grief, there was always a reckoning.

"Come along," she said. "I don't have all day."

He reached for the back of his brim and bumped his hat low on his forehead. "I was given to believe you had quite a bit of free time these days."

"You are no gentleman to remind me."

"You bring out the scoundrel in me."

A light sleeper, Tomasina woke to a disturbance. Hushed voices sounded in the corridor, and feet pattered by her door. She considered ignoring the commotion then discarded the idea just as quickly. She'd always had more than her fair share of curiosity. Awake now, she dressed quickly in the dark and tugged on her boots. She tiptoed down the stairs and discovered the lobby empty.

The noise sounded again. Muted laughter and the thump, thump, thump of a lively drumbeat.

The front desk was deserted, though a lamp remained lit. She stepped outside, and the faint music and laughter grew louder. The boardinghouse for men, Drover's Place, was located directly across First Street from the Cattleman Hotel. A crowd of people had gathered on the boardwalk in front of the building.

Tomasina crossed the distance. Lights shone from every window. Music from a crude band along with raucous talk and laughter spilled onto the boardwalk. It was clear the boys were having a real whopper.

She recognized the sheriff and one of his deputies, along with Daniel Gardner, Simon, Mr. Rumsford, the hotel manager, and, of course, Will. A disturbance near the hotel would not go unnoticed or unattended.

The sheriff scratched the stubble on his chin. He'd obviously dressed in a hurry. He'd forgone his coat, and one of his suspenders hung loose across his back. "I say we let 'em wear themselves out. If we go storming in there, we'll only cause more problems."

"What do you think?" Will asked the man to his right.

She recognized Daniel Gardner, the gentleman who owned the stockyards.

"Shut them down," Daniel said. "They're drunk. It's only a matter of time before someone starts a fight."

Will turned toward one of the deputies, caught sight of her lurking in the shadows and waved her forward. "Tomasina."

She scuttled from her hiding place. "I heard the noise."

The sheriff shot a glance at her and hastily stuffed his shirttail into his trousers. Though not as disheveled as the sheriff, Will had not donned his coat, either. He wore no tie, his sleeves were rolled up and the top few buttons of his shirt were undone. He didn't carry his cane, either.

Seeing him this way was oddly intimate. Without the armor of formality between them, he seemed much more accessible. Her surreptitious gaze was drawn to his corded forearms. She pressed a hand against the strange quivering sensation in the pit of her stomach. Why did the mere sight of him weaken her knees and turn her thoughts into jelly?

"They'll have the whole town awake before long." Will rested his hands on his lean hips. "They've been up for hours. How long before they wear themselves out?"

"They can go like this for days," Tomasina added helpfully. "Once those boys get started, they don't quit."

"I was afraid of that."

The sheriff had set a lantern at his feet, and the light cast long shadows across the men's faces.

Daniel peered up at the building. "What if we give them another hour or two before we bust up the party?"

Will caught Tomasina's gaze. "You know them best. What do you think? Shut down the fun or let them wear themselves out?"

She carefully considered her answer. "Wait them out. Those boys are like a box of dried tinder. Anything we add is fuel to the fire."

A crash sounded, interrupting Will's reply. Glass shattered, and shards rained down on the group. Something stung her arm. Suddenly knocked aside, she landed hard in the street. Pain blasted in her hip. Will sheltered her with his arms, his back to the commotion, surrounding her with his warmth. A wooden chair splintered inches from her head.

Springing upright, Will grasped her hands and pulled her up. "Get back to the hotel!"

Glass shattered once more, this time from the lower window. Two brawling men landed at her feet. Will shoved her behind him, protecting her yet again. Daniel and the sheriff each grabbed a drover by the scruff and yanked them apart.

Bracing a hand on Will's arm, she peered around him. The party had turned into a melee. Pairs of men exchanged punches. Whiskey bottles crashed, and the hollow thumps of fists against flesh filled the still night air.

The sheriff reached for his gun, and Tomasina froze. This was getting out of hand quickly. Someone was liable to wind up dead. She placed two fingers in her mouth and gave an ear-splitting whistle. A universal sign among drovers, the whistle halted the men in their tracks.

Daniel and the deputies used the distraction and waded between the fighting pairs. They pulled people apart, gradually restoring order.

Something dripped on her arm and she gasped. Will's shirt had darkened along his sleeve. "You've been hurt."

He clutched his arm. "It's nothing. I'll finish here and visit the doc."

"You'll go this instant."

Rubbing his knuckles, his expression grim, Daniel approached them. "Visit the doc, Will. We'll take care of the rest."

He hesitated another moment before nodding. "I'll wrap

it back at the hotel. You know where to find me if you need anything else."

Will took a limping step, and for the first time Tomasina recognized the extent of the injury to his leg. He obviously relied heavily on his walking stick.

She looped her arm around his waist. "I was wrong. I shouldn't have told you to wait out the boys."

The feel of his muscles beneath her fingers invoked a strange, prickly sensation.

He stiffened and moved away. "I hurt my arm. I can walk on my own."

"But your leg…"

She knew immediately she'd said the wrong thing.

He scowled, and a muscle ticked along his temple.

Simon arrived and stepped between them.

He handed Will his walking stick. "You left this in the lobby, sir."

Nausea pitched in her stomach. She'd been raised around men the whole of her life. A man didn't like appearing weak. Though she didn't view his injury as a disability, she doubted he wanted her opinion at that moment.

She cleared her throat and looked away. "I'll fetch the doctor. Might be more injuries. Not much I can do here, anyway." She paused, wanting to smooth out the moment. "Thank you for protecting me back there."

"I'll have to start charging you for the service soon."

"I'll keep a running tab."

Tomasina fetched the doctor, rousing him from his sleep. Accustomed to late-night calls, he was dressed and ready before she figured he'd even fully woken.

When she returned to the hotel, Will was sitting on a banquette while Simon clumsily wrapped a bandage around the cut.

She waved the young porter aside. "I'll finish."

Clearly grateful for being relieved of his duty, Simon scurried away. She took the seat beside Will and reached for his arm. He didn't protest.

"You remind me of my pa," Tomasina said softly. "I miss him."

Fatigue had weakened her defenses. She wanted to sleep beneath the stars with the clatter of cattle horns in the background. She missed the aroma of coffee brewing over the campfire. She wanted to wake up and know where she belonged.

"What was he like?" Will asked. "Your father?"

"He was stubborn." It was odd talking about her pa in the past tense—he was very much alive in her thoughts. She hadn't yet relegated him to history. "He was smart."

"Promise you'll tell me more about him one day." Will glanced at the clock. "When it's not three in the morning. Stories about your father deserve my full attention."

"I'd like that."

For the next few minutes she concentrated on staunching the bleeding and securing the bandages. With only the lamp on the front desk for light, she struggled with the task. When she finished, he smoothed his hand over the bandage.

The corner of his mouth tipped up in a weary smile. "Do you think we'll ever have an encounter that doesn't end in bloodshed?"

"Your peaceful town needed a little mayhem."

"When I decided to put Cowboy Creek on the map, this wasn't exactly what I had in mind," he said ruefully.

"The town may never recover."

Will pushed off from his knees and stood. "*I* may never recover."

She sighed. Just once she'd like to end an encounter between the two of them without someone bleeding. Maybe then he'd see her as a person separate from the rowdy drovers.

Then maybe he'd see her as a woman. She wanted him to look at her the way the men at the bank had gazed at Pippa Neely.

He reached for her hand. "I'll walk you to your room. We should make the distance in one piece even without an armed guard." A smile softened his words. "Try and stay out of trouble for the next few hours, okay? You'll be the death of me before long."

"You survived a war." Some dreams weren't meant to be. "Surely you can survive Texas Tom."

"Time will tell, Tomasina Stone. Time will tell."

Chapter Nine

In an effort to restore peace Will sought out Tomasina in the dining room the following morning. Since she tended to avoid him, he'd recruited Simon in the effort. The request had garnered him a speculative stare.

"Tomasina," he said, his voice suddenly too loud. "Ava and I are visiting Hannah at the boardinghouse. If you're not busy… If you wouldn't mind…could I interest you in a walk?"

Her fork stilled midair. "Uh, I suppose. Can I finish breakfast?"

"Certainly. I'll join you." He cleared his throat. "May I join you?"

"Take a seat."

He pinched the bridge of his nose. Always before he'd prided himself on his ability to maintain a cool head while those around him lost theirs. With Tomasina, his skill had deserted him. He shoved his hand through his hair. He sounded like an idiot.

The previous evening he'd done more than sound like an idiot. He'd looked like one. She'd seen him walk without his cane.

At the rodeo he'd been able to mask his disability. Last

night she'd seen the true nature of his injury. She'd offered to help him. And though her intentions were kind, it rankled the way she'd rushed to his side, acting as if he was a man who needed assistance crossing a room.

Will scowled. He refused to be treated as an invalid. If she considered him less of a man because of his injury, he'd accept the consequences. Living in ignorance of her judgment only exacerbated the problem. He'd chosen to assess the damage immediately.

Since their last few encounters had been stressful, he wanted a meeting on neutral ground. There was no possible way for this encounter to end in injury. Especially with Ava chaperoning.

Tomasina devoured her eggs and polished off his bacon. They'd almost drained their coffee when Mrs. Foster met them in the dining room with Ava.

The housekeeper handed over the bundle. "You need a pram. Booker & Son has a catalog."

"Excellent idea," Will said. "I'll order two."

Tomasina tilted her head. "Two?"

"A gift for Mrs. Gardner. A friend of mine who's expecting a child."

He cradled Ava against his chest and held his cane in the opposite hand. As they set off for the boardinghouse, he glanced at Tomasina askance. She didn't offer to take the baby or spread her arms as though waiting to catch him if he stumbled. An excellent sign.

She wore her usual placket-pocket shirt and dungarees, her hat fastened beneath her chin.

He inhaled the fresh spring air and admired the recently graded street. All signs of the most recent cattle drive had been cleared away.

Will quirked an eyebrow. "No guns this morning?"

"Ava will protect us." Tomasina grasped the boardwalk

pillar he'd hidden behind when the cattle had spooked and swung around. "Who is Hannah? You said we were taking Ava to visit her."

"Hannah Taggart arrived on the first bride train. There were four ladies in all. Leah Gardner married Daniel. Prudence works at the newspaper. And Hannah came with her father, the preacher. She chose to stay at the boardinghouse rather than move to the vicarage." He tucked the blanket beneath Ava's chin then said, "She's offered to watch the baby today. She usually watches Ava at the hotel, but she sent a note saying she's catching up on her sewing. Apparently, she'd rather watch Ava at the boardinghouse where her supplies are handy."

"What brave ladies. That must have taken a lot of courage to come to Cowboy Creek."

He lifted a brow and gave her a droll look. "I didn't expect that reaction from you. I thought you valued independence, Miss Stone."

"I value survival, Mr. Canfield." Tomasina playfully skirted around the glass front window of the hotel. "We've done well so far. No stampedes. No falling glass. No charging bulls. I think we've broken our plague of trouble."

"I'm cautiously optimistic."

The day was perfect for a stroll along the boardwalk. Wispy clouds stretched across the sky, and sunlight danced off the hills in the distance. Horace and Gus were in their usual spot, sitting on a bench in front of Booker & Son, their constant prattle littered with town gossip.

Will paused before them and made the introductions.

Old Horace peered around him. "It's been awfully quiet at the jail."

"Don't worry," Will said. "We've hired plenty of extra security."

"We'll keep an eye out, as well. If we see any of them Murdochs, we'll send up the alarm."

"I'm sure Quincy appreciates your vigilance."

Old Horace elbowed Gus. "I think Zeb is faking. He's not as sick as we think. He don't want nobody thinking he can talk."

"Either way, we'll keep an eye on him."

As they continued on, Tomasina glanced over her shoulder. "What a pair. I bet they know the comings and goings of everyone in town."

"The town wouldn't be the same without them."

He cast her a glance out of the corner of his eye. "You were right about our string of bad occurrences. We've gone three whole blocks and nothing has happened. Not a single runaway bull or inebriated drover. I think we might survive this day without even a flesh wound."

"Speaking of flesh wounds, how is your arm?"

"Sore," he said, grimacing slightly. "I let Simon change the bandages today."

"I'm sure you were very brave through your ordeal."

"He's better suited as a porter than a doctor."

Tomasina held out her arms. "Let me carry her for a spell. We'll look like a proper family."

He passed the baby over then casually slipped his free hand into his pocket. "You promised to tell me stories about your father."

"Not yet. The memories are too choppy. If I wade in too soon, I'll drown in them."

"Then we'll wait for calmer winds."

She smiled at him over the baby's head. "Storms never last forever. Aren't the preachers always telling us that 'this too shall pass'?"

Tomasina was a natural with the infant. She'd probably consider those maternal qualities as a weakness, but he considered her caring a strength. If a perfect stranger could become attached to the child, what had happened to her mother? The question raised his concerns for the child's future once more. He'd been putting off the inevitable, but the time was fast approaching to make a decision about her future.

"Are you brooding about the past again?" Tomasina asked. "You've got that wrinkle between your eyes again."

He rubbed the spot with his finger. "I wasn't aware I was frowning."

"Not frowning so much. You have a way of looking focused sometimes."

Will supposed there was no harm in sharing his growing concerns. "The more time passes without word from Ava's mother, the less likely she is to return for her daughter."

"Is that very important? Having her return?" Tomasina covered Ava's tiny ears. "I mean, if her mama doesn't want her, maybe that's not the best place for her."

"You're right, of course. Except I can't shake a feeling. A feeling that her mother should be with her."

"Feeling or not, there's only so much you can do if she doesn't make an appearance."

They'd arrived at the neat clapboard building. It wasn't a fancy structure but was two stories with an abundance of windows and two sets of stairs, one leading to a balcony that covered the front of the whole upstairs and a set on the side leading to a second floor entrance. The building was freshly painted, and someone had planted fledgling rose bushes on either side of the entrance.

Aunt Mae ushered them into the parlor, and they waited another fifteen minutes. As he checked his watch for the second time, Hannah Taggart appeared in the entry. Her cheeks were slightly flushed, and her fawn-colored hair was pulled back from her face. Though not as flamboyantly beautiful as Pippa, she shouldn't have any trouble finding a husband.

Yet as far as he could tell, she seldom left the boardinghouse. He rarely saw her except when she cared for Ava, and he certainly hadn't seen her out with any of the gentlemen in Cowboy Creek. Though he respected her right to make her own choices, the ladies had come here seeking husbands. He'd expected more of an effort.

Hannah smoothed her hair and brushed at her skirts. "You're early. I wasn't expecting you."

Actually they were right on time. Come to think of it, this wasn't the first time the young woman had gotten the time wrong. "I sent you a note. I thought we agreed on eight thirty?"

Two dots of color appeared on her cheeks. "I must have written down the time wrong."

"If you're busy, I can have Mrs. Foster watch Ava instead. I'm sure she won't mind. The hotel doesn't have many guests this week."

"No, no. I'm ready now." Ava fussed, and the preacher's daughter took her from Tomasina. The child quieted immediately. "Sorry to make you wait."

"Not at all," he assured her. "Ava has taken a shine to Miss Stone."

Hannah blanched. "Really? That's, um, that's wonderful."

"She's a baby." Tomasina rolled her eyes. "She wants to be fed and loved. I'm no one special to her."

"You're the favorite, Hannah," Will assured her. The girl appeared nervous and out of sorts. Did she think her job was in jeopardy? "Ava favors you most."

A broad smile spread across Hannah's face. "She is an absolute darling. I'm pleased I can help."

There was something different about Hannah today. Will looked between the two women, searching for the source of the change. Perhaps it was Hannah's style of dress. She tended to favor layers of ruffles and voluminous flounces.

Maybe because they'd caught her unaware, today she wore a simple calico shirtwaist with little adornment. While he wasn't exactly an aficionado of fashion, he appreciated the less fussy look.

Hannah was an accomplished seamstress and had tentatively indicated she wanted to open a dress shop in town. At the time he'd been somewhat reluctant to encourage her in the endeavor. He kept picturing the women of Cowboy Creek traipsing around town like walking Christmas trees and stacks of animated doilies.

Yet she'd made Leah's wedding dress and tailored Leah's other dresses for her increasing figure. There was obviously more talent in Miss Taggart than he'd given her credit for at first blush. If she wanted to open a dress shop, he'd speak with Leah to ensure she was satisfied with the work before investing. Either way, he made a mental note to pursue the issue.

"Have you ladies had the pleasure of meeting?" he asked. "Hannah, this is Tomasina Stone. Miss Stone, this is Hannah Taggart."

The two women exchanged a greeting. "We saw each other at the mercantile the other day," Tomasina said. "While I was purchasing more clothing."

"Hannah is considering opening a dress shop," he offered.

"I sure hope she does," Tomasina chimed in. "There's not much of a selection here in town."

The baby fussed and Hannah cooed softly. "Cowboy Creek needs a dress shop. And a milliner, as well."

Will reached for his pocket watch, flipped open the lid and checked the time once more. "Let's speak about your shop when you drop off Ava this evening. I might be able to help you."

"I'd like that. Also, I had a favor to ask." Hannah tugged her lower lip between her teeth. "The other ladies have mentioned the noise when Ava fusses. The walls are like paper here. I wondered if I could bring my sewing supplies to the hotel?"

"I have a better plan." He didn't know why he hadn't thought of such an obvious solution before. "Why don't I arrange a room at the hotel? You can stay there. Just until we find a new home for Ava."

"That arrangement would be lovely." Hannah's face lit up then darkened once more. "I don't know if my father would approve."

"How come you aren't living with your pa now?" Tomasina asked, crossing her arms. "He's the reverend, isn't he? Why stay at the boardinghouse? That parsonage looks big enough for the both of you."

Though bluntly stated, Will was curious about the answer himself.

The shy woman absently pleated the folds of Ava's blanket between her fingers. "My dad will have to get used to me being gone eventually. I came as one of the brides."

"You picked a fellow yet?" Tomasina asked.

Will made a strangled noise. "Miss Stone. That's private."

Although, truth be told, he was just as curious about that answer, too. As a gentleman, he was bound to respect her privacy.

"I'm not badgering her," Tomasina declared. "I'm just asking a question."

"It's all right," Hannah replied softly. "I haven't found a fellow yet."

The way her eyes grew misty snagged Will's attention. There was a hint of unrequited love in that longing gaze. Had she fallen for someone who didn't return her attention? He couldn't think of who that might be. Daniel was the only gentleman who'd taken a bride thus far. Will didn't see how Hannah could develop feelings for a man she'd only met once or twice. That was a stretch by any standards.

That led to another obvious question. Was there a gentleman in her past? Was she pining over a lost love? Although how she'd managed to conduct an affair of the heart beneath Reverend Taggart's watchful eye was beyond him. Either way, there was something telling about that wistful look in her eye. He shoved a hand through his hair and sighed. Of late he'd realized that women were creatures beyond his understanding.

When he found the time to question Leah about Hannah's skills as a seamstress, he'd ask if she had any insight into the younger woman's romantic life. He wasn't above dropping a few hints in the right direction if need be.

None of which solved his most pressing issue. "Why don't I speak with your father? I can assure him of the propriety."

Tomasina planted her hands on her hips. "Why don't you stay with me? There's no place safer. This fellow over here says I can keep my guns. Any fella gets out of hand, we'll shoot him. Your pa can't argue with you on that account."

"I'll, uh, I'll ask him. I'm not sure what he'll say."

"Well, I guess we won't know until we ask, will we?"

"Don't browbeat the poor girl," Will admonished. "Hannah, if you'd like to stay with Tomasina at the hotel for a couple of weeks and help out with Ava, I'd be eternally grateful. If your father doesn't agree, we'll find another solution."

"Ava and I get on well together, and I like having something to do all day." Hannah nuzzled the top of Ava's head. "Until I have my own dress shop, that is." Ava groped at her chin with an open mouth. "As long as my father knows I'm well chaperoned, I'm sure he'll see the value of such a plan."

"Who knows," Will said. "Little Ava's parents may come for her tonight, and this whole conversation will be for naught."

Hannah's expression turned guarded. "Perhaps."

"Either way, why don't you think about what you'll need for your dress shop? There are several empty buildings at your disposal. If Cowboy Creek needs a new seamstress, we'll give the town one."

"Th-thank you."

"By the way, the town business leaders are holding a dance this Friday evening to celebrate the town's founding." And to give the prospective brides a chance to meet more eligible bachelors. An opportunity Hannah sorely needed. "Everyone is invited. I hope to see you and the reverend at the event."

"I'll let him know." She smiled shyly. "He's eager to meet more people."

"The event is formal. If you don't have anything suitable to wear, I can make arrangements at Booker & Son. I owe you a great deal for your help with Ava."

"No need, though I thank you kindly for the offer. I have the perfect dress for the occasion. It's one of my own designs."

Excellent. Another chance to see if she was the right

choice for seamstress of Cowboy Creek. There was no use opening a shop if no one patronized the business.

After a few more pleasantries, Will and Tomasina set off for the hotel once more.

She bumped his shoulder with her own. "You still have that worried look."

"I'm not worried, I'm formulating a plan."

"Huh. Because it looks like you're worried when you're formulating a plan."

He was used to trusting his instincts, and they'd been wrong this time. "Ava is a loose end. I don't like loose ends. If we don't hear from her mother in another week, I'll have to speak with the circuit judge about putting her up for adoption."

"You ever think of keeping her yourself? Someone left her with you. Maybe you're supposed to keep her."

Will stepped wrong and grimaced. He'd been leaning more heavily than usual on his walking stick. His leg was stiffer than normal from his fall. Tomasina wasn't slowing her pace for him. A good sign.

"Ava deserves loving parents," he said. "If she stayed with me, she'd spend her life with a succession of nannies. That's no life for a child. Trust me, I know."

Tomasina canted her head. "How's that?"

"Back before the war, that's how things were done among our set. The men worked long hours and the women hired help for the children. I suppose that was a sign of prosperity, having hired help. The parks were filled with nannies and prams."

"Wasn't that lonely?"

"No." He glanced down at her. "Don't paint me as a tragic figure. I can assure you, my parents adored me. My upbringing aside, Ava needs two parents."

Despite his reassurance, he didn't relish the idea of putting this sweet little girl up for adoption, but he wasn't certain what else he could do. Ava couldn't stay with him indefinitely. She deserved a proper family. A mother and a father. Even the chance at siblings. Except something held him back each time he considered approaching the circuit judge. An uneasy feeling he couldn't shake.

Tomasina's laughter drew him from his reverie.

"I'm sorry, I can't concentrate anymore." She smothered a giggle. "I'm having a hard time picturing you with a bonnet tied beneath your chin."

"Then don't." She wasn't the least bit cowed by his fierce expression. "Whatever happens, I'll see that she's well cared for."

Tomasina scuffed at the ground. "I know."

They'd reached the ornate brass double doors of the Cattleman Hotel, and Will paused. "If you need another job, I'm sure I could find something for you at the hotel."

She stuck her hands into her back pockets. "No fooling?"

"Nope."

And now he had two bad feelings.

Hiring Tomasina Stone was either an inspired idea or a terrible mistake. She'd occupied far too many of his thoughts lately. He'd noticed a gradual shift in the routine of his day. He sought her out on the flimsiest of excuses. This morning's walk was only one example. He simply enjoyed hearing her laugh or watching her lovely, expressive face when he goaded her. Her happiness had become vitally important to him. Except he knew what she wanted—she wanted out of Cowboy Creek.

He wasn't ready to make her *that* happy. "Then you accept my offer?"

"I do."

"Magnanimous of you." He was living on borrowed

time with her. Sooner or later she'd leave. She was a drover at heart. He'd simply enjoy the time they had. "Try not to kill any of the guests."

"I'm not making any promises."

Tomasina stared at Mrs. Foster. "Are you joking? Please tell me you're joking."

Mrs. Foster pinched her lips together as though gathering herself before she spoke. "I can assure you this is a very serious matter. Mr. Finley's room must be cleaned."

"But he's disgusting." Tomasina pinched her nose against the putrid stench. "Have you looked in there? What kind of person lives like that?"

"Mr. Finley lives like that, as you've taken great pains to specify. And it is your job to clean up after Mr. Finley. That is the job Mr. Canfield hired you to do."

Tomasina grimaced. Did Will have something against her? Work as a maid was difficult and thankless. Was this job punishment for defying his mandate about the rodeo? This must be a veiled reprimand of some sort. There was no other reasonable explanation.

She snuck a peak at the mess once more and reared back. "Is this the usual type of cleanup?"

"Mr. Finley is perhaps more extreme than most of our guests. He also pays his bill on time and doesn't cause a ruckus. Because of that, Mr. Rumsford allows a certain degree of leniency."

"Mr. Rumsford should get a whiff of this odor the next time he decides to be lenient."

"Be that as it may, Mr. Finley is a guest, and we are required to straighten his room and change his linens."

"If you say so."

"I do say so. If you'll excuse me, I have my own work to do."

Tomasina wrinkled her nose and entered the room. She was used to cleaning up after animals, but picking up after human folks was an entirely different story. At least animals were predictable in their messes. She plucked a coffee cup from the side table and grimaced at the contents. She'd never seen coffee turn furry before.

A half an hour later she'd straightened Mr. Finley's room and started on the next. After seeing how people lived behind closed doors, she'd developed some personal judgments about the folks living in the hotel. A lot of them could use some basic instruction on hygiene and organization. Even living on the trail for the better part of her life, she'd had some standards. Standards a few more folks residing here should embrace.

A miniature bed frame and wardrobe sat in the corner. Furniture samples. She should have known this guest was a traveling salesman. No self-respecting cowboy would be caught dead wearing the shade of burgundy coloring the trousers draped over the bed frame.

She stripped the linens and her toe bumped something beneath the bed. Kneeling, she raised the dust ruffle. Gracious, the man even had dirty dishes beneath the bed. They'd have all manner of vermin in here before long.

Crouching lower, she stretched out her hand and reached for the plate.

A sharp smack landed on her bottom.

Tomasina yelped and started, cracking her head on the bed frame. Heart pounding, she scooted out and whipped around.

A man sporting a dandified three-piece suit and a horseshoe of fluffy gray hair stared down at her. He was as round as he was tall, with the shape of an enormous egg.

The man leered at her. "Don't forget the fresh water,

love. The last maid was always forgetting my fresh towels, as well."

Tomasina rubbed her backside and glared. "You lay a hand on me again, and I'll wrap that towel around your neck and squeeze."

The lecherous grin widened. "You're a feisty one, aren't you?" Rubbing his hands together, the man took a menacing step forward. "You know what I like to do with feisty little morsels like you? I like to teach them a lesson."

Narrowing her gaze, she focused her attention on the man. He had at least two hundred pounds on her. She'd have to use her wits against his brawn.

Groping behind her, she reached for the lamp on the side table. "Oh, yeah? I'd like to see you try."

Chapter Ten

Will heard the commotion all the way on the third floor. He set aside the sheriff's report and stood. Stretching his back, he considered the news the sheriff had provided. The Cowboy Café had been robbed. *The Cowboy Café*. What sort of outlaws robbed an eatery? The Murdoch Gang was desperate if they were stealing slices of pie.

He swung open the door and discovered Simon dashing toward the stairs.

"What's going on?" Will asked.

Without pausing, the porter called over his shoulder, "Trouble with one of the guests. Don't worry, Mrs. Foster and Mr. Rumsford have been fetched."

"Then why are you needed?"

"I'm not needed. I just don't want to hear about this secondhand."

"A little decorum, please. This is a hotel, not a sideshow."

Since he'd finished his ledgers already, Will reached for his coat and walking stick and followed the sounds of excited chattering. He turned the corner of the second-floor landing and halted.

Rubbing his forehead, he studied the strange scene. A

rather overweight patron was flat on his back in the center of the corridor. He'd been trussed up like a calf, his hands and feet tied to each other and strung together in the middle. The hotel staff had formed a crescent around the odd sight.

Mrs. Foster knelt beside the man and struggled with the ropes. "Be still, sir. You're making the knots tighter."

Will frantically searched for the obvious culprit. Tomasina stood with her arms crossed and one shoulder propped against the wall. She didn't appear any worse for wear, and the air whooshed from his lungs.

"I wouldn't get too close to that one, Mrs. Foster," Tomasina said. "He's got busy fingers."

In his weekly report Mr. Rumsford had indicated several complaints lodged against Mr. Daniels. Will's annoyance flared. Though he didn't know the guest personally, he recognized the traveling salesman by reputation.

"This is outrageous!" The man tipped back his head and caught sight of Will. "Help me! This woman tried to kill me."

Pushing off from the wall, Tomasina planted her hands on her hips and glared down at the man. "You'd know if I was trying to kill you because you'd be dead. I was teaching you a lesson. You seem big on lessons, fellow. You remember promising to teach me one? I was returning the favor, is all."

Though shaken, the man appeared uninjured. His pride was more wounded than his physical person. And who could blame him? The gathering crowd of hotel workers and guests didn't help the situation. The salesman deserved a little humiliation, but there was no benefit in letting the situation spiral out of control.

Will braced both hands on his cane and widened his stance. "What exactly happened here, Mr. Daniels?"

"This woman trussed me up for no reason."

Tomasina inhaled sharply, and Will silenced her with an almost-imperceptible shake of his head. Let the man dig his own hole. "Are you telling me this wee maid overtook a man of your size and stature all alone? You must have two hundred pounds on her. How did she manage? Did she have an accomplice, perhaps?"

"She caught me by surprise, she did."

Will turned toward Tomasina and hoisted an eyebrow. "I assume there's a reasonable explanation for this."

"I'd rather tell you in private."

He waved her nearer. She leaned forward and whispered her explanation in his ear. With each subsequent word, his wrath grew.

"Mr. Daniels," Will declared, "I believe it's time for you to check out of this establishment. The Cattleman Hotel is no longer interested in your business."

Mrs. Foster, who appeared no closer to unraveling the knots, heaved a sigh. "It's about time."

Will reached into his pocket for the collapsible knife he'd carried since his days in the army and stepped toward the prone man. "You're going to slink quietly back into your room, pack your belongings and check out of the hotel. If you cause another ruckus, I will tie you up myself and dump you at the edge of town. Do we have an understanding?"

Despite his predicament, the man remained unrepentant. "I'm reporting the lot of you to the sheriff."

"That's a superb idea." Will snapped his fingers. "Simon, fetch Sheriff Davis. While you're out, run by the newspaper offices and summon D.B. Burrows. He can write up a story for the morning edition. I'll request a front-page article. If you don't mind waiting, I'll even have the photographer, John Cleve, set up his equipment. A photo for your scrapbook."

The man scowled. "That's blackmail. I won't have my name dragged through the mud."

Will neatly sliced through the ropes. "One more word and I'll drag more than your name."

Mr. Daniels sprang upright with surprising agility for a man of his size and girth. He rubbed his wrists and glared. "This is an outrage. My superiors at Baker Furniture will get a full accounting of this incident."

Will ignored the furious muttering and faced the crowd of cooks and bellhops. "The show is over. Everyone back to work."

When a certain trouble-making redhead turned away as well, Will caught her arm. "Except for you and Simon."

Mr. Daniels slammed the door behind him with a last furious curse.

Will bade Simon keep an eye on the man. "Make sure you escort him out of the hotel. I'll contact Sheriff Davis and see that Mr. Daniels leaves town on the first train. In the future, let's be more discerning of our guests. There's no reason the maids have to put up with this nonsense."

Simon touched his cap. "Will do, boss."

The mere idea of someone laying a hand on Tomasina filled Will with rage. While he admired her actions, he wasn't leaving her vulnerable again. She'd been here less than a week, and the woman was giving him gray hairs. She was a magnet for trouble. There weren't enough guns in the county to keep her from disaster.

Tomasina sidled toward the stairs.

"I'd like a word with you, Miss Stone."

"Don't go blaming me for what happened back there," she seethed. "That fellow had it coming."

He propped his walking stick against the wall and

limped the distance. "Your actions with Mr. Daniels were warranted, and I rather admire your restraint. I don't believe he realizes how much worse things might have gone for him."

"He has no idea."

"It's clear this position isn't a good fit." He rubbed his forehead with a thumb and forefinger. "You might be more suited for kitchen work."

Something behind the scenes where she didn't cross paths with lecherous guests. The hotel was better than the laundry. There'd be no more pink shirts. There'd be no more cleaning guest rooms. He'd find a nice, peaceful solution to her employment dilemma.

She swallowed. "Kitchen work?"

"I don't think housekeeping suits you."

"Agreed."

"Don't forget, the staff has Friday off for a dance celebrating the town's founding." He searched her animated face, drawn toward the smudge of dirt on her nose. "I trust you're attending?"

"I don't dance, but Hannah is looking forward to attending."

"I'm glad the two of you are getting along well."

"Like a house on fire."

She had one foot propped on the stairs as though she might flee at any moment. He placed a hand on the door frame and leaned forward. The enchanting smattering of freckles beckoned him, and he touched her nose.

"You have a smudge."

Her gaze dropped to his mouth. "Oh."

The air between them crackled. She had only to duck under his arm and slip away. She didn't move.

This was madness, and yet he couldn't resist dropping a chaste kiss on her forehead. He immediately liked the feel of her warm skin beneath his lips but forced himself to pull away.

"Stay out of trouble," he said, his voice thick.

With a swish of her skirts she was gone, leaving his heart clattering against his ribs. He'd only been near her for a moment, and yet he could map each and every freckle on her delightful, troublemaking nose.

Straightening his lapels, he turned away from the stairs. Kitchen work better suit her, because he was running out of other options. Having her near meant more to him than he cared to admit to himself.

The little firebrand was burrowing her way into his affections, and she didn't fit his plans any more than he fit into her future. As much as he admired her pluck and those luminous green eyes, they weren't suited for one another. She'd never stay put. She'd never settle for the staid life of a politician's wife. She'd wither beneath the restrictions. She was a wild thing, that one. His chest burned with the truth.

Wild things weren't meant to be tamed.

Fifteen minutes later Tomasina dumped her load of linens in the rolling hamper, glanced up and realized the next room on her list belonged to her and Hannah. In deference to her new roommate, Tomasina knocked softly. The living arrangement had been working out well enough thus far. She'd never had much privacy beyond the basics in her life. Hannah, on the other hand, put great stock in her time alone.

The only child of a preacher was probably used to being alone. Since Tomasina didn't spend much time in her room anyway, after a few missteps, they'd become accustomed to one another.

Hannah had also been watching more and more of Ava recently. Because Will's office was also located in his suite, he'd moved them to a larger room with an adjoining parlor that they'd turned into a nursery. Only one lingering concern nagged at her.

Having watched her in close quarters, Tomasina had begun to worry that Hannah was growing too attached to the baby. Will's self-imposed timeline was about to lapse, which meant placing the child with a permanent family in the very near future. When that happened, Tomasina feared Hannah's reaction.

The door opened, and Hannah waved her inside. "I've got Ava this afternoon, but she's not sleeping. There's no need to be quiet."

"Thank goodness."

Tomasina entered the room and flopped on the bed. Ava was lying on her back on a blanket spread over the floor, cooing and clasping her hands. Hannah brushed her skirts aside and knelt beside the baby.

"You going to the dance?" Tomasina asked.

"I don't think so. Someone has to stay and watch Ava."

"Mrs. Foster already volunteered. She said she's far too old for dances and she can't stay up past nine anymore. She also said..." Tomasina assumed a falsetto voice. "'The band plays far too many reels. It's not dignified, a lady of my age, hopping about.'"

Hannah giggled and smoothed her hair from her face. "Do you think the drovers are invited?"

"Pretty girls and free food? They'll show." Tomasina linked her fingers behind her head. "Any particular drover you were hoping to see?"

Hannah blushed. "No. Of course not. I just wondered."

"You're one of the prospective brides. Makes sense you'd want to check out all the possibilities. I've seen you turn down two of the fellows from town already. I just thought maybe you had someone particular in mind."

Tomasina paused. "Why do you want to get married anyway?"

"I don't want to stay in my father's house forever. I want my own home. My own things. I want my own family."

Rubbing her chin, Tomasina considered her new roommate. "I guess that makes sense."

She'd always considered her and her father a team. She'd never much thought of them as a family. Her and James and her pa. Now that the team had parted ways, she realized how much she'd taken for granted. They *had* been a family. Maybe not in the traditional sense, but they'd cobbled together a reasonable imitation.

Somehow she'd thought they'd go on the same indefinitely. She'd never much considered the future. How naive she'd been. Things couldn't stay the same forever, yet she'd given no thought to what she'd do if her life changed.

Tomasina raised her head. "At least you have a skill. You can sew. A lady who can take care of herself doesn't need a fellow."

"There're other reasons to have a fellow. Love. Companionship. Children."

Will would be a wonderful father. He was patient and kind. He wasn't afraid to be vulnerable. He was different from her pa in that regard. Her father had loved her, but he'd preferred her once she was able to care for herself. He'd never had much use for helpless things.

"I'd rather be you." Hannah braced her hands behind her and leaned back. "You're independent. You can do whatever you want. Fall in love with whomever you want."

Tomasina narrowed her gaze. "What are you getting at?"

"What if you fell in love with the wrong man? What would your father have done?"

"Probably shot him."

"Oh, my."

"Not to kill, of course. Just to maim. Pa was a good shot." Tomasina stared at the ceiling. "What about your pa?"

"I don't know. It's never come up." She sighed. "You're right. At least I have my sewing."

For a woman who wanted a family, she didn't appear interested in a suitor. The two things Hannah seemed to enjoy were Ava and sewing. When not busy with Ava, the woman sewed fiendishly. She spent much of her time with a measuring tape slung around her neck and a needle in her hand. While Tomasina didn't know much about women's fashion in general, she preferred Pippa's style to Hannah's. Though flamboyant, Pippa's mode of dress was far less fussy than Hannah's flounces and ruffles.

Then again, Hannah hadn't been wearing those awful dresses much lately.

"Say," Tomasina began, "how about we go to Booker & Son to see if they have anything fancy I can wear to that party? Maybe you could buy some fabric or ribbons, as well."

"About that…" Hannah stood and approached the wardrobe. "I have an idea."

While Tomasina's belongings remained in a knapsack under her bed, Hannah had filled the wardrobe to overflowing with her dresses.

Hannah riffled through the ruffles and bows. "I've been reworking some of my old dresses. Now that we're out West, I've discovered my fashion is woefully overdone."

You could say that again. "I hadn't noticed."

"Anyway, I pored over all the fashion plates in Booker & Son and drew up some of my own sketches. I had plenty of fabric in my old gowns to rework the designs. And, well, since I haven't been taking care of my father and Ava naps most of the day, I've had a lot more time on my hands. What do you think of this?"

Tomasina gasped. Pushing up with her elbows locked behind her, she leaned forward. Entranced by the dress, she swung her legs off the bed and gingerly touched the silky fabric.

The design was elegant and simple. The fabric was satin in a shade the color of new spring grass. The design featured a scooped neck with cap sleeves and a modest bell skirt. Hannah had decorated the neckline with an embroidered ivory-silk ruffle. She'd created a matching embroidered silk overlay for the skirt with scalloped edges in the same fabric.

"Why, this is absolutely beautiful, Hannah." The young woman had real talent. Tomasina admired the elaborate craftsmanship of the stitching. "You did this all by yourself?"

"Yes. I learned from my mother." She took Tomasina's hand. "I thought…well, I thought that if some of the ladies in town wore my dresses, it would be an advertisement. Once Mr. Canfield realizes how many orders I can arrange, he might consider investing in my shop."

"You wouldn't have to talk anyone into wearing something this beautiful."

"I designed this one for you. I was hoping you'd wear it to the dance."

"I couldn't." Tomasina reverently touched the gossamer fabric. "It's too pretty."

"But you have to! It's the exact color of your eyes. I knew the minute I saw you that this dress would be perfect."

Dropping her arms to her sides, Tomasina backed away. "I'll look silly all decked out in something that fancy."

"You won't. We'll have Pippa fix your hair." Hannah moved behind her and grabbed the mass of red curls, piling them atop her head, then angled her toward the mirror. "Look how pretty that is. With a few strands hanging down to frame your face, you'll be the belle of the ball."

Tomasina held the dress in front of her and examined her reflection. "Forget about convincing Mr. Canfield. I'll be your first investor."

With a shake of her head, Hannah let the red curls tumble free. "Opening a shop is quite expensive. I need fabric and another sewing machine. Not to mention trims, beading and buttons. I couldn't ask that of you."

"Don't worry about me. I have a lot of money. More than I can spend on myself."

"Then why are you working as a maid?"

"What else would I do? Sit around and twiddle my thumbs?" Tomasina opened the wardrobe door wider. Her work as a maid was finished after today anyway. She doubted she'd have much success in the kitchens, though she'd give the opportunity a try. There was no use sitting around bored. "How many more of those dresses do you have? You know, like that one. Not like the other, uh, fluffy ones with all the bows and stuff."

"I've reworked this one and started on another."

"If you and me and Pippa each wear one, that'd be a good start." Tomasina rubbed her chin. "If Daniel Gardner's wife wore one as well, we'd have you swimming in orders in no time."

"I know Leah would help." Hannah tugged her lower lip between her teeth. "I made her wedding dress, and she seemed quite pleased with that gown. I've also been letting out her other dresses."

The news kept getting better and better. "Leah is married to one of the town founders. We'll convince her that it's important for Cowboy Creek to support a local business. Especially if that business is owned and operated by women." Tomasina glanced at the clock and shot to her feet. "I have to get back to work. The dance is less than a week away. You make up a list of what you need, and we'll get started right away. I'll talk with Pippa and you speak with Leah."

Distracted by her new project, Tomasina practically skipped to her next room. That's what she'd been missing in her life since arriving in town. She'd been missing a goal. Normally by now she and Pa would be traveling back to Texas or taking on work with another outfit. Until now she hadn't realized how much of her future had depended on her pa and where he chose to work next.

She paused at a smudged mirror and grasped the rag she'd tucked into her sleeve. Absently wiping the surface, she considered her life until this point. Everything she knew about herself was a lie. She wasn't independent. She'd never been respected. The men had shown her deference because of her pa. She wasn't a free spirit; she was a camp follower. Her entire upbringing had been dependent on her father's whims.

Even the money tethered her to her pa, to the past. He'd saved that money because he'd known she'd relied on him for her future.

The image in front of her blurred.

For once she was in control of her own destiny. Assisting Hannah with her shop felt good. Why shouldn't women help each other out instead of always counting on the men?

She wanted real respect, not the shelter of her pa's reputation.

Opening the door to the next room, she wrinkled her nose. Clothing littered the floor, and dirty dishes covered every available surface.

She threw herself into cleaning the space.

A sound caught her attention, and she glanced up. Will leaned on the door frame, his arms crossed.

Her cheeks flooded with color. She wasn't used to men who wore their clothing with such casual charm. For a cowboy, shirts were loose, often mended and rarely without stains.

Though not flamboyant, Will's clothing spoke of impeccable tailoring and expensive materials. On closer inspection, she noted threads of black and forest green woven through his wool suit. The fawn colored embroidery of his waistcoat along with his crisp, white shirt contrasted nicely with the darker fabric.

She'd always considered men who wore suits as stamped replicas fashioned from the same mold.

Not so with Will Canfield. He was in a class alone.

She sat back on her heels. "Don't you have your own work?"

"I was patrolling the corridors for hog-tied guests."

"Very funny." She fisted one hand on her hip. "You're checking up on me."

"Is that so bad?"

"I suppose not. A good trail boss always takes care of his crew."

There was something comforting about having him near. He didn't treat her as though she was helpless. He looked out for her, same as he would Simon or Mrs. Foster. She was part of his team.

All the loneliness of the past few weeks came flooding back. She should be happy. She should be relieved. She should be grateful she'd found a new team.

She'd gotten exactly what she wanted only to discover she craved more. She didn't just want to be part of a team, she wanted to be a vital member. Indispensable. Not simply an interchangeable part.

Assisting Hannah with her new shop was just the thing to get her mind off her problems. She also liked the idea of snatching the project from under Will's nose. He'd hesitated too long. That man was too used to getting his own way around town.

It would do him good to lose out to a woman once in a while.

"You don't have to finish the day as a maid," Will said. "Take the afternoon and relax. Leave the mess. Living in squalor will build character for this hotel guest."

"Nope. This is my job. I'll see it done properly." She wasn't living off her pa's reputation anymore. She'd earn her own respect. "Now leave me alone. I have work to do."

"Tomasina?"

"Yes."

"Try not to kill any of the guests."

She chucked her towel at him, and he ducked out of the way. "I'm not making any promises."

One day she'd get the upper hand on him. One day soon.

Chapter Eleven

Two days following the hog-tying incident, Will called entrance to the knock on his door.

Tomasina appeared, a stack of towels in her outstretched hands.

He raised his gaze from his ledger. "They're not pink."

"I didn't wash them. I'm only delivering."

"How is kitchen duty?" he asked.

"Never ending."

He absently tapped the letter resting on his desk. "I forgot to apologize the other day for what happened with Mr. Daniels."

"That wasn't your fault."

"I've given Mr. Rumsford more latitude in refusing guests in the future."

"Mr. Rumsford is only happy when the hotel is full of guests." She lowered her chin and gazed at him from beneath her hooded lids. "Which means he turns a blind eye to all sorts of things."

"Really."

Tomasina stacked the towels on a chair for him to put away later. "Don't mind me. I shouldn't be gossiping. Forget I said anything. Don't fire Mr. Rumsford over my silly comment."

"Never apologize for honesty." He sat back in his chair and slid one hand into his vest pocket. "Any other observations you might share?"

"Oh, no. I'm not falling into that trap." She bustled around the room, straightening pillows and opening the curtains with a snap. "I'm not a snitch."

"You're not a maid anymore, either. Quit fussing with the knickknacks."

She heaved a sigh and flopped onto a chair set in front of his desk. "Are you worried about something or planning something? I can't tell with you."

"Worried."

"A burden shared is halved."

"I did something I regret, and now I have to face the consequences."

"This is getting interesting." Tomasina rubbed her hands together. "Spill your guts."

"You might take a little less delight in my suffering."

"I might. But I'm not gonna." She flashed a teasing grin. "What's got your chaps in a twist?"

He slid the letter across the desk. "Daniel and I sent away for a mail-order bride."

"So what? I heard you sent away for twelve of them, plus the four that came last month. What's the big deal?"

He heaved a sigh. "This bride is for one particular man. She's coming to meet Noah."

"Noah Burgess? The recluse with the half-wolf dog who only comes into town for supplies?"

"That's the one."

She arched a brow. "Does he know you sent away for this bride?"

"No."

"You are in trouble." She threw back her head and chortled. "He'll have your hides for pulling this stunt."

"The news only grows worse." Grimacing, he tapped the letter with his index finger. "Read this."

She dutifully took the paper and scanned the contents. Expressions flitted across her face: humor, confusion and dawning sympathy. Whether for him or for the prospective bride, he wasn't certain.

Reaching the end, she folded the letter and slid it back across the desk. "What are you going to do?"

"Nothing. Yet. I'll speak with Daniel and we'll find a solution."

"You owe that woman an apology. Consider all the things she wrote. Constance Miller is a flesh-and-blood person. She has hopes and dreams, and she's looking forward to a new life. With Noah. I've never even met the man, but from the rumors I've heard, he isn't sociable in the best of circumstances."

Will raked his hand through his hair. "I know."

"Can you fess up real quick like? Before she makes the trip?"

"Too late."

Tomasina pursed her lips. "Then you'd better tell Noah."

"I will. After I speak with Daniel. There's no use saying anything too soon. Once we tell him, Noah will stew. Since she's already on her way, my friend might as well live in peace for a few more days."

"Oh, I see. It's Noah you're worried about." She smirked. "You wouldn't be wanting a few more days of peace for yourself now, would you?"

"I gave up on peace the minute a certain redheaded rabble-rouser dropped into my life."

"That's fine thanks for saving your life."

"Maybe we're worrying for nothing. Constance has

never met Noah. She's never met anyone in town. There's no reason she won't find a husband." Will tipped back his head and studied the dangling crystals of the chandelier. "For all we know, they may even fall in love."

Tomasina snorted. "Not likely. From what I've heard, Noah isn't looking for a bride. He won't be happy when one arrives for him unannounced."

"It's too late now."

"Why don't you marry her?"

"Me?" A cold sweat broke out on his forehead. "That's ridiculous. She's coming for Noah."

"Just a minute ago you were passing her off to any eligible bachelor in town. You're an eligible bachelor, Will. Why not you?"

"Because…because I don't want to court her."

The idea was hardly far-fetched. Up until a few weeks ago he'd been looking forward to settling down and starting a family. Dora had seemed a perfectly reasonable companion at the time. He was no longer willing to settle. His heart hadn't been engaged before. Their breakup had revealed the truth.

"You still think Noah will like her." A wry smile stretched across Tomasina's face. "You're a romantic."

Oh, thank goodness. Her conclusion was better than anything he might have invented.

Will discreetly blotted his damp forehead. "I'm not a romantic."

She stood and sashayed toward the door. "Will Canfield is a hopeless romantic."

"Say one more word and I'm firing Mr. Rumsford."

"You wouldn't dare."

"I might."

"Don't worry. I'm sure Constance Miller will step off the train and Noah will fall madly in love with her at first sight. When Constance sees him, little hearts will appear over her head and stars will shine from her eyes." Turning, Tomasina placed her hands in prayer beneath her chin and fluttered her eyelashes. "They'll marry each other and live happily ever after."

She made a few annoying kissing noises for good measure. Will took her ribbing in stride. At least she hadn't scolded him as Leah had. As was her habit, Tomasina cut to the heart of the matter. There was little chance of this situation ending well, and a very good chance Noah would never speak with him again.

"Tomasina," Will called, "when is your next shift in the dining room?"

He was only being polite. He certainly wasn't planning his day around her work schedule.

"Tomorrow morning. I'm serving breakfast. Why do you ask?"

He ate in the dining room quite often. Tomorrow was as good a day as any other for eating downstairs. "I'll keep watch for rowdy guests. Someone has to save them from you."

She stuck out her tongue. "Be nice to me or I'll tell Noah your little secret."

His gaze lingered on the swish of her skirts as she exited the room. With her sharp mind and quick wit, she was wasted at the Cattleman Hotel. What was her father thinking—raising her as a drover? Mr. Stone must have known she'd never survive in the profession without him.

Tucking the letter into his breast pocket, Will blew out a heavy breath. His own behavior was not above reproach. Who was he to judge others for their poor decisions? Mr. Stone hadn't expected to die. Perhaps he'd had other plans for Tomasina's future.

Either way, Will was on borrowed time with her.

Too bad, really. She was far more entertaining than facts and figures.

How would she feel about formal dinners and endless campaigning? His hands grew cold and he recognized the familiar dread that always preceded a fruitless battle. He pictured the future he'd built for himself, only this time something was missing.

He imagined the next months, the next days, even the next hour without her, and each second stretched before him with endless gray monotony.

What an irony. He'd decided to run for office because he missed the adrenaline of working toward an important cause.

Running for governor was tame compared to battling wits with Tomasina Stone.

Tomasina faced the hotel cook. "I wonder if we could keep this latest development between the two of us."

The man gave her a look she was becoming all too familiar with lately—an expression that landed somewhere between anger and exasperation.

"You were on a trial period as part of the dining room staff. Your actions this morning have nullified that agreement."

"Those children drove me to it."

"The children were rather unruly, yes. I agree with you. We cannot, however, compel them to scrub the floors."

"I don't see why not." Tomasina took a seat on a stool in the corner of the kitchen. "If someone makes the mess, they ought to clean it up."

"That's not the way things work around here."

She lifted her chin. "It should be."

The moment the family of four had come through the door, two of the older boys had begun taunting her. They'd deliberately tossed crumbs on the floor when their father wasn't looking. One of them had even tripped her. The little beast had pretended it was an accident. When a plate had mysteriously slid off the edge of the table, she'd had enough.

Though she hadn't boxed their little ears, she'd threatened the punishment. And she'd been more than willing to follow through on that threat.

"You can't go boxing people's ears and threatening violence toward the patrons, Miss Stone."

The cook leaned over a vat of soup. The scent of chicken broth sent her stomach rumbling. The boys hadn't been ornery enough for her heated reaction. She'd been short tempered of late. The conversation with Will had festered in her thoughts. The idea of him getting hitched to one of the mail-order brides had stuck in her craw. That was ridiculous. Of course he'd marry. He seemed the type of fellow who was building an empire. Folks who built empires needed a legacy, and children were an obvious solution. Her anger bubbled back to the surface.

The cook glanced at her. "You'll find something you're good at, but working with people doesn't suit you."

"You might be right." Tomasina slumped on her perch on the kitchen stool and sighed. "It's frustrating, you know? I'm already good at something. I'm good with animals. I know how to rope, ride and shoot a gun."

"Well, that's a place to start." The cook chucked her on the shoulder. "You'll find something you enjoy. Preferably something that doesn't require contact with the public. Keep looking."

"It's no fair, being a woman," she grumbled.

Mrs. Foster pushed her way through the swinging doors into the kitchen then patted her hair into place. "What is it now? I was having a rest when Simon alerted me to another disturbance."

"I'm not cut out for work in the dining room," Tomasina said.

"I'm shocked. Shocked, I say."

"Me and the cook were trying to figure out if I was good at anything."

"You drove cattle before, I believe," the older woman remarked. "There must be skill involved in that."

"Yeah. But who wants to see someone rope a calf? There's no pay in that."

"I disagree. When Mr. Foster was alive, we attended a show in Abilene. Mr. Foster had a sister living there. Fussy woman. Anyway, they had a fellow who did tricks with a rope. He'd make it twirl around and jump in and out of the ring."

Tomasina's eyes lit up with interest. "And people paid to see that?"

"They most certainly did."

"Rope tricks are easy."

Tomasina and the other cowboys often tried to show up one another with their tricks. It had never occurred to her that someone might actually pay to see that dubious talent.

"I don't know," she said, biting her lip. "I don't think I can turn roping into a whole career. I'm not fit for anything respectable."

Mrs. Foster harrumphed. "Crying about your lot isn't going to change things, young lady, that's for certain. A body has to make their own way in this world, by and by. When Mr. Foster was alive, I never worked. After he passed, there simply wasn't enough money. The children were grown and gone. They had families of their own. I read an advertisement for a housekeeper. I'd never been farther west than the Mississippi, but I figured I'd been comfortable for long enough. It was time for me to try something different. I don't regret the decision."

She raised her eyebrows and tipped her head forward. "I don't regret that decision even the past few days, when your employment here has been a singular challenge. I enjoyed seeing Mr. Daniels all trussed up. That lecherous old coot will think twice before he smacks another bottom. You must be good with a rope, because I don't know how you managed to get the better of him."

Tomasina smothered a laugh. "I caught him by surprise."

"You'll find your way, Miss Stone. Nothing ever stays the same. People think change is bad. Sometimes it is. But oftentimes change can open up a whole new world of possibilities."

Planting her chin on her hand, Tomasina sighed. There was a difference between choosing to make a change and being forced to change. Maybe she'd given up on riding as a drover too soon. Maybe she'd given up on convincing James of starting up their own outfit too soon. Maybe, maybe, maybe…

Her hand strayed to her forehead. Recalling the gentle pressure of Will's lips after the incident with Mr. Daniels, the strange feeling returned. That fluttering that began in her stomach and spread through her limbs.

The gesture had meant nothing to him. A comforting peck. Yet the sensations he stirred lingered. Rubbing her hand against her cheek, she felt once more the rough wool of his coat when he'd held her at the drover camp. She closed her eyes and heard the beating of his heart against her ear.

To him, she was nothing more than an annoyance. A nagging difficulty he'd yet to solve. One way or another, she'd solve her own problems.

She'd redouble her efforts in locating a solution. Sometimes the best way out of a difficulty was to circle back around to the beginning.

She knew right where to start.

"You're right, Mrs. Foster." Tomasina stood and untied her apron. "I'm good at roping and riding. Roping and riding is what I should be doing."

"That's the spirit, dearie." Mrs. Foster pumped her fist. "What's your plan?"

"I'll let you know as soon as I have one!"

Chapter Twelve

Will tugged on his coat sleeves and straightened his collar. The planning committee had outdone themselves. A temporary stage had been constructed in the center of town. Lanterns had been strung from the upper beams, and red and white bunting decorated the lower railings.

After the success of the county fair a few weeks back, the town council had planned a smaller, more intimate gathering for the business owners and townspeople. He'd initially been skeptical of hosting another event so soon after the fair, but the business leaders had been adamant. For the past two weeks they'd been busy on a construction project located in front of the bank at the corner of First and Eden Streets. The project had been shrouded in secrecy, and Will anticipated the reveal.

Passing Booker & Son, he tipped his hat to Horace and Gus.

Gus spat his tobacco and cackled. "Folks around these parts sure do like a party."

Will paused. "I didn't notice you complaining when you won the horseshoe tournament at the last party."

Horace elbowed his friend. "Came in first and second, the two of us. I'd have won except the sun was in my eyes."

"The sun was in my eyes just as much," Gus declared. "And it didn't make me no never mind."

"Oh, shut up, you old coot. You know I've always been sensitive to the sun."

Will shook his head. These two never changed. They were always arguing and gossiping. They especially enjoyed sitting across from the jailhouse. Nothing made the two happier than watching a prisoner transfer.

"Are you going to the dance this evening?" Will asked. "There should be a good turnout."

"Mebbe," Horace said. "I was quite the dancer in my younger days."

"You were a dancer in your drinking days, anyway." Gus chortled.

"Haven't touched a drop in twenty years."

"And we're all grateful." Gus threaded his fingers over his rounded stomach. "Any word on the next bride train?"

"Arrangements have been made for the next twelve women," Will replied. "We'll run out of eligible bachelors before long."

"You're turning Cowboy Creek into a regular thriving me-trop-o-lis." Gus exaggerated each syllable.

"That's the plan."

"What are you going to do after that?"

"I have an idea or two." Will leaned one shoulder against the boardwalk support beam and stared down Eden Street. "There's an election next year. Might consider running for governor."

"You don't think small, do you, Mr. Canfield? Or should I call you Governor Canfield?"

"Somebody has to run for governor. Why not me?"

"Fair enough, fair enough." Horace rocked back. "A man like you always has a plan. You ought to be more like Gus and me. Just float on the wind like a feather."

"More like a buffalo," Gus badgered his friend. "Your backside is practically nailed to that chair. You only move for breakfast, supper and dinner. Some feather."

"No more talk of the future." Will held up his hands in surrender. If he let those two keep blabbering, they'd talk his ear off. "Tonight, I plan on enjoying the evening. Nothing more, nothing less. You should do the same."

The two kept up their good-natured bickering long after he walked away. Their voices drifted above the familiar sounds of the thriving town. Crossing the street, Will paused in front of Aunt Mae's boardinghouse and savored the wafting scent of fried chicken. While he enjoyed the fare served at the restaurant in the Cattleman Hotel, no one prepared comfort food quite like Aunt Mae.

Distracted by the enticing aroma, he nearly collided with Prudence Haywood as she exited the newspaper office. She caught sight of him and started, clutching the cameo at her throat. Will narrowed his gaze. Two weeks before, the Murdoch Gang had robbed the church in broad daylight. They'd stolen Leah's wedding ring, Pippa's ruby earrings and the men's wallets. He was certain Prudence had gotten her cameo stolen, as well.

"Mrs. Haywood." He paused, leaning on his walking stick.

She had a way of carrying herself that left him on edge, though he couldn't put his finger on the source of his unease. With no way of avoiding her, he tipped his hat in greeting.

She was one of the brides from the first train. Neither she nor the reverend's daughter had courted any of the men in town. When Prudence had immediately taken a job at the newspaper, he'd thought there was something brewing between her and D.B. Burrows, the newspaper editor.

Yet weeks had passed with no sign of a romantic attachment between the two.

She was a full head shorter than Will, with wavy auburn hair and hazel eyes. He couldn't help but picture a cap of wild curls and stunning green eyes. While Tomasina was pure spitfire, Prudence was much less animated. She had one of those faces that tended to look disagreeable.

"Lovely evening," he greeted her. She'd been widowed. He really should be more charitable in his thinking. The war had taken so many men. Perhaps she simply wasn't ready to marry again. "Is Mr. Burrows available?"

As though prompted by the inquiry, D.B. appeared in the doorway. He flipped the sign to read Closed, stepped outside and set about locking the door.

"Mr. Canfield," he said, throwing back his shoulders. "Come to play king of the party, have you?"

Will stifled a groan.

Though he carried a slight paunch, D.B. dressed sharply and was well-spoken. Charming, even, in an oily sort of way. The man's appearance didn't help the slightly unpleasant impression he inspired. He looked like a black-and-white daguerreotype come to life. He tended to wear dark suits with bright, white shirts. His bushy dark muttonchops highlighted his pale complexion, and his jet-black hair only emphasized his disquieting façade.

Since D.B. had taken over as editor of the newspaper, there'd been a prickly quality about the man. He'd seemed eager enough when they'd hired him some months back. Since that time, the newspaper editorials concerning Cowboy Creek had been less than flattering. While Will respected the man's right to organize the paper as he pleased, the stories had lacked balance recently.

"There are no kings in America, or hadn't you gotten the word?" Will kept his tone neutral. There was always a challenging edge about D.B. "I'm here to enjoy the festivities. Same as everyone else."

"And yet we have you to thank for the success of the town, don't we? Without you, Cowboy Creek is just another watering hole in the middle of nowhere."

"We have the Union Pacific depot to thank for that." Will shrugged. "It was the luck of the draw."

Out West, having a railroad depot almost guaranteed the success of a town. Though a few stagecoaches remained in operation, that mode of transportation was becoming a thing of the past. Railroad cars were full of untapped potential. They were pulling the country together like a thousand threads, and he'd be a fool to squander that potential.

Mr. Burrows puffed up like a bantam hen guarding an egg. "I don't believe in luck. Wouldn't surprise me if a few palms were greased in the process."

"Not by me," Will said easily.

This wasn't the first time he'd heard rumors of corruption surrounding the Union Pacific railroad. Towns lived and died based on the route of railroad lines and the placement of depots. When there were great sums of money in the balance, bribery always thrived.

"We won the depot," he reiterated, "fair and square. This route was the most direct."

"If you say so."

Mrs. Haywood and the man exchanged a glance. Fidgeting, she touched the cameo at her throat once more. If he didn't know better, he'd think the two of them had met each other before settling in Cowboy Creek. They'd certainly formed a comfortable working relationship in a short amount of time. They also had a silent way of signaling each other.

Yet if they knew one another, why would Mrs. Haywood travel as a prospective bride? Why hide their relationship—

whatever it may be? Obviously he was letting his imagination run away with him.

D.B. flipped back his suit coat and stuck one hand in his pocket. "The new wave of prosperity must suit you. You own half the buildings in town, after all."

Since the man was determined to be rude, Will said, "You've been running a lot of front-page stories about the Murdoch Gang lately."

"They robbed a church. Zeb is on his deathbed in the jailhouse." The man guffawed. "That's news. My job is selling papers."

"Might have been nice if you printed a story about the success of the county fair."

"Except it wasn't really a county fair, was it?" the gentleman retorted. "You and your lot decided Cowboy Creek was the county center. Never mind about everyone else."

"I'd think you'd be pleased at the success of the town. It's your home, after all."

"What an honor it is to live here." D.B. flushed. "Positively warms my heart to be a part of such a thriving community."

Prudence snickered.

Will glanced between the two. There was most definitely an undercurrent he didn't understand. Was D.B. simply capitalizing on the recent troubles caused by the Murdoch Gang to sell his papers, or was there something more sinister at work? With the ever-present danger hovering around them, this town sure didn't need any more negative publicity.

He'd speak with Daniel and Noah at the next opportunity and make a few inquiries about the man. And Prudence, as well. Following his instincts had served him well in the past.

His instincts called for a change of subject. "Are the two of you attending the dance this evening?"

"Wouldn't miss it." D.B. offered a smile that didn't quite reach his eyes. "I paid ten dollars for the privilege."

"The event is free." Will tilted his head. "I don't follow."

"Remmy Hagermann demanded ten dollars from all the businesses in town. They're putting together a presentation for you, Daniel and Noah. Didn't you wonder what all the fuss was about? They're building some sort of monument in your honor with a plaque and everything."

Will smothered his annoyance. "Not much of a surprise anymore now, is it?"

"I hope I didn't ruin the grand unveiling." D.B. laid a hand over his chest and assumed an expression of mock remorse. "At least now you have time to prepare a speech."

The man clearly wanted a rise out of him.

"Your donation is greatly appreciated. I'll be sure and call you out personally."

"You do that."

The cameo caught his attention once more. "What a lovely piece of jewelry, Mrs. Haywood. Is it new? I thought your broach was stolen."

Prudence's mouth opened and closed, giving her the appearance of a fish out of water. "I hid it when the robbers arrived."

"But you claimed it was stolen. I was certain I heard you lamenting the loss."

She'd done more than lament. She'd demanded reparations for the lack of security in town. An order she'd made in no uncertain terms.

"The other ladies had lost their jewelry." Her eyes flashed with challenge. "I was embarrassed I'd hidden mine."

"There's no law against hiding a piece of jewelry from

outlaws," D.B. blustered. "If you'd been protecting the town properly, we wouldn't be having this conversation."

"I'm pleased Mrs. Haywood was able to save such a precious heirloom." Will tipped his hat once more. "Mr. Burrows."

There was definitely something odd about those two. As he pondered the strange encounter, he caught sight of Amos Godwin and his heavily pregnant wife, Opal.

The Godwins owned the boot and shoe shop in town and lived above their store. Mrs. Godwin was eight months pregnant and painfully thin apart from her rounded belly. She was never particularly hearty, and the pregnancy had taken its toll. Though a kind woman, there wasn't much color about her. She tended to dress in drab shades that washed out her complexion. Though her eyes were a lively shade of brown, the dark circles beneath them distracted from the color. Today she'd pulled her brown hair back in a tight bun at the nape of her neck. The severe style only highlighted her thin neck.

She rarely worked beside her husband in their shoe shop these days, though she often had her feet up in the corner in deference to her condition. Outside of the shop, Mr. Godwin seldom left his wife's side, hovering over her and ensuring she was comfortable. The pair were hardworking and devoted to each other. All in all they were a fine addition to the community.

"Mrs. Godwin, you're looking well," he said. "Is that a new lace collar you're wearing today?"

"It is." His compliment drew some color into her sunken cheeks. "Thank you, Mr. Canfield."

"I trust you're feeling well. Won't be long before the population of Cowboy Creek increases by one."

Mr. Godwin took his wife's hand. "Not long at all. She insisted on coming out for the celebration tonight." He cast a concerned look at his wife. "Promise you'll tell me if you get tired."

"I will. I've been feeling ever so much better since Leah—I mean Mrs. Gardner—arrived. She's given me all sorts of help and advice."

Her husband wrapped an arm around his wife's shoulders. "Leah will make a fine midwife for the town."

Opal blushed again. "She's become a good friend."

"I don't mean to bother you on such an occasion," Mr. Godwin began, "but I wondered if you'd look into something for me."

"Anything," Will replied amicably.

"As you know, when Opal and I purchased our shop, we bought the space next door, as well. Opal's father lent us the money. He thought it was a good investment, and he was correct. Someone has approached us to rent the building."

"That's wonderful."

"Yes. Except the bank is questioning our deed."

Will stilled. "What do you mean?"

"Just that. The bank refuses to go forward with the transaction until they authenticate the deed."

"There has to be some mistake." Will and the town founders had been scrupulous with their transactions. Every business deal had been overseen by lawyers and filed with the county. There was no reason for the bank to question the deeds. "I'll speak with someone at the land offices first thing Monday morning and straighten out the problem."

Relief flitted across Opal's wan face. "I knew you'd help."

"Absolutely. You shouldn't be worrying about anything in your condition, Mrs. Godwin. I promise you, I'll get to the bottom of this." Seeking to distract the young couple from needless worry, he asked, "And who is looking to rent the shop?"

"Hannah Taggart."

"The preacher's daughter?"

"Yes. She wants to open a dress shop in town. With all the new brides arriving, we'll need a milliner before long. I have a cousin who might be interested. She works in a shop in St. Louis."

"Of course, um, yes. A lady can never have too many hats."

How was Hannah getting the money for the shop? She'd approached him about the idea a few days ago, but he'd been reluctant to give her an answer until he saw more of her designs.

Mrs. Godwin cleared her throat. "I believe Miss Stone is partnering with Hannah in the business."

"Tomasina Stone?"

A hesitant nod. "Yes."

He'd obviously assumed a fierce expression, because Opal was looking absolutely terrified.

Will relaxed his features. "I think that's wonderful. I'll look into the deed and contact Miss Stone and Miss Taggart personally. I'm happy to hear the women in town are banding together in their endeavors."

"I thought so, too."

A certain redheaded spitfire might have mentioned her intentions earlier.

Mr. Godwin shook his hand. "I appreciate your help straightening out the deed."

"Anything." He bent in a shallow bow. "Mrs. Godwin, I hope you'll save me a dance."

His offer was hollow. She'd never accept and, because of his injured leg, he didn't dance anymore.

She stifled her giggle with one hand. "What a pair we'd

make. Me with my stomach and you with your walking
stick."

He ignored the touch of melancholy her words inspired.
He'd survived when others hadn't. If he never danced
again, it was a small price to pay.

"We'd clear the floor."

With a touch on his brim he set off for the spot where
the stage had been set. Unlike at the fair where comfort
was the order of the day, the few ladies present were decked
out in their finest attire. The enormous bell skirts popular
before the war had been tamed by practicality. The war
had sobered the nation. Nothing was quite as flamboyant
as before. In this one instance he was grateful. The enormous hoop skirts had bordered on ridiculous with ladies
barely able to navigate doorways. He much preferred the
more restrained silhouette.

A glimmer of red caught his attention, and he halted. A
tumble of curls cascaded down the back of a shimmering
pear-green gown with a gossamer-embroidered overlay.

The vision turned, presenting him with her profile. His
breath caught. Blinking, he tugged on his tie and swallowed around the lump in his throat. Feeling as though
he'd been kicked in the gut, he took a step back.

Tomasina.

He couldn't think. He couldn't breathe. He couldn't even
move. Here was the indomitable Tomasina Stone as he'd
never seen her before.

Chapter Thirteen

Will had seen Tomasina in chaps. He'd even seen her in a dress. He'd seen her in a simple calico shirtwaist during her short-lived employment as a laundress. He'd seen her in the severe black dress and white lace cap of the hotel maids.

However, he'd *never* seen her like this. Her curls were partially piled atop her head in a delightful halo, with a few pieces artfully arranged around her face. The length in the back had been gathered into a waterfall of corkscrew curls.

The dress featured a modest scooped neck lined with a ruffle in the same material as the overlay of the skirt. A wide satin belt with a gold buckle highlighted her tiny waist.

He'd always thought her lovely. Even that first day he'd been captivated by her luminous eyes. This was different. This was beyond anything he could have imagined. She didn't even seem real. If he reached out and touched her arm, he feared she'd shatter like a porcelain doll. The man standing beside her said something, and she laughed. A light, lyrical sound.

But this was no porcelain doll. She was flesh and blood. Her dress floated around her in an ethereal green shimmer. He admired once more how the delicate material draped her shoulders and nipped in at her waist.

She caught sight of him and glided forward. His gaze dropped and his fingers trembled. He longed to caress the auburn curl grazing her collarbone.

"Mr. Canfield," she said, "you're looking quite dashing tonight."

Everything faded into the background. People pushed and jostled around them, and he willed them away.

"You are… You're beautiful."

She gently waved herself with an ivory-handled fan he hadn't noticed before. "Don't look quite so surprised. It's rather ungentlemanly of you."

"That dress. Your hair." He was babbling. "How? When?"

"My goodness. I never thought to see you so put out by a drape of fabric and a bit of rice powder." The fan ruffled those delightful curls. "I enjoy seeing you speechless."

Everything about her was different. Her voice. Her carriage. Normally she leaned slightly forward, as though preparing for a race at every turn. Today she stood straight and proud, her shoulders thrown back, her head held high. The transformation was astonishing. *Breathtaking.*

The years melted away, and it was as though he was whole again. As though the war had never happened. As though he was still that naive bright-eyed fool who had no idea of the horrors in store for him; a green youth worshipping at the feet of a beautiful woman.

He savored the feeling.

A cowboy who'd started celebrating a little too early tripped into Tomasina. The man's drink sloshed from his tin cup and splattered onto her pristine skirts. The cowboy groped for her arm and mumbled a slurred apology.

Tomasina's lips whitened.

Will lunged. The cowboy stumbled again and the remainder of his drink splashed over her satin shoes.

Tomasina fisted her hand and socked the man in the shoulder. "You've ruined my best dress, you drunken oaf."

The man tripped in reverse, caught his heel on an uneven tread and landed hard on his backside. His empty cup tumbled from his limp hand.

Partygoers gasped and murmured.

Tomasina caught Will's astonished gaze, her brilliant green eyes wide with horror. With sudden insight Will recognized how important this evening was for her. All the changes he'd noticed hadn't come easy. As the folks around them tittered, a fury of color spread across her delightful décolletage.

Grasping her arm, he gently hustled her toward the double doors of the Cattleman Hotel and away from the curious townsfolk. She didn't deserve to have her evening ruined because of that clumsy fool.

Thankfully the lobby was far less crowded. She didn't protest as he led her toward a banquette near the far wall.

Hannah Taggart was staring into the lobby mirror and pinching color into her cheeks when she caught sight of them. "Oh, my. What happened?"

"A little accident," Will offered quickly. "Can you help?"

"I'm so sorry." Tomasina reached for her roommate. "I know how much work you put into this dress. I wanted everything to be perfect."

Hannah hustled over and knelt then grasped the damp skirts and wrinkled her nose. "Beer. Trust me, this isn't the worst thing I've ever seen. Don't worry. We'll have you fixed up in no time."

Simon appeared, straightening his cap, his gaze scanning the room.

He caught sight of Will and rushed over. "You're needed, boss. They can't start the ceremony without you. Everybody is waiting."

"Then let them wait."

He clasped Tomasina's hand, massaging warmth into her icy fingers. He wanted to fix this for her. He wanted to turn back time and let her have her moment.

Tomasina glanced up. "Don't worry, I'll be all right."

Only a slight sheen of tears revealed her distress.

He hesitated between his two commitments. Though she was in capable hands with Hannah, he was reluctant to leave.

Hannah pulled Tomasina to her feet, away from Will, and ushered her into the parlor.

Facing Will, Hannah spoke softly. "It's best if you go. She's been practicing her walk and her speech all day. She wanted everything to be perfect."

"She is perfect. I mean, uh, she looks perfect."

Hannah offered a rare smile. "We'll meet you at the ceremony."

He paused, staring at the younger woman.

Her smile.

That's what had been missing. Hannah rarely smiled. The only time he'd ever seen her truly happy was when she was caring for Ava. Come to think of it, he'd assumed she was watching the baby tonight. When he'd mentioned the dance before, she hadn't appeared interested in attending.

"Who's watching the baby?" he asked.

"Mrs. Foster. I wanted… I was hoping to attend the dance. You don't mind, do you?"

"Of course not. Enjoy yourself, Hannah. If you need anything, let me know."

Thank goodness. She was a prospective bride, after all. This was the first time she'd showed any interest in socializing. He should have noticed sooner that she was wearing a new peach-colored dress, as well. Her usual flounces and bows were gone, replaced by a modest bell skirt and V-necked bodice. Her hair was braided into an elaborate chignon, showing off the graceful curve of her neck.

"You look lovely," he said. "Your skill as a seamstress is apparent. Is Tomasina's dress your work?"

"Yes."

"The design is inspired. You're quite talented."

Her smile was tinged with pride. "I sewed new dresses for several of the ladies attending this evening. I'm advertising for the new shop."

Her shop. The Godwins. His whole brain had been muddled by the sight of Tomasina, and he'd forgotten all about his other worries. "Mr. Godwin told me about the difficulty with the deeds. I'll speak to the bank and visit the land office first thing Monday morning."

Simon cleared his throat. "You have to go, sir. You're supposed to give the opening speech."

He lingered a moment longer.

Hannah pushed on his shoulder. "Go. She'll be fine. I'll have her out dancing in no time."

He followed Simon out the doors, his thoughts jumbled. A sweep of tenderness filled his heart. He'd kept a distance from Tomasina. Not physically, certainly, he'd ensured she was always underfoot. But he'd kept the distance in his thoughts. She was part of the prairie lands he'd grown to love. Exotic, wild and free.

He'd thought to protect her untamed spirit and to shelter her from the encroaching world. Yet she'd sidestepped all his boundaries, effortlessly crossing all the safeguards he'd imposed. She was neither drover nor sophisticated lady— she was an enchanting mixture of both worlds.

She navigated the gulf between classes with effortless

ease. Despite her well-deserved outburst this evening, he admired her ability to speak with diverse groups of people. She wasn't untamed; she was authentic.

She was captivating.

Simon tugged on his sleeve. "They're waiting, Mr. Canfield."

Tomasina easily fit into his world. Could he ever fit into hers?

Tomasina pounded her fist against her thigh. "I was doing so well. You woulda been so proud of me. I was pronouncing all my words and everything." Hannah and Pippa had spent their free time over the past few days giving her lessons on decorum. As long as she spoke slowly and didn't move too quickly, she could pass as a real lady. Except she didn't suppose real ladies punched people. "That drunken fool ruined everything."

Who could blame her for losing her temper?

"Nothing is ruined," Hannah said in a soothing voice. "The dance hasn't even started yet. There were only a few people who saw what happened. Rest assured Mr. Canfield will deal with that rowdy cowboy."

"That clumsy oaf better not be around when I get back. I'll trip him into the punch bowl."

"Now, Tom. A lady always ensures her conduct is such that her inferiors may respect her."

"He was inferior, all right. Especially after I socked him."

Hannah gasped. "You didn't."

"Sat him right down in the dirt, I did."

"Well, obviously he deserved what happened. A slight hiccup. Nothing more."

"The kind of hiccup where you can hold your breath until it passes?"

"Something like that."

While they'd been speaking, Hannah had wiped down her skirts with a damp towel. She sat back on her heels and waved them dry with her ivory-handled fan.

After a few minutes Hannah stilled her fanning and surveyed her work. "You're good as new. We will begin again as though nothing happened."

Tomasina planted her elbows on her knees and cupped her chin in her hands. "It's too late. Will already seen me acting rough and tumble."

Tonight of all nights she'd wanted him to see her as a lady. As someone who deserved respect. Not that he'd ever disrespected her. Far from it. He'd always treated her like a lady. That's why she wanted to act like one.

"Mr. Canfield already *saw* you acting rough and tumble." Hannah folded her fan. "A gentleman would never remark on a lady's misfortune."

Tomasina snorted. "A drover would never let me live it down."

"Drovers are rude." Hannah snapped her skirts aside and stood. "Drovers are uncouth, ungentlemanly, pig-headed fools."

"Have you spent time at the stockyards? You described them just right."

A gentle knock sounded, and Pippa appeared. "Come along, ladies. The town is absolutely swimming with eligible bachelors and, thanks to Hannah, we're the belles of the ball."

Hannah had chosen a daring shade of black cherry for Pippa's dress. The bold color highlighted her strawberry-blond hair and brought out the flecks of gold in her hazel eyes. Because of her slight frame, Hannah had added a peplum hem to the bodice and belted it with an embroidered sash. The neckline was draped a bit lower than

Tomasina's, with bows at the caps of her cutaway sleeves. The dress was as striking as her personality.

Suddenly shy, Hannah ducked her head. "I didn't do anything very special."

"Do be serious." Pippa patted her elaborate coiffure, a mass of looped braids tumbling from a knot at the top of her head. "You did everything. There's nothing I detest more than false modesty." She flounced toward the door, gesturing over her shoulder. "Now come along, you two. No long faces. I'm not wasting this hair. We're young, we're unattached and this town is full of rich, eligible men."

"Pippa!" Tomasina admonished. "We're not cattle going to market."

"All right then, we're princesses at the ball."

Tomasina frowned. "I don't follow."

"Didn't you read fairy tales growing up?"

"No. My pa told me stories."

"What kinds of stories?" Pippa asked.

"Like the time he was fetching water from the creek when he came across a mountain lion. That mountain lion chased him back to camp and up a tree. But the only tree he could find was barely taller than a buffalo and the mountain lion caught his boot and tugged. Then he'd say, 'That mountain lion was pulling my leg, just like I'm pulling yours.' That was a good one. That was one of my favorites."

"Fascinating." Pippa appeared slightly bewildered. "Let's not waste any more time, ladies—we're not getting any younger and neither are those cowboys."

With her skirts dried and her decorum back in place, Tomasina threw back her shoulders and followed the other two outside once more. To walk like a lady, she simply had to think about her actions. The extra effort slowed her progress, which actually turned out to be a good thing. Evidently ladies did not gallop from place to place. Pippa had driven that point home several times. Tomasina had begun to wonder how ladies ever got anything done with all the rules they had to follow and the sedate pace they were bound to keep.

Most of the town had turned out for the event, and everyone had dressed in their finest. Even the drovers had come. She recognized several of the fellows and realized most of them had even bought new suits. With their hair washed and their beards trimmed, some even looked almost respectable. Tomasina caught a glimpse of James in his beaded vest with his tan Stetson. The moment he saw her he turned away.

Tomasina bit the inside of her lip until the pain replaced her angry betrayal. Really. The man was impossible. She was done trying to make peace with him. Will never turned his back on her. Even when he was angry after the trick riding show, he'd sought her out. And tonight. She pressed her trembling hands together. He'd been looking out for her tonight.

She shook out her hands. He looked out for everyone. She was nothing special to him, and she'd best remember that. He'd accepted her as a temporary resident of Cowboy Creek and he was watching out for her the same as everyone else.

The three women took their place in the crowd standing in front of the makeshift stage. Several of the men elbowed each other out of the way, doffing their hats and stepping back a proper distance. Tomasina patted her hair in an imitation of Pippa and glided toward the front of the stage. Some of the perks of dressing like a lady weren't half-bad.

The three town founders took the stage, and her chest swelled. Will stood strong and tall, his hands clasped together over the handle of his walking stick. He didn't stare at the crowd; his gaze remained fixed on the horizon. Her heart went out to him. He'd clearly rather blend in, but he was doing his duty as a town founder. While Will hid his unease, Noah fidgeted and tugged on his collar. Of the three men, Daniel appeared most comfortable, his hands stuffed in his pockets and an easy grin on his handsome face.

The three of them had the proud bearing of soldiers. The crowd grew hushed, and the town council presented the three men with a plaque.

Remmy Hagermann gave a long-winded speech about the future of the town. By the time he'd finished, the rest of the council waved off their opportunity to speak. With the sun sinking low on the horizon, the town council whipped off the sheet with a flourish and unveiled a brick monument at the corner of First and Eden in front of the bank.

A simple obelisk with a pointed tip nearly fifteen feet tall, the council had affixed a brass plaque featuring the three names of the town founders, with Noah's name first. The three men shuffled their feet and admired the monument. John Cleve Parker set up his camera. After he'd arranged the men, he ducked beneath the black fabric drape and took the men's photograph in a burst of flash powder. The crowd hollered for speeches from the men.

Noah declined to speak, instead thanking those assembled with a smile and a quick wave.

Daniel stepped forward. "Well, I'm sure glad we located this town by Cowboy Creek and not Skunk Valley." As the crowd roared with laughter, he paused. "I served with Noah Burgess in the War Between the States, and I am proud to call him a friend. He settled here first and wrote letters describing the fruitful plains and fertile valley.

"I have to admit, when I got here, I thought he was

drinking his own moonshine." More laughter met his words. Everyone knew that Noah didn't drink and he certainly didn't own a still. "I've grown to love this place. I appreciate the land and the people who have the courage to settle this land. Thank you for this honor. May we prove worthy of your esteem."

Enthusiastic applause followed his exit from the stage.

Will took his place and cleared his throat. "Towns like this are like families. We see before us the past, the present and the future. With each new generation, we will remember the folks who came before us. We will honor the sacrifices they made, and we will carry their spirit with us. A hundred years from now, a family will pass by this monument and recall our names, and the legacy of Cowboy Creek will live on. Because the future is built on the ruins of the past. May we inspire the dreams of those who look upon this enduring legacy. As long as we always dream a little bigger than the generation before us, Cowboy Creek will survive and thrive."

Raucous applause sounded at his words. Tomasina blinked rapidly. Will Canfield was a man building a legacy. Her enthusiasm waned, and when Pippa and Hannah left for the dance floor, she stayed behind.

As dusk fell low over the horizon, the men lit hanging lanterns, bathing the scene in a soft glow. At first the men and women lined up across the dance floor from each other like children at a school dance. Two or three lively reels later the floor was full. Tomasina fended off a few ardent suitors before taking a seat on a bench in the shadows.

Bracing her hands behind her, she watched the dancers from a distance, her toes tapping the cheerful rhythm.

"Why aren't you dancing?" A familiar voice spoke. "Surely you're not lacking for partners."

Tomasina glanced up. "I don't dance. Pippa and Hannah offered to teach me, but there's only so much a body can learn in a few days. I was busy trying to walk and talk properly. Adding the dancing was too much. I don't mind. I like watching everyone else."

Will indicated the empty seat beside her. "Do you mind if I join you?"

Scooting a little, she made more room. "Of course not. Have a rest."

"The old injury is worse at the end of the day." He sat, one leg bent, the other stretched out. "I was quite the dancer before the war."

Tomasina elbowed him. "You're fooling me. I can't picture you dancing."

"Not at all. There's no better way to woo a pretty girl than sweeping her around the dance floor." He absently rubbed his thigh. "Look at that. Miss Ewing is dancing with Mr. Gardner."

"Who are they?"

Will pointed out the couple. "Miss Ewing has been assisting Daniel and Leah until their baby arrives. Oliver is Daniel's father. A widower. We may have another wedding before long."

"Cowboy Creek is bringing romance to the West."

"One couple at a time."

"You *are* a romantic, Will Canfield. Quit denying it." Still feeling like a first-rate heel for reminding him of his injury, Tomasina stared at her satin slippers. "You could still dance now, if you wanted."

"No. Those days are gone. Before the war I'd never have imagined I'd miss something as simple as a turn around the dance floor. I took so much for granted."

Pippa swept by in a lively jig with a handsome drover. The two attacked the dance with more enthusiasm than grace.

"What do you miss most of all?" Tomasina asked softly. "From how life was before the war?"

"My family, I suppose. I was an only child. My parents were older. I think they'd given up on ever having children. I must have been quite a surprise to them." He exhaled slowly, hesitating a moment before continuing. "I was always self-conscious growing up. The other children assumed my parents were my grandparents, and I rarely corrected the mistake. I was too selfish to understand how much that hurt them. They doted on me."

"They're gone, then?"

He nodded. "My mother died shortly before the war began. My father soon after. Daniel and I had already enlisted. My father was proud of me, but worried. I assured him the war would be over in a matter of weeks. He died without knowing how wrong I was."

"Why didn't you go home again?"

"Home is family. My family was gone. I had served with Daniel and Noah. Noah was here, and Daniel and I followed. I haven't been back east since." He turned toward her, his dark eyes searching hers. "What about you? Where did you grow up?"

"Nowhere. Everywhere. My mother died when I was young. Me and Pa lived with his sister for a spell. Then she found a fellow of her own and got hitched. She offered to take me with her, but Pa wasn't having any of it at first. He tried his hand at farming, but he wasn't much good. Eventually he left me with my aunt and her new husband and joined a cattle drive."

"Left you behind? And how did you feel about that?"

"How do you think?" she asked with a scowl. "I was just nine years old, but I refused to wait around for my pa. Rode my little pony six miles to catch up. The other fellows thought it was funny, having a little girl on the trail.

They looked out for me. That's how it's been ever since. Me and him."

"I heard your father passed away recently. You promised to tell me about him."

"I miss him." The hollow pang was there, though not as strong as before. "His death was peaceful. He went to bed one night and didn't wake up come morning. He's home now."

"It's difficult, losing someone. I'm sorry for your loss."

"People think grief is a wound and, when the wound heals, you go on like before. I think it's more like losing a limb. The pain eases, but you're never the same. You have to figure out a different way of doing things. You have to learn a new way of surviving." Her voice faltered, and she swallowed hard. "You go on, but there's always something missing. Take what happened to your leg. You healed, but there's always a hitch in your step. Grief is the same way."

"Is that a weakness? I've always wondered."

"It's a strength. Only broken men thrive out West. Because broken men know how to survive."

"You're a survivor. Does that mean you're broken, Miss Stone?"

Chapter Fourteen

"No," Tomasina replied wistfully. "I'm not broken. I was protected. Sheltered."

"I'm glad someone protected you. There are enough broken folks since the war. We don't need any more." Will stood and propped his cane against the bench then held out his hand. "Dance with me."

Tomasina tipped back her head. "I told you, I don't dance."

"Neither do I. That's why we're perfect together."

She cautiously stood and took his hand. Her insides were trembling wildly, and her chest was tight. He wrapped his other arm around her waist. She was acutely aware of him—his scent, his warmth, his touch. Urging her closer, his chin brushed her temple. Swaying a little, she followed his lead.

Barely shuffling their feet, Will whispered his instructions. "This is a waltz, the dance of romance. It caused quite a scandal when it was first introduced in Austria. Like most things in life, the steps are deceptively simple and incredibly nuanced." He guided her with a gentle pressure against her back. "Back, together, side. Back, together, side."

His breath whispered against the sensitive skin behind her ear, stirring the hairs on the nape of her neck.

The fiddle player spun a tune, and Tomasina gradually relaxed into the rhythm. As the other dancers swirled around the floor, the two of them barely moved from their place in the shadows. Where his hands touched her, a tingling sensation feathered over her skin. She was surrounded by his warmth and his strength. Her pulse quickened. She'd never been this vitally aware of a man before. With every breath her senses were assailed with the heady scents of his starched shirt and bay rum cologne.

His hand engulfed hers, and she felt calluses on his palm and fingers, a testament to his physical labor. Though he spent much of his time with office and managerial duties, she'd seen him hoisting bags of flour and supplies with ease. His rugged features were far more attractive than mere handsomeness. Beneath his civilized exterior, there was something primitive and raw. His masculinity made her acutely aware of her own femininity.

All her life she'd fought against the restrictions of being a woman. Anything feminine was considered weak. In Will's arms, she felt powerful. He was exciting and tempting... and frightening.

She'd mastered her emotions in all other aspects. She never showed fear and she gave as good as she got when the cowboys were taunting each other. This new awakening was both alluring and terrifying. She'd unleashed a power within herself she had no idea how to control. If she gave in to her feelings, she worried she'd regret it. There was a rash part of herself she didn't trust.

When the music ended, Will cleared his throat and stepped back. "You have a natural grace, Miss Stone. You're ready to take your place on the dance floor."

Clinging to the moment, she pressed her hand against

his chest and felt the rapid beat of his heart. She swayed forward, her face upturned. His head lowered, blotting out the moonlight. A restless need drew her forward.

"My, my, my. What is all this?" a feminine voice chided. "What will the chaperones say with you two hiding in the shadows?"

Tomasina took a guilty step aside. Will caught her around the waist and eased her protectively against his side.

"Miss Edison. You're looking lovely this evening," he said, his hand resting heavily on Tomasina's hip.

Tomasina recognized Dora Edison from meals at the hotel restaurant. She was one of those patrons who rarely acknowledged the staff beyond placing her order or demanding additional service. Mr. Wilson, one of the bankers from the Western Savings & Loan Bank of Kansas, stood beside her.

Dora's dark, curly hair was arranged in a smooth chignon, enhancing her heart-shaped face and blue eyes. She ran her finger over the daring neckline of her gown. "It's so nice of you to let the kitchen help attend the evening's festivities. I'm certain such charitable causes will assist your bid for the governor's mansion." She leaned forward with a broad wink. "But I'm guessing you knew that already, didn't you?"

"Governor's mansion?" Tomasina asked weakly.

Dora smiled; an odd, square-lipped smile that revealed her lower teeth. "Surely you realize Will Canfield would never be content with some place as common and coarse as our dear Cowboy Creek."

Tomasina glanced at his profile. A vein throbbed in his temple. Dora wasn't speaking of Cowboy Creek, and everyone standing in their tight circle understood the implication.

"Dora," Will said, a warning in his voice. "You've over-stepped your bounds."

"But we were engaged, Will. Surely that affords me some latitude?"

A vise tightened around Tomasina's heart. *Engaged?*

She must have made a noise because Dora fixed her gaze on her. "He was engaged to Leah Gardner at one time, as well. Since the two of you appear cozy, surely you knew that! He can't even settle for one woman, let alone one place."

"Mr. Canfield," Simon called from the path. He glanced around, his gaze flitting over Dora with a grimace. "You're needed back at the hotel."

"I'll be along shortly. Enjoy your evening, Miss Edison," Will said. "Mr. Wilson."

Dora clung to the banker's arm. "Too bad you have to leave, I'm sure Miss Stone will have plenty of company in your absence."

She flounced off, all but dragging the banker behind her.

Will lifted his hand from Tomasina's hip and offered her his bent arm. "Pippa will wonder what happened to you. I'll see that you're settled before I leave."

She placed her hand in the crook of his elbow. Considering Pippa had stood up for every dance, Tomasina doubted she'd given her a second thought.

"I'd rather go back to the hotel."

"Then I'll walk you the distance."

Grateful for the distraction, she pressed her free hand against her thumping heart. She'd made fun of the boys for getting all moon-eyed over girls before. She'd never understood their single-minded adoration. She owed them an apology. She'd never experienced the pull of attraction before. She was growing increasingly aware of Will. She sensed his moods, she sympathized with his difficulties. For the love of little green apples, she was even beginning to soften about some of his rules. The mere thought of him left her insides quivery. Agitated.

She was intensely aware of him, and yet he was completely oblivious to her. He'd been engaged to Dora Edison. He was on his way to the governor's mansion. He'd never settle for some place as common and coarse as Cowboy Creek.

Or *someone* as wild and untamed as her.

They stepped from the shadows, and light from dozens of lanterns lit their path. The encounter with Dora had shaken her fragile sense of belonging. She wanted so badly to believe she could fit into his world, but doubts assailed her at every turn.

She glanced at Will's unyielding profile.

A governor needed a lady as a wife. Her transformation had been superficial only. She hadn't become a lady; she'd fooled them all with Pippa's instructions on decorum and Hannah's fancy dress. Once again her respect was borrowed. On the inside, she was still a drover.

Ahead of them, the lights from the Cattleman Hotel spilled over the boardwalk. Will squeezed her hand in a reassuring manner. "Are you certain you wouldn't rather stay and enjoy the dance? Dora is right. You'd have plenty of partners."

"I'd rather have a little quiet. I'm not accustomed to so many people."

"When will you learn that I'd rather risk a thousand embarrassments than miss the chance at seeing your beauty one more time?"

"What are you saying?"

"It's the moonlight." He made a sound of frustration. "I

never should have let you stand in the moonlight. Those copper curls shall forever be my undoing."

He pulled her to him and placed his mouth on hers. She answered by slipping her arms inside his coat, clinging to his warmth, assailed with the comforting scent of his linen shirt and bay rum cologne.

The calloused pads of his thumbs brushed gentle circles over the tender skin on the back of her arms. Amazed at the electrifying shock of his gentle touch, she shivered.

Her reaction broke the mood.

He sprang away, then rubbed his hands down his lapels.

His expression shifted to an unreadable mask of stone. "I beg your forgiveness, Miss Stone, for my unpardonable behavior."

He pivoted on his heel and melted into the shadows.

Tomasina touched her trembling lips. What had she done wrong?

An all-encompassing dread seeped into her soul. She didn't belong here. She didn't belong anywhere.

Chapter Fifteen

His throat tight, Will struggled to focus. He'd kissed Tomasina. And not a chaste kiss on the forehead. A searing kiss that branded her lips.

Simon fell into step beside him.

"What's this emergency at the hotel?" Will asked a bit impatiently.

He suspected the boy's interruption had been planned. Simon had never had much use for Dora.

"It's the baby, sir. Something is wrong with Ava. Mrs. Foster needs you back at the hotel. That baby has been crying and crying. She won't quit."

Furrowing his brow, Will gave Simon his full attention. "Have you sent for the doctor?"

Probably all the fuss was for nothing. Ava had been known to keep the whole hotel awake until all hours of the night. As Tomasina had so aptly pointed out earlier, that little one had a mind of her own. Ava had already picked favorites, as well. While she tolerated Will and was somewhat fond of Tomasina, she was most content when Hannah was near.

Simon tugged on the hem of his jacket. "We called for the doctor first thing. Can't track him down."

"Keep looking. Meanwhile, see if you can locate Mrs. Gardner. She's the next best thing we have."

Will turned and nearly collided with Tomasina.

"I saw Leah earlier," she said. "She was sitting with a lemonade on the far side of the dance floor. I can fetch her."

Of course they were traveling in the same direction. They both lived in the hotel.

With events escalating around them, there was no time for an apology. Dora had been inexcusably rude. Her blunt announcement of his past engagements hadn't helped matters. He'd seen the disappointment in Tomasina's eyes. Reaching out, he touched her arm, but words escaped him. Had their shared kiss meant anything to her? He didn't know. Though he'd never considered himself a cowardly man, he'd rather face a firing squad than the uncertainty of her answer.

"We'll spread the word that Doc Fletcher is needed," Tomasina said. "And meet you back at the hotel."

She moved away and he fought the urge to tuck her against his side once more. He wanted to comfort her and to protect her. To assure her that Dora's words were full of spite against him and had nothing to do with Tomasina. This wasn't the time or the place.

Instead he let her go. "I'll relieve Mrs. Foster. You two search for the doc."

They had little chance of locating him. With the party in full swing, there were too many bodies milling around. Hoping his earlier suspicions were correct and the child was merely exercising her preference of caregiver, Will returned to the hotel. He took the stairs two at a time and heard the squalling by the second landing.

Mrs. Foster was red faced, her hair disheveled, beads of perspiration visible on her forehead. Her gown was damp in the front and there was a distinct, unpleasant odor in the room.

"I haven't been able to quiet the wee thing," she said. "Just hearing these pitiful wails is breaking my heart."

Equally red faced, Ava squalled and shook her tiny, fisted hands.

Sensing Mrs. Foster's growing distress, he held out his arms. "I'll take her. You need a break."

"I couldn't. She's been spitting up, as well. You'll ruin your best suit."

"I'll buy another." Will shrugged out of his coat and tossed it over a chair. "Mr. Lin already owes me several new shirts to replace the pink ones."

Will took the infant, and Mrs. Foster breathed a gusty sigh. "Simon sent for the doctor ages ago. I don't know why he isn't here."

"Patience, Mrs. Foster. The cavalry is on its way."

True to his word, Tomasina arrived a short time later with Leah and Daniel in tow.

"Must you live on the third floor?" Daniel grumbled. He guided his wife toward an overstuffed chair. "Sit. You've worn yourself out climbing all those stairs."

"I'm fine," Leah replied as she gratefully sank onto the chair. "There's no need to fuss."

As was usual these days, Leah appeared radiant. Since marrying Daniel, there was an inherent vivacity that had nothing to do with her pregnancy and everything to do with the adoration Daniel showered on her. He was grateful his two childhood friends had found love together.

Leah reached for Ava. "Let's see if we can figure out what's wrong with this little one."

For the next few minutes she peppered Mrs. Foster with questions and gave the baby a thorough examination.

Daniel paced behind her. "It's not contagious, is it? I don't want you exposed to something contagious."

He rested a hand on Leah's shoulder, and she reached across her chest and grasped his fingers. "There's nothing to worry about. It's a simple case of colic."

"Colic?" Will questioned. "What is that? How is that treated?"

The term was familiar—a stomach ailment—but he didn't know much else.

"Colic is a fancy word for a bellyache," Leah explained. "These little ones have sensitive tummies. Even the slightest change in her diet can cause an upset." She wrapped the blanket around the squirming baby once more. "There's not much to do but wait and ease her discomfort as best we can. We can give her a bit of peppermint tea. I wouldn't suggest anything more. Time is the best remedy. We're in for a long night."

"Not *we*." Daniel absently ran the backs of his knuckles along Leah's cheek. "Absolutely not. You've already had a busy evening. I'm taking you home, and you're putting your feet up. You've already been dancing. Not to mention all those stairs."

He shot another accusatory glance at Will.

"I'll stay," Tomasina offered. "Ava is accustomed to me."

Mrs. Foster nodded. "I'll stay, as well."

Will surveyed the group. "You've done enough, Mrs. Foster. Perhaps Miss Taggart can assist."

"She's at the dance." Mrs. Foster tsked. "First time the girl has shown any interest in something social. I refuse to drag her away."

With a mischievous grin, Leah held the baby against her shoulder and patted her back. "I don't mean to gossip, but I saw Miss Taggart dancing with a certain handsome drover."

"Who?" Tomasina demanded. "What did he look like?"

Will glanced between the two. Did Tomasina have a crush on one of the drovers?

"Oh, what was his name?" Leah bit her lower lip. "You remember, Daniel. We had him for supper. He's been helping out with guard duty, as well. He was on watch the night I injured my ankle. He wears that distinctive vest with beading on the back."

Daniel nodded. "That'd be James Johnson."

"Oh, yes. James!" Leah exclaimed. "Nice young fellow."

With everyone's attention focused on Ava, Will studied Tomasina's reaction. She appeared more speculative than jealous. Not that it was any of his business. Not in the least. He was merely curious as to her interest in James Johnson and Hannah Taggart.

The young drover seemed a decent enough fellow, and they'd be well chaperoned. The reverend was also in attendance at the dance, although Will wasn't certain if his presence was good or bad news for the young couple. The reverend didn't strike him as the sort of man who'd endorse the pairing. Drovers tended to be rough around the edges, not to mention their vagabond existence. Though father and daughter no longer lived beneath the same roof, the reverend kept a close watch on Hannah. If there was an attraction brewing between the young lady and the handsome cowboy, he doubted Reverend Taggart would approve.

Simon touched his cap. "I'd best get back downstairs. You want I should send for Hannah?"

"No. She's worked hard enough these past weeks caring for Ava and sewing dresses for all the ladies. Let her have some fun and relax for once." Will caught Simon's sleeve. "Can you send up a tray? I don't know if the ladies have eaten supper."

With a plan in place, the room quickly cleared, leaving only Will, Mrs. Foster and Tomasina.

Mrs. Foster's wrists dangled over the arms of her chair. "Ava seems to like it best when you walk with her. You let me know when it's my turn. I'm going to rest my eyes for a wee moment."

Twenty minutes later a knock sounded on the door and Simon appeared with a tray containing a teapot and cups, along with a selection of sliced meats and bread.

"You're a dear, Simon." Tomasina thanked the boy. "I'll take that."

As Will paced, she poured three cups of tea. He declined cream and sugar. Mrs. Foster accepted her cup and set the saucer on the table beside her chair. After experimenting with several positions, Will discovered that if he let Ava rest her stomach on his forearm, her arms and legs dangling, her head cradled in his hand, she quieted.

Tomasina shook her head. "That is the oddest way of carrying a baby I've ever seen."

"Shh. It's working. I don't care how it looks."

With Ava content, he heard another noise. A low, rumbling sound. Glancing around, he discovered Mrs. Foster had nodded off.

Seeing where his attention was focused, Tomasina stood and motioned him into the private parlor off the sitting room they'd converted into a nursery. She pulled the double doors closed behind them.

"Poor Mrs. Foster," she whispered. "She's had quite an evening. We might as well let her sleep for a bit."

"She was worried sick when I arrived." He paced in front of the fire. Though spring, the nights were chilly. "How do you like working in the kitchen?"

Tomasina straightened her arms, locked her elbows and stared at her blunt fingernails. "About that… I am no longer in your employ."

Will halted. "What did you do this time?"

"Me? Why must you assume that I did something?"

"What did you do?" he repeated, narrowing his eyes.

"I threatened the Ferguson boys with bodily harm if they didn't clean up the mess they'd made in the dining room."

Ava fussed, and he resumed his pacing. "I know those children. They can be rambunctious."

"They spilled a glass of milk on purpose, and then they deliberately tripped me."

"I'll speak with Mr. Ferguson. His boys have been a handful since their mother died. Mr. Ferguson can be distant. He lived in South Carolina. Lost his farm when he was away fighting."

"All that killing and dying," Tomasina said. "And for what? Nothing. We fought a war to keep the southern states part of the union, and now they're starving. Overrun by carpetbaggers. Most of the folks still farming after the war owe their souls to the mercantile."

"There didn't have to be a war."

The glint in her eyes warned him. A Northerner should never start a debate about the war with someone nicknamed Texas Tom.

She set her jaw and leaned forward.

There was absolutely no chance of an argument between the two of them about The War Between the States ending well.

Tomasina pinned Will with a mutinous glare. "Are you one of those folks who think the South needs to suffer? That we let them starve? Punish them?" She made a sound of disgust. "I don't know why Texas ever joined the union in the first place. We were better off before the war. Texas doesn't even have an elected representative in the federal government anymore."

"You can't blame President Johnson for that. Texas hasn't exactly met the requirements for reconstruction."

"Some reconstruction."

"Everyone knew reconstruction was going to be difficult. President Lincoln knew that better than anyone did. He paid with his life. A lasting peace might have been different had he lived."

"I guess we'll never know, will we?" She grimaced.

"The healing will take a generation. Nothing will happen overnight."

Tomasina had known this debate was a bad idea from the beginning. Will was a Union soldier, born and raised in the north. He didn't understand. For good or for ill, the Southern way of life had been destroyed. He was right about one thing: people didn't change generations of tradition overnight.

"There's healing and then there's punishment," Tomasina said. "Folks are punishing the South."

Why did everyone think starting over was easy? Folks who spent generations living a certain way weren't prepared to be upended. She needed to find another outfit. Once she found a trustworthy crew, she'd go back to the way things were. The key was James Johnson. He'd know the dependable cowboys from the rest. Except James had been dancing with Hannah Taggart earlier that evening. If he settled down with a wife, he wouldn't be going on the trail anymore.

No. James wasn't one for settling. There'd been rumors of a girl in Harper, Kansas, as well, and he hadn't settled down that time. There was no reason to think he was changing his ways now. It was a dance and that was all. No need to read anything into his actions. She and James were two of a kind. A couple of loners who'd never settle down. Like her pa before, she'd live and die on the trail.

Ava fussed for a moment then settled down once more. Simon arrived with the peppermint tea Leah had recommended, and Tomasina filled a bottle with the warmed brew. Ava fussed in Will's arms and eventually took a measure of the cure.

He grinned at Tomasina. "Success! We're parents in the making." He realized what he'd said, and tension stretched between them. "I didn't—"

"It's all right." She glanced away. Was the idea that unpalatable? "I know what you meant."

His pensive expression remained. Her chest grew so heavy she couldn't breathe. He'd make a wonderful father. Seeing his unabashed devotion to Ava, a child for whom he had no obligation, she knew he'd be a doting father to children of his own.

Her pa had never been particularly demonstrative. He'd loved her, but his work had been his life. He'd channeled his affection through his teaching. He'd always been a man who needed a student. He'd trained her to rope and ride, and then he'd trained James to do the same. Most of the younger men had learned from his vast wealth of knowledge. He'd certainly never treated her as a child. They'd made that agreement on her first trail ride. If she wanted to ride with the men, there'd be no coddling.

She didn't regret her upbringing. Not for a minute. She'd seen sights that most folks only dreamed about. She'd met Indians and trappers; she'd seen buffalo trails cut into the earth a hundred years ago.

Thinking back on all the places she'd been, all the people she'd met, she couldn't recall ever feeling this overwhelming sense of comfort and peace. The sensation was a panacea, tugging her toward its depths yet always out of reach. Having Will near, she felt utterly protected and safe. She'd heard Daniel call him "the captain," and she understood the designation. She had no doubt he'd give his life for her.

He was an arm's distance and a lifetime away from her.

He rubbed his nose against Ava's, drawing a coo from the tiny baby. There was no trace of boyishness in his features. The hard planes of his face had been shaped by battle and loss, tragedy and grief, yet he appeared younger in that moment—lighter somehow.

He was an affectionate man, and she wasn't used to affection. She'd never realized the comforting assurance of human touch—the cupping of her elbow as she'd traversed an uneven patch on the boardwalk, the way he'd rested his hand on her hip when he'd sensed she was upset. The gentle pressure of his lips against her forehead.

A tremor of pure emotion vibrated through her. She wanted to fling herself into the warmth of his solid embrace and crush her cheek against the linen of his shirt. She wanted to feel safe and protected. She wanted to feel as though she belonged someplace.

Instead she held herself in check.

How was putting that burden on Will any different than depending on her pa? She needed to build her own life, her own future. She was no better than Dora. She'd seen how the dark-haired girl had clung to the banker's arm. Tomasina might have lived on the trail most of her life, but she had a fair understanding of how the world worked for a woman. Hitching her wagon to a rich man guaranteed Dora a better future. Yet she'd always be beholden. Trapped in a cage of her own making.

Will glanced up, his expression concerned. "Are you all right?"

She stood and glanced at the door. Why stay when there was nothing for her here? A shiver rattled through her body. In an instant Will was on his feet. After resting Ava in the bassinet, he reached for the coat he'd discarded over a chair.

Wrapping the material around her shoulders, he guided her toward the settee once more and then urged her toward the spot nearest the fire.

He caught her hands, massaging warmth into her fingers. "You're like ice. You should have said something sooner."

"When were you engaged to Leah?" she blurted.

The question had been eating away at her. She'd watched them together this evening and sensed nothing but friendship between them. That observation had fueled her curiosity.

Something flickered in his gaze. "Ages ago. Before the war. We were young. Naive. It seemed the thing to do. I saw her as a friend, as a companion. But Daniel had always loved her. Truly loved her. Things worked out exactly as they should. Eventually."

"And Dora?" The name quivered on her tongue.

His expression grew shuttered, and her heart sank. Why must she always charge into things without thinking first? Pippa had admonished her more than once for being too direct. Evidently, ladies didn't pry. According to Pippa, ladies didn't gossip, either. Instead they "shared" the news of the day. The rules of being a lady were complicated. But Tomasina wasn't a lady. Not really.

Will stared into the fire, and the crackling flames cast shadows over the planes of his face. "She decided we didn't suit."

"You're lying." She might not be a lady, but that didn't mean she lacked feminine intuition. "Dora wanted a piece of your hide. You broke off the engagement, didn't you?"

There'd been a distinct venom behind Dora's toothy smile.

"I can't say."

Tomasina sank her fingers into the plush velvet tufting of the wine-colored settee. "She was after your money, wasn't she?"

He made a choking sound, and she slapped him on the back.

He coughed and sputtered. "Why do you think that?"

"The way she was hanging on that banker. He's not nearly as handsome as you." She cleared her throat. "I mean to say, there's no reason she'd have chosen Mr. Wilson over you."

"Mr. Wilson is a fine gentleman. They suit each other."

A rush of relief surged through her. His gentlemanly answer was all she needed. He had most definitely ended the engagement and not the other way around. The truth struck her as a triumph. She much preferred Dora as a gold digger and not the source of Will's unrequited love. Judging by his tone, he wasn't too broken up by the loss.

"I'm not as fickle as I appear." Appearing abashed, he raked his fingers through his dark hair. "You don't think the worst of me, do you?"

She ruffled the velvet against the grain then smoothed it back in place once more. "What does my opinion matter?"

"It matters."

Her heart pounded with sudden painful jerks. She ached to stroke her finger down the sandpapery length of his jaw. She tugged his coat tighter around her shoulders.

Ava squalled, breaking the mood around them.

Will straightened with a rueful laugh. "I declared victory too soon."

Tomasina turned away, hoping he hadn't seen the flash of sorrow in her eyes. He'd make a fine father one day. She stood and backed away from the realization, physically and mentally. Her hip bumped against the buffet, rattling the supper dishes.

He'd make a fine husband. Just not hers.

Chapter Sixteen

Will woke with a start. The hand shaking his shoulder retracted.

Simon stared down at him. "Time to get up."

Blinking, Will rubbed the heels of his hands against his eyes. "What time is it?"

"Half past ten."

He bolted upright. "That late? I'm meeting Mr. King at the land office."

He rose and glanced around the room. The last he recalled, Tomasina had fallen asleep on the couch, his coat wrapped around her shoulders. The space was empty now, his coat folded and draped neatly over the arm.

He'd known immediately she was gone. It felt as though all the life had gone out of the room with her.

His porter turned toward the door. "Mrs. Foster is resting. Ava is better this morning. Hannah is watching her in her room. After last evening, no one wanted to disturb you."

Yanking open the curtains, Simon bathed the room in sunlight.

Will shaded his eyes against the glare. He discovered his shaving kit had been prepared and a dark charcoal suit had been pressed and hung on the back of the door. Simon had been busy this morning.

The young porter had been up late the previous evening, as well. Maybe not as late as Will and Tomasina, but late all the same. Tomasina's subtle accusation rang in his ears. Simon worked far too hard for a boy of his age.

Will reached for his shaving blade. "Simon, do you ever take a day off?"

"Why would I do that?"

After splashing his hands in the washbowl, Will dried them on the dangling towel. "You didn't attend the dance last evening, either."

"Someone had to watch the front desk."

Will lathered his face then scraped the blade along his chin. "Take a few days off. Relax. Mr. Rumsford and Mrs. Foster can handle the extra work."

The boy's face crumpled. "Have I done something wrong?"

Will flicked the foam off his blade into the washbowl and turned. "No, of course not. You're my best employee. It's just that you work too hard. Take some time for yourself."

"I can't. I'm saving money."

That gave him pause. "For what?"

"Schooling. Mr. Rumsford went to a fancy college back east. He talks about it all the time. I'm going to study the law someday."

Will's chest constricted. He'd never known Simon's aspirations. In all the years they'd worked together, he'd never thought to ask about his plans—or anything else of a personal nature. He'd been treating the boy as a fellow soldier when he should have been regarding him as a younger brother or a son. Shame heated his face. The habits he'd formed during his years in the war had transferred into his civilian life. He'd kept a distance from the men fighting beneath his command out of necessity. There was no room for sentiment in war. Only with Daniel and Noah had he let down his guard. The war was over, and it was time for a change.

"I'll make you a deal," Will said. "I'll pay for your schooling, with one condition."

Simon frowned. "Why would you do that?"

"This town needs more lawyers. Every time I buy a parcel of land or sell a property, the lawyers are involved. I'm starting to wonder if the last fellow knew his job. There's trouble with the deed to the Godwin's store. Not to mention I'll be asking the town for investors in the Union Pacific soon. You can hardly cross the street these days without consulting a lawyer. I'd consider your schooling an investment."

"An investment? How so?" the lad asked.

"I'd ask that you stay in Cowboy Creek for five years after your graduation in return for my investment."

"I'm honored, sir." Simon's voice was filled with awe.

"Think about it, Simon. That's a big commitment. The years of schooling in addition to five years in Cowboy Creek. I can't promise the town will make you rich, but it's growing. You'll always have business."

The boy's eyes glimmered, and his Adam's apple bobbed. "Thank you. I wish my ma was around. She always said I was smart."

"Your mother would be proud. You're smart. You're a hard worker. I've come to rely on you. I've also taken you for granted. You're trustworthy and dedicated, and you're growing into a fine young man full of potential." Will exhaled a slow, ragged breath. "I should have realized sooner that you were meant for something more. I was selfish. I couldn't imagine running this hotel without you. While I might lose you as an employee, I hope I can keep you as a friend."

"A friend?" The same wonder infused Simon's words. "Thank you. I'd like that."

"You're welcome," Will replied, his voice gruff. "It's settled then."

The war was over, and it was time to stop shutting people out. Dora was a prime example. He'd enjoyed her company, but his feelings for her had been shallow. The paltry sentiment had been mutual. Dora was more interested in a comfortable life and the chance at being the first lady of Kansas. Her esteem for him had not stretched beyond those goals. She'd merely been a convenient choice for a spouse. With neither investing too much of their heart, the choice had been safe for both of them.

Since enlisting in the Union Army, he'd kept his feelings tightly contained. With great love came great loss, and he'd seen too much death already. The practice no longer served a purpose. There would be losses to come. No life remained untouched. But he'd been denying himself the joy of close friendships. Even his connection with Daniel and Noah had suffered. He'd held a part of himself back, fearing that if something ever happened to one of them he'd never be whole again.

"Thank you for this opportunity." Simon interrupted his musings. "I won't let you down."

Will chose his next words carefully. "I was a grown man when I lost my parents, and I miss them every day. You never told me what happened to your folks."

"The war," Simon replied simply. "I didn't like the orphanage. I wound up here."

There was more to the boy's story, but he decided not to press him. The shift in their relationship was too new, too fragile. There'd be time enough for questions later.

"You have made your parents proud. You're a fine young man."

His throat working, Simon approached and held out his hand. "I wish they could have met you."

"And I them." Will clasped his fingers and slapped his shoulder. "Take the day off and start making plans."

"Tomorrow. I'll take tomorrow off and rest up for Friday." Simon grasped Will's charcoal-gray coat and shook it out with a flick of his wrists. "Friday is an important day for Cowboy Creek. Gideon Kendricks is arriving, and the town council meeting is that evening."

A knock indicated another visitor.

Simon crossed the room and swung open the door.

Sheriff Davis doffed his hat and stepped inside.

Will offered him a drink, which he declined, and a seat, which he accepted.

The sheriff propped his hat on his bent knee and rested his hand on the brim. "You better do something about those cowboys, Canfield, because I'm running out of jail cells."

Anticipating a lengthy conversation, Will dismissed Simon, and the boy promised to fetch him when it was time to meet Mr. King at the land office.

Will took the seat across from Sheriff Davis. "What happened?"

"The usual. After you left the dance, the boys got rowdy. Drinking. Fighting…"

Will clenched his hand on his thigh. "I should have stayed."

"Nothing you could have done." Quincy waved off his concern. "It was late. Most of the ladies and the families had left already. I'm thinking we ought to clear out the tent city. If there's not enough room for them to stay at Drover's Place, then it's time for them to move on."

"That's Daniel's decision. It's his property."

"You better speak with Mr. Gardner real quick like then, because I'm running out of room in the drunk tank."

"I'll speak with Daniel." This was an unfortunate turn of events. They walked a fine line with the drovers. While the town would survive without the cattle drives, many of the local businesses would suffer. "In another month or two, most of them will move on anyway."

"If we make it that long." The sheriff cleared his throat. "There's something else." He swallowed hard and then cleared his throat again. "If the drovers were occupied, they might cause less trouble."

The few ways of entertaining cowboys that came to mind were hardly suitable.

"You think I should set up a quilting bee?" Will joked.

The sheriff coughed and sputtered. "Not a quilting bee, no."

Will stood and poured a glass of water, offering it to Quincy. "If you have a suggestion, don't beat around the bush. I'm all out of ideas."

"A rodeo," Quincy announced. "Let's plan a rodeo."

Will gaped. "After what happened before?"

"That was an accident."

"You really think a rodeo will help?"

"At this point it sure can't hurt."

Tomasina's words came rushing back. She'd warned him. She knew those drovers better than anyone. They worked hard and they played hard.

"I'll speak with Texas Tom." Will cast a baleful glance toward the door. "I'll ask her to consider more roping contests and less bull riding."

"It's a good idea."

She was never going to let him live down his change of heart. "Time will tell."

Quincy stood and replaced his hat, running his thumb

and forefinger along the brim. "I'll be at the meeting on Friday."

"Excellent. I'll need all the support I can get." He followed the sheriff out the door. "I'll walk you out. I have a quick stop to make at the land office."

His quick stop turned out to be singularly frustrating. The office was torn apart and stacks of deeds had been pulled for authentication. The deeds to the Godwins' shops had been discovered as forgeries.

Mr. King scurried around the office. The land officer was slight and balding with a wisp of hair he'd coaxed over his forehead.

The older man placed the two Godwin documents side by side on the table. "As you can clearly see, sir, the signatures don't match."

"I know my own signature."

"Then you realize this deed is a fake. Along with several others."

"I see *what* you're saying, I don't understand *why*." Will shoved a hand through his hair and scowled. "What is the purpose of stealing the real deeds?"

"It ties up all the sales in court, doesn't it? You can't sell the property without a clear deed. All the sales of property in Cowboy Creek are in limbo until further notice."

"All of them?"

"All of them." Mr. King spread his hands. "I can't risk a sale. Not until we discover which deeds are authentic and which are fake. If you think we're in a mess now, wait until the bank is involved."

"I know the original documents were legal. Which means they were altered after we filed the paperwork," Will said slowly. "I don't recall hearing about a burglary at the land office. When do you suppose this happened?"

"Whoever did this was smart. There's no way to tell

when the forgeries started, which means all the deeds are in question."

"The Cowboy Café was vandalized recently. Everyone assumed the Murdochs were stealing supplies. What if we were wrong? You've complained before about the noises and smells. The buildings are connected. What if the land office was the real target, and robbing the café was merely the cover?"

"The Murdochs are wily. They can rob a church in broad daylight and slip into town a few weeks later to dump Zeb." Mr. King's expression turned speculative. "But why break into the land office and replace the deeds with forgeries when there are thousands of dollars in the bank across the street?"

"Excellent question." Will surveyed the documents once more. "Think about this from the Murdochs' perspective. For starters, no one has assigned this crime to them."

"True. None of us even realized a crime had been committed."

"Exactly." Will stuffed the Godwins' forged deeds into his breast pocket. "I'll speak with the Godwins this afternoon. What should I tell them?"

"They can't rent the shop unless we can prove they own the building." Mr. King straightened a pile of papers. "There are legal ramifications."

Will massaged the spot between his eyes with two fingers. He certainly didn't need this trouble right now. With Gideon Kendrick's arrival in town, he didn't need any additional complications.

"Sort out the fake deeds from the real deeds," Will said. "We can start from there."

At this rate he'd best get Simon through law school quickly. There was already a legal mess for sorting. First the Murdoch Gang, then the trouble with the drovers, now the deeds.

What else could go wrong?

Having slept late, Tomasina snagged several slices of bacon and a mug of coffee before taking a seat in the empty dining room. Moments later Simon crossed through toward the kitchen, whistling a merry tune.

Tomasina did a double take. "What's put the song in your step this morning?"

"I'm going to law school back east," he said, straightening his cap.

"Just like that?"

"Just like that. Mr. Canfield is paying for my schooling so long as I start my practice in Cowboy Creek."

She peered at him over the rim of her coffee cup. "He is? What brought that about?"

"We talked this morning. Different than we normally talk. We talked as equals. He listened to what I had to say. Really listened."

Her chest swelled. Will had listened to Simon. He'd listened to her. Instead of ignoring her criticism when she'd questioned his handling of Simon, he'd actually taken her advice and talked with the boy. He actually respected her opinion.

Meaning to thank Will for his generous offer to Simon, and since she was currently between jobs with no place to be that day, she watched for him until he returned. When he crossed the lobby, she froze. Suddenly nervous, she stood from the banquette and called his name.

He turned, his expression unreadable.

There were no guests in the lobby, and the front desk was empty. There was an awkwardness between them that hadn't been there the night before.

She rung her hands together. "Uh… Ava is doing well this morning."

"She's a tough little scamp," Will said. "How are you? No ill effects from your sleepless night?"

"Nah. It's the same as having a late watch on the trail. I'll catch up on my sleep tonight." She ducked her head. "Simon said you talked with him this morning. He told me about becoming a lawyer."

"That's all your doing. I didn't give you the proper credit when I spoke to the boy. I'll correct the oversight the next time I see him."

"No. Don't tell him." She flashed an impish smile. "I don't think he'd like feeling beholden to me."

"I'm beholden to you and grateful for it. I'm ashamed I didn't approach him sooner."

"Then you're not mad at me for being too honest?"

He barked out a laugh. "Never apologize for plain speaking."

"You don't mind my honesty?"

"This town needs more people like you. I'll tell you something I learned in the army: the higher a man moves up the ranks, the less likely folks are to tell him the truth. The same holds true in civilian life. I don't want to be surrounded by people who tell me what I want to hear, I want people who tell me what I *need* to hear."

Her chest expanded. Praise had been rare in the Stone family and given only grudgingly.

The clock in the lobby chimed, and Will's gaze turned toward the sound. "I have a meeting this afternoon. How goes the job hunt?"

"Still looking."

"You're wasted in menial tasks, Miss Stone."

She arched a brow. "Do you have a better idea?"

"No. But I'm thinking."

"If you think of something, let me know."

Their goodbye was as awkward as their greeting. Will continued on to his meeting, and Tomasina remained motionless. The staff bustled around her. Everyone had someplace to be. Everyone had something to do. Everyone but her.

At loose ends, she wandered outside. She rounded the corner and caught sight of the picturesque church in the distance. Gazing up at the impressive structure, she couldn't help but admire how the shiny bell in the tower caught and reflected the afternoon sunlight. She walked down Second Street and approached the white frame church building with its soaring steeple and fresh paint. Reverend Taggart, Hannah's father, knelt beside the front stairs, a trowel in hand. When he spotted Tomasina, he waved her over.

"Miss Stone. How are you this fine morning?"

She'd met the reverend on two previous occasions. He was a kindly man with neatly trimmed brown hair and a stature that, though not rotund, tended toward paunch. He sported a narrow mustache and a smile that creased the corner of his eyes. His affection for his daughter was obvious. Tomasina had caught him gazing at her a time or two, his expression troubled.

Having been raised by her pa, she understood his apprehension. He clearly wanted the best for Hannah, but his attitude around her was uncertain. He treated his daughter with kid gloves, gingerly asking her questions, then retreating, as though he feared the answers. The two of them shared an obvious affection, but there was distance between them she didn't understand.

The reverend wiped his forehead with the back of his hand. "I thought I'd plant some roses. The missus always liked roses. Hannah never took to gardening like her mother."

"I was never much for gardening myself."

A pang of longing surprised her. Before, when Pippa had mentioned a garden, the idea had felt suffocating. Seeing the reverend with circles of dirt marring the knees of his trousers and soil beneath his fingernails, she had a sudden desire to sink her hands into the dark earth.

"Have you seen the inside of the church?" he asked.

"I haven't."

Her pa had been a God-fearing man, and he'd carried a worn Bible on all their travels. He hadn't been much for crowds, though, and he'd never been comfortable attending church.

The reverend led the way. He held the door for her, and she stepped inside. The interior of the church smelled of new wood and plaster. Twelve stained glass windows lined the east and west walls, six on each side. The morning light streamed through and reflected colorful rainbows on the polished wood pews and floor.

Tomasina gazed in awe. "This is beautiful."

"The town council did a fine job with the design."

She sank onto one of the pews and ran her hand along the polished wood. "You must be real proud of this church."

"I am." He took a seat in the row ahead of hers, rested his arm on the back of the pew, then spoke over his shoulder. "Thank you for being a friend to Hannah. She speaks highly of you."

"She's been a good friend to me, too."

"She didn't warm to the other ladies as quickly as I'd hoped. The first few weeks here, she barely left her room at the boardinghouse. Since she's been staying at the hotel, she's more social. Did my heart good to see her at the dance last night."

"Hannah is wonderful with Ava." Tomasina gushed with the compliments. "I don't know what Mr. Canfield would have done without her help."

"How is the wee one this morning? I heard she had a rough time last evening"

"She's fine." Word of Ava's illness had sure spread quickly. "No worse for wear. I wish the rest of us could say the same. We didn't get much sleep last night."

"Yes. I was sorry Hannah couldn't enjoy the rest of the dance. She told me that after she left, the two of you were up all night pacing the floors with the baby."

Tomasina blanched. Hannah had stayed the night with her pa. At least that's what she'd said when she and Hannah had arrived back at their room at the same time this morning.

Snatching her hat from where she'd rested it on the pew, Tomasina slid into the aisle. "It was nice seeing your church, Reverend Taggart. It's a real beauty."

"I hope to see you here next Sunday. All are welcome in the house of the Lord."

"I'll take you up on that offer."

Fearful she'd give something away, Tomasina stumbled outside, blinking against the blinding sunlight.

If Hannah hadn't been with her father, where had she been all night? And who had she been with? Tomasina replaced her hat. She had a real bad feeling she knew the answer to both those questions.

Chapter Seventeen

Will paced the platform of the train depot, anxious for the arrival of the Union Pacific representative.

Simon stood beside him, his hands clasped behind his back. "Don't worry, boss. Everything is in order."

"Any word from the jail?" Will asked.

"Zeb is still laid up. He ain't talking. The doc thinks the fever may have done something to his brain. Something permanent."

"Gus and Old Horace think he's faking."

Simon shook his head. "I trust the doc over Gus and Old Horace.

"Either way, tell anyone and everyone who will listen that Zeb is in no shape to travel. The Murdochs won't come for him if he's a hindrance."

Will wasn't sure whom to believe. He trusted the doc, but the Murdochs were a wily bunch. As long as Zeb was in the jail cell, the town was in peril. He'd speak with the doc about transferring the prisoner to a larger town. Cowboy Creek didn't have the resources for jailing a fugitive beyond a week or two.

The steam whistle blew, scattering the chickens pecking along the tracks. Moments later the train chugged to a halt. Passengers disembarked, emerging through the steam vapors.

A tall gentleman stepped onto the platform. He was young, not yet thirty, with slicked-back blond hair. His mustache and goatee were neatly trimmed. Though he'd been riding the rails all morning, his dove-gray suit was impeccable. There wasn't a whisker of stubble on his cheeks or a single hair out of place. The man's gaze scanned the crowd before landing on Will.

He cut a direct path across the platform with singular purpose. His presence was such that people scooted out of his way.

The man paused in front of Will and Simon. "Will Canfield, I assume?"

"You must be Gideon Kendricks."

"I am. Good to meet you, sir."

Will clasped the man's hand in greeting. "How did you know who I was?"

"You have the bearing of a man accustomed to giving orders."

"I'll take that as a compliment," he said with a wry grin.

"As it was intended."

The man was a politician in the making.

"Have you had a noon meal yet?" Will asked.

"Not yet."

"Then let me invite you to the Cowboy Café. Nels Patterson makes the best chicken salad this side of the Mississippi. He also serves an excellent steak, if you'd prefer."

Gideon patted the flat plane of his stomach. "I never turn down a good meal."

"Then you've come to the right place. Simon, here, will see to your luggage. If there's anything you need during your stay in Cowboy Creek, let me know. My porter and I are at your disposal."

"Thank you." The gentleman tipped back his head and studied the cloudless sky. "I've been sitting on the train for hours. A stretch of the legs will do me good. How about a tour of Cowboy Creek before we eat?"

"Excellent." Will was impressed with the man already. He was direct without being rude, curious without being aggressive. "We'll take Eden Street to Zimmerman's and walk back on the opposite side. Most of the established business are along Eden Street."

"A good investor is always on the lookout for prosperity."

Gideon proved to be remarkably quick-witted. His questions were astute and his manners above reproach. They strolled down Eden Street past the bank, and Will made a point to skirt past the monument. While he appreciated the sentiment, he found the whole thing rather embarrassing. They passed the barber and the jail, sketching a wave to Old Horace and Gus across the street. He peered into the window of the *Herald* and caught sight of D.B. with his head bent over the typeset, Prudence by his side.

He didn't linger. Those two weren't exactly the best ambassadors for Cowboy Creek. His concern over Prudence and her mysterious, reappearing cameo returned with force. Following Zeb's capture and the trouble with the drovers, he'd forgotten to confide his concerns with Noah and Daniel. He made a mental note to do so later.

Pausing at Aunt Mae's boardinghouse, he caught sight of a very familiar redhead sitting with Pippa Neely on the porch. His heart stuttered in his chest. It was as though an invisible thread joined them, tethering them despite whatever physical distance separated them. She brought out a tenderness in him; a fierce urge to cherish her and to protect her. The sensation was unlike anything he'd ever experienced.

Certainly he'd felt affection for the women in his life. He considered Leah a friend. He and Dora had shared mutual interests. However nothing had prepared him for this soul-deep yearning. He felt as though his whole life had been leading him toward this moment.

A part of him balked at the attachment. The attributes about Tomasina that he admired were the same things that made a relationship between them impossible. Whereas he was bound to the town, she was a free spirit. Whereas he'd built a solid foundation, a house and a thriving business, she let her heart lead her. He was an oak tree, putting down roots, growing slow and steady. She was a tumbleweed, as wild and beautiful as the vast prairie surrounding them.

Gideon stared at him expectantly, and Will shook off his romantic musings. He'd never been a sentimental fellow, and this was no time to change. Pippa and Tomasina were deep in conversation and didn't immediately notice the two men. Will cleared his throat, and they sprang apart.

He braced his boot on the bottom tread and rested his elbow on his bent knee. "Miss Stone, Miss Neely, allow me to introduce you to Gideon Kendricks. He's visiting Cowboy Creek on behalf of the Union Pacific Railroad."

Gideon climbed the shallow stairs and leaned over Tomasina's hand. "A pleasure."

He repeated the gesture with Pippa.

Pippa smoothed her skirts and gave a coquettish grin. "Where are you two gentleman walking this fine afternoon?"

"The Cowboy Café." Gideon looked over his shoulder for confirmation from Will. "I've been trapped on a train all afternoon."

"That's an odd thing for a railroad man to say." Pippa tilted her head. "I doubt your superiors at the Union Pacific would appreciate the allusion to being trapped."

"Merely a turn of phrase."

"A telling one."

The air between them crackled, and Will suppressed a grin. They were both absurdly good-looking, and both well aware of their charms. Those two had met their match in each other, and sparks were bound to fly.

Without letting his composure slip, Gideon offered Pippa his wide, charming smile. "Mr. Canfield's tour of your lovely town has worked up my appetite."

"Dining at the Cowboy Café, you say?" Pippa stood and patted her hair, straightening the wisp of a hat balanced atop her head. "Isn't that a coincidence? We were planning to eat there as well, weren't we, Tomasina?"

Tomasina started to say something and then yelped.

The two exchanged a speaking look.

"Uh… I could eat," Tomasina said after a lengthy pause. "Let me tell Aunt Mae we're leaving."

The screen door banged behind her. She returned a moment later, a pert straw hat adorned with a cluster of daisies set at a rakish angle upon her head. Any other lady would have worn the hat low on her forehead. Not Tomasina. She created her own, unique style.

Pippa sashayed forward and held out her hand, letting Gideon assist her down the stairs. He turned almost immediately and offered Tomasina a hand, as well.

The move left Will standing beside Pippa, and he offered her his elbow. A hint of a pout skittered across her face before she mastered her emotions. She slipped her hand through the crook of his arm and glanced wistfully over his shoulder. He'd have been amused by her dismay if he wasn't experiencing his own stab of jealousy.

"You must travel quite a lot, Mr. Kendricks," Tomasina said. "For your work."

"I have a home in Omaha. I spent exactly thirty-two days there last year."

Pippa batted her eyelashes. "Surely you exaggerate."

"I'd never lie to a lady," he replied, his eyes twinkling.

Tomasina gazed up at the handsome blond man, and Will suppressed the urge to yank her away. If she brought out his tender side, she'd also unearthed a jealous, brutish side he hadn't known he possessed until now.

"You must have seen a great many amazing sights," Tomasina said breathlessly. "I envy you."

A thread of possessiveness wound around his heart. Why hadn't he seen the obvious right off? Gideon was the perfect sort of man for Tomasina. She adored an adventure, and his job provided a constant source of travel.

Except this Gideon fellow's smile was far too toothy. His hair was too well kept and his suit a touch extravagant; a sure sign of vanity. Gideon's exaggerated lack of interest in Pippa was suspect, as well. The man probably had a sweetheart in every town he visited. He wasn't good enough for Tomasina. Far from it.

Pippa tugged on Will's sleeve and flashed an overly bright smile. "Is Mr. Kendricks staying long in Cowboy Creek?"

"A week or two. Maybe more if his work requires."

Tomasina laughed at something Gideon was saying near her ear.

"Hmm," Pippa's lips turned down in a pout. "Those two have certainly struck up a quick friendship."

Will gritted his teeth. Gideon was not perfect for Tomasina. He was perfect for Pippa. Or someone else. Anyone else. Anyone but Tomasina.

A short while later Nels Patterson seated the four of them at a square table in the center of the Cowboy Café. From Will's spot across from Tomasina, he swallowed his sour mood and admired her fresh beauty instead. She'd donned a dress today instead of her chaps. A simple green calico that brought out the luster in her luminous skin and sparked golden highlights in her red hair.

She caught his gaze and smiled shyly. Their relationship had altered the previous evening, and he was only beginning to understand the implications.

Because if Gideon Kendricks touched her sleeve one more time, he was going to lay the man flat.

Tomasina stared at Pippa, who'd obviously taken leave of her senses. Eating lunch at the Cowboy Café had not been part of their afternoon plans.

Her encounter with the reverend had been weighing on her mind, and she'd sought out Pippa's advice. If Hannah had not stayed overnight at her father's house, then where had she been? Since Pippa had remained at the dance, she might have a clue as to Hannah's whereabouts the previous evening. If one of the drovers was playing fast and loose with Hannah, Tomasina vowed to find the man. She considered Hannah a friend, and no one took advantage of her friends. Especially not a fellow drover.

Seeking Pippa's guidance on how to proceed proved to be impossible without revealing Hannah's identity. That left Tomasina no closer to a solution than before.

The Cowboy Café was homey and welcoming with enticing aromas wafting from the kitchen. A glass-fronted display case filled with mouthwatering pies lined the back wall. Most of the tables were occupied, and friendly chatter lent a festive backdrop to their conversation.

Gideon Kendricks touched her sleeve, and she started. "I'm sorry, I didn't hear your question."

Will bumped the table, rattling the dishes. Tomasina shot him a curious stare.

"I was asking how you came to settle in Cowboy Creek," Gideon said.

"I haven't settled." Caught off guard, she fumbled for a reply. "Not yet at least."

"You have me intrigued."

"I arrived on the cattle drive." She glanced at the gingham napkin in her lap. "I'm a drover. I was riding point."

Gideon leaned forward. "That's fascinating. You drive cattle?"

Since he didn't appear shocked, she warmed to the subject. "All my life. Brought in almost four thousand head on this last drive."

"You have my undying admiration, Miss Stone. Such difficult work."

Will snapped his napkin onto his lap. "Miss Neely is the director of the new opera house. She's planning an inaugural performance next Friday."

"How delightful," Gideon declared, his rapt attention focused on Tomasina. "Will you be participating, Miss Stone?"

"I will be singing," Pippa announced. "I can sing."

Her tone had taken a desperate edge, and Tomasina looked between the two. She'd never seen Pippa flustered. Then again, she'd never seen a man who didn't fawn all over himself when speaking with her. Except maybe Will. He was polite toward Pippa without showing her any deference. Pippa didn't seem to mind Will's indifference.

Gideon was clearly upsetting her. While the railroad executive wasn't exactly ignoring Pippa, he wasn't singling her out, either. And Pippa was accustomed to being the center of attention.

Gideon tossed Pippa a cursory glance and smiled politely. "I hope I have the opportunity to hear your beautiful voice."

"Since you're staying through the week, Mr. Kendricks," Will interjected smoothly, "I hope you can attend."

"I wouldn't miss it."

Nels Patterson interrupted Gideon's next question and took their orders. They each chose the house specialty—chicken-salad sandwiches with lemonade.

The conversation ebbed and flowed. Gideon was charming, and he appeared to be equal with his flattery, but Tomasina sensed a growing unease from Pippa and Will. If her fellow drovers had been acting oddly, she'd have called him out. Drovers were known for their plain speaking. Since that tactic clearly wasn't appropriate in this setting, she'd have to find another way.

When the sandwiches were all but eaten, Tomasina stood. "Pie."

Both men automatically stood.

Gideon tilted his head. "Pardon?"

"Aunt Mae, who runs the boardinghouse, provides pies for the Cowboy Café. They're the best in town. Come look."

Though mildly surprised by the offer, Gideon followed her to the glass case at the back of the restaurant.

She pointed to a particularly scrumptious peach pie. "Are you flirting with me, Mr. Gideon?"

His ears pinkened. "You're a lovely lady, Miss Stone."

"Well, stop it. I don't flirt. Pippa flirts. Flirt with Pippa."

"I take it your affections are engaged elsewhere."

"Where my affections are engaged is none of your concern." She indicated another pie. "Some people enjoy a lemon meringue, but I'm partial to apple or peach." She pinned him with a stare. "I think Pippa likes you, and you're driving her mad."

"Good."

Tomasina hoisted her eyebrows. "Why is that good?"

Gideon had the grace to appear abashed. "I have a feeling Miss Neely is used to getting what she wants."

Dawning understanding softened Tomasina's annoyance. "Oh. I get it now. You like her, but you don't want her to know that you like her."

"I don't know if I like her," he grumbled. "I've only just met her."

"You like her. Same thing happened to me at the schoolhouse in Abilene when I was eight. Tim Twohig used to put tacks on my chair because he liked me. Ignoring Pippa is just another way of putting tacks on her chair."

"Are you always this forthright?"

Tomasina shrugged. "Usually. I've had to be more careful lately. The rules of being a drover are different than the rules of living in town."

Nels approached the counter, wiping his hands on the towel tucked into the strings tying his apron around his waist. "Can I serve you folks some pie?"

"Four slices of apple," Tomasina said. "You like apple pie, Mr. Kendricks?"

"I adore apple pie."

"Excellent," she said.

"You're quite unusual, Miss Stone."

She pursed her lips. "That doesn't sound like a compliment."

"It was a great compliment. Your candor is refreshing." Gideon motioned her back toward the table. "I apologize for my earlier behavior. In my line of work, I've become accustomed to playing games. I forget that not everyone understands the rules."

"What is the point of playing games? Why not speak your mind?"

"The usual reasons. To test the waters. To save face."

"I hope you know what you're doing with Pippa," Tomasina stated archly. "She has her choice of men in town, you know."

"I know. And that's the whole problem."

Along with Nels' assistance, they delivered the pie to the table. The rest of the dessert passed with little drama. Gideon took on the role of storyteller and regaled them all with anecdotes from his travels. He and Will staged a mock fight over the check and everyone left the restaurant in a chipper mood.

Once outside, Pippa managed a maneuver that neatly forced Gideon into presenting his elbow. Grinning from ear to ear, the gentleman flashed a triumphant look over one shoulder.

Tomasina shook her head. Gideon must know what he was doing. Pippa was practically hanging on his arm.

Will let the space stretch between the couples. "Gideon was certainly friendly."

"He's very handsome."

Will squinted at Gideon's back. "In an average sort of way."

"He's quite well traveled."

"Anyone can sit on a train. How is that interesting?"

Tomasina warmed to her subject. She might not know the game as well as Gideon, but she was learning. If she didn't know better, she'd think Will was a little jealous. And not of Gideon's attention to Pippa.

"He's well spoken," she said coyly.

"If you like that sort of thing."

She glanced across the street and caught sight of the boarded windows of the Drover's Place. The recollection of the rumors floating around town dampened her good mood.

There was talk of running out the drovers, and the mood

among the men was tense. "What is Sheriff Davis doing about the cowboys?"

"He believes they need a distraction."

"What sort of distraction?" she asked.

"I suggested a rodeo. Maybe a sharpshooting contest."

She gasped and faced him on the boardwalk, her hands on her hips. "Are you serious?"

"I was wrong, Tomasina Stone." He grinned at her outrage. "You were right."

She took his elbow once more. "Can I have that stamped into the brass plaque honoring the town founders?"

"No. You may not. That blasted monument is embarrassing enough."

"They only meant to honor you."

"I appreciate the sentiment." He offered a crooked grin. "Not the execution."

She enjoyed their verbal sparring. Thoughts buzzed around her brain, and as many scattered emotions chased around her heart. She'd always considered herself tough. Over the past few weeks she'd discovered an unexpected thread of vulnerability in her heart.

She felt the play of muscles beneath her fingertips. More and more she feared he had the ability to pierce her guarded heart. What kind of future could they ever have together? Despite her instructions from Pippa this week, she was still the same person. The evening of the dance, though delightful, had only cemented her concerns. Will had ambitions and she wasn't fit for the governor's mansion.

In politics, everything was a chess game. Moves and countermoves. She preferred plain speaking. Only moments before Gideon had been flirting and playing a game, a game everyone at the table had understood but her. How would she ever survive in Will's world? She was a bigger fool for even worrying about the agonizing pain of his rejection. She'd tested the waters, and she'd saved her dignity if not her heart. He'd been engaged to two women—two beautiful, accomplished ladies. Though Dora's motives had been suspect, the truth was there.

Consider how Mrs. Lincoln, the former first lady, had suffered. Her husband's position had only sheltered her so much. Tomasina had yet to earn her own esteem in this world, and she was tired of borrowing respect from someone else.

The rest of the walk passed in companionable silence, and they soon reached the hotel. Since Will was leading the meeting of the town council that afternoon, Gideon offered to walk Pippa to the boardinghouse.

Tomasina stepped into the lobby and discovered James Johnson slouched in one of the chairs.

He stood when he saw her and crossed the distance. "We need to talk. Alone." He cast a pointed glance at Will. "I've been thinking about what you said."

"Don't mind me." Will released her arm, his expression closed. "I should prepare for the meeting."

Ever the gentleman. Even if he was curious, he'd never intrude on a private conversation. Her throat tight, she followed his ascent to the third floor.

James grunted. "I never thought you'd be walking out with someone like Will Canfield. He's beyond your reach, Tom. He owns half the town."

"Thanks for your concern, James, but I wasn't walking out with him. We're acquaintances, nothing more. Not that my relationship with Will Canfield is any of your business." She adjusted her reticule over her wrist. Only days before she'd considered Pippa's beaded bag a frivolity and now, here she was, wearing one of her own. How quickly times changed. "You said we needed to talk. What do you want, James?"

"I thought about what you said. About getting the Stone outfit back together. I think we should try."

Her stomach twisted. She'd have the chance she'd been craving—a chance at earning her own respect in a job she knew well. No more floundering around, trying to find her place. James was offering her a chance at regaining a bit of her old life, her old confidence.

However, something in his expression gave her pause. "Why now, James? she asked, nervously biting down on her lower lip. "Why the change of heart? Does this have anything to do with Hannah Taggart?"

"No!" He reared back. "Why would you even ask that?"

"No reason. No reason at all."

Chapter Eighteen

The next hour was agony for Will. He spoke his lines at the town-council meeting with practiced ease. He listened to Gideon Kendrick's speech, nodding in all the right places, clapping at the correct time. All the while his thoughts were focused on Tomasina. He'd always known she'd leave Cowboy Creek. He'd assumed the date was off in the distant future.

He wasn't an idiot. James Johnson was a fellow drover. The cowboys were moving on. If James was putting together a new crew, Tomasina was an obvious choice. There was no doubt in his mind about James's motivation for seeking out Tomasina. The boy was ready to move on, and he needed her help.

His gaze kept drifting in her direction. She'd joined the meeting and taken a seat in the back, her mood inscrutable. Imagining her leaving with James Johnson wrung his insides into a knot.

When Remmy Hagermann elbowed him in the side, Will stood and cleared his throat. "We've given you all the information to the best of our knowledge. In conclusion, while any investment has risks, I believe an investment with the Union Pacific railroad is in the best interest of

Cowboy Creek merchants and business leaders. Mr. Kendricks will be staying at the Cattleman Hotel for the duration. He's available to answer any questions you might have." He paused for a moment, looking out at the crowd, then went on. "I will be collecting your funds personally. Can I see a show of hands for those considering an investment?"

Every hand in the room raised.

Will nodded. "Excellent. There's one more item on the agenda. As you all know, we've had some difficulty with the drovers in town."

A collective groan erupted from the audience.

"There's been a motion put forward to sponsor another rodeo and sharpshooting contest."

The meeting descended into chaos. People both for and against the measure raised their voices. Amos Godwin sat in his chair, his arms crossed, shaking his head. Mr. Irving and Mr. Hagermann argued over him. Clusters of men formed, with people shouting and gesturing.

A familiar, ear-splitting whistle silenced the room. All heads turned toward Tomasina.

She smiled. "Gentlemen. The drovers are vital to the success of this town. Correct?"

The men mumbled their agreement.

"The drovers bring cattle. They also bring business. Money. They pass through every town from here to Texas and spread gossip along the way. Would you rather they praised or criticized Cowboy Creek? And don't forget, eventually, those drovers will settle down and buy land. Wouldn't it be beneficial if they settled in this fine town?"

Mr. Livingston guffawed. "Not if they come to drink and carouse."

"I don't believe they will," she said matter-of-factly. "You want them to feel a part of your community. If they feel as though they are a part of something, they'll change their ways."

"Can you guarantee that?" Remmy demanded.

"No. I can't."

More grumblings followed her words.

"I can, however, guarantee that this town and your businesses will suffer if they decide to spend their money elsewhere."

No one disputed her words. An uncomfortable silence filled the room.

"Help invest them in your community," she said. "And they will care for that community."

Mr. Livingston snorted. "They don't buy anything from my store. Cowboys don't need furniture."

"They don't buy any of the furniture you currently sell. But what if you sold something they needed? One of the fellows I know has a collapsible chair. The hinges fold in half. The chair fits on the chuck wagon. You could make a whole business out of building those chairs."

"That's all fine and good for Mr. Livingston." Remmy stood and leaned his hands on the back of his chair. "How do the rest of us go about interesting them in our stores?"

"Mr. Hagermann is an excellent example of forward thinking. When the town founders sent for brides, what did you do, Mr. Hagermann?"

The owner of the mercantile puffed up. "I stocked the things women like to buy in my stores."

The men laughed.

"Remmy sells stockings," Timothy Watson hollered. "How does that help with a bunch of drovers?"

Remmy scowled. "You wouldn't be laughing if you saw my books. My business has increased. I'll be expanding before long."

His words quieted the crowd.

Tomasina beamed. "Follow Mr. Hagermann's example. Stock things the drovers buy. Run specials. Sales. You know what they purchase, the items they prefer. Place signs in your store windows advertising these items." She spread her hands as though unfurling a banner. "Have a special on tinned peaches."

Mr. Booker of Booker & Son rubbed the back of his neck. "That's not a bad idea."

Tomasina moved toward the front of the room. "Take advantage of your specialties. The items that make your business unique. Consider the Cowboy Café. Everyone loves Nels's chicken-salad sandwiches."

"Don't drag me into this." The older man crossed his arms over his chest. "I already have cowboys eating in my restaurant."

"Then cater to the cowboys who *don't* eat in your restaurant. Sell the sandwiches in a bag, with a pickle, wrapped in wax paper. Call it the Drover's Special. That's only the beginning. Why stop with the drovers? Down South, a clever group of ladies who call themselves waiter-carriers bring meals right to the trains. The ladies line up on the tracks and folks plan their route just for a taste of those meals. Nels could fix sack lunches for the folks on the train who don't have time for a sit-down meal."

Rubbing his chin, Nels nodded. "Might work. Course, I'd have to hire more help."

"If you make more money, you can afford to hire more help. That means Cowboy Creek is creating jobs. The more jobs, the better. Am I right?"

"Jobs bring people," Will offered. Her ideas were inspired. They were all intelligent men, and yet none of them had considered these opportunities. "Jobs bring families."

"Waiter-carriers for the railroad are only the beginning." She paced in front of the group. "Nels can sell his sandwiches between shows at the opera house. Serve them with lemonade."

Owen Ewing placed a hand to the side of his mouth and leaned toward Remmy. "People are sure gonna get sick of those sandwiches." He spoke in a whisper loud enough the others could hear.

Remmy laughed.

"Use your imaginations, gentlemen." Tomasina threw up her arms. "If people tire of one kind of sandwich, then make another. All of these ideas are simple, and many of them can be undertaken with little or no planning or cost. The cowboys living out of their tents need a shower and a shave at least once a week. The barber can run specials. The bath house can run specials."

"The jail is already running enough specials," Sheriff Davis called out.

Discordant voices vied for attention once more. Will withheld any words of support. If the men thought he was favoring Tomasina because she was a woman, they'd eat her alive in the meeting. She had to hold her own among the business leaders. Thus far, she'd been magnificent.

Tomasina let their good-natured ribbing continue for another moment before quieting them once more. "Put signs in your windows that welcome the drovers. The saddle shop can run an advertisement on leather repairs and cleaning. We don't want to run the cowboys out of town—we want them to stay. The longer those fellows stick around, the more money they spend. Every dollar in Cowboy Creek is a dollar in your pocket."

"What about the rodeo?" Mr. O'Neill called out, his mouth set in a hard line. "We all know what happened last time."

"I don't know." Her voice faltered. "That wasn't one of my suggestions this time around."

Will's heart went out to Tomasina. Mr. O'Neill's son had been injured that awful day, and clearly she still harbored guilt over the incident. Seeing his opportunity, Will stood.

"We all know the truth about what happened." He held his hands in a placating gesture. "The Murdoch Gang was responsible for setting that bull loose. If we cancel the show, we let the Murdochs win."

Shouted denials drowned out his words. Will exchanged a glance with Quincy Davis over the heads of the protesting men. When Tomasina started to speak, he touched her arm, quieting her.

"Let them argue it out," he said quietly. "The tide is turning."

His instincts were correct. The business owners had latched on to the plan. They recognized the value of having the drovers spend their pay from the cattle drives in town. The few dissenters were gradually outnumbered by the supporters.

When their voices quieted once more, Will resumed his place at the front of the room. "We can schedule the rodeo and the sharpshooting events in the spring and summer when the drovers are passing through town. I propose that we hold an event every Friday and Saturday during that time. If those cowboys are roping and riding and practicing their shooting, they won't be drinking."

"And they won't be fighting and breaking out the windows at Drover's Place," Quincy Davis added.

"Exactly." Tomasina grinned. "Instead of driving the cowboys away, let's figure out how to make them belong."

Remmy patted Tomasina on the back. "You got any ideas about how we can get more settlers in this town?"

"I do, as a matter of fact," she shot back immediately. "Hire someone who speaks Slovak."

Remmy's eyes widened. "That's not a half-bad idea."

"People want a taste of the old country. There's a bakery in Morgan's Creek that sells kolaches. Settlers come from miles around for those pastries."

D.B. Burrows, the editor of the *Herald*, rocked back on his heels and crossed his arms over his chest. "Why should we cater to a bunch of foreigners? If they want the old country, they can go back to where they came from. It's not our job to change, it's theirs."

Mr. Irving scowled. "We were all foreigners at one time. Or did you forget that, Mr. Burrows?"

"I like kolaches," Remmy added. "A few of those foreign customs are tasty."

Some of D.B.'s bluster waned. "You can sell your peaches at a discount and bake your foreign pastries. You're wasting your time. Those cowboys will still drink and carouse and cause trouble."

His words were drowned out by the men's excited chatter. When D.B.'s protests were ignored, he replaced his hat and stomped out of the meeting.

Ignoring his exit, the other business owners circled their chairs. Planning committees were formed and ideas exchanged. Tomasina circulated around the room, answering questions and offering additional suggestions.

Will followed her progress, and his chest expanded. He was proud of the business owners of Cowboy Creek. He was proud of Tomasina. Not only had she thought up ideas for keeping the drovers in town, she'd convinced the town council.

Gideon shook Will's hand. "The Union Pacific made a good choice in placing the railroad depot in Cowboy Creek. Miss Stone is a singular asset to your community. Her ideas are inspired, and she even managed to get a bunch of rowdy men to agree with her."

"I know." Will admired the way the light played off her lustrous hair. "She's one of a kind."

Gideon followed his gaze. "If I had ten men like her, I'd run the Santa Fe line out of business and rule the railroads."

Will listened to the praise with a touch of melancholy. How many more days did he have with her? He felt time slipping away. He felt Tomasina slipping away.

"What did you think of Pippa?" Will asked abruptly.

"I think the next few weeks in Cowboy Creek are going to be very entertaining."

At least someone was looking forward to the future. Will recalled sitting in his study all those weeks ago, facing the coming cattle drive with dread and anticipation. He'd had no idea a certain redheaded firebrand would touch his heart.

If his time with Tomasina was limited, then he'd best savor the time he had left.

The following morning Tomasina donned her drover's gear and set out for the livery. She needed something to ground her before she met up with James. After saddling and bridling her horse, she made her way to the stockyards. The corral fence had been repaired, and she went through her paces. Soon her muscles ached at the exertion. The pain was welcomed, reminding her of her past. As though her muscles had a memory all their own, she'd soon mastered her skills once more.

Though a dry spring, the day was clear and bright, the temperature ideal. A few of the men recognized her and called greetings. Another drive had brought more cattle, and she trotted through the pastures.

A couple of the cowboys were searching for strays, and she spent the rest of the morning tracking. Impressed with her skills, the drovers thanked her before riding away. It wasn't much, but their respect buoyed her. She'd always been an excellent tracker.

The sights were familiar, the smells comforting. Even the pungent scent of the cattle was welcome. She rode past the town toward a slight rise in the distance. When she'd reached the top of the small slope, she turned and studied the town.

A train whistle blew in the distance, a plume of smoke heralding another arrival. All her plans were falling into place once more.

She caught sight of James riding toward her.

He reined in beside her. "There's a ranch in Colorado looking for an experienced crew. They need ten men, and the pay is good."

"Do they know about me?"

Few ranches welcomed a female hand.

"Nah," James said. "We'll work that out later. I've got Dutch and Butch signed on already. We'll have a full crew before the week is out."

"You never really answered my question before. Why the change of heart?"

"I know I've been a jerk lately, Tom. I'm sorry about your pa. Truly, I am. He was a good man. He taught me everything I know, and I owe him."

"Is that why you want me as part of your crew?" She studied his face. Always blessed with boyish good looks, the lines around his mouth had deepened, lending him an air of maturity he'd lacked before. "Because you owe Pa?"

"Nah. It ain't that. I've been watching you. We're the same, you and me. We can't settle down. It ain't fair, folks trying to change us. You and I accept each other for who we are—a couple of drovers. You don't expect me to build a fancy house like Will Canfield and settle down, and I

don't expect you to go dressing up and acting like girl."
He glanced out at the horizon, his hands resting on his
pommel, then turned back toward her. "We don't belong
in Cowboy Creek, Tom. Let's go back to what we know.
We already found what we're good at, why fight it?"

The solution was ideal. He'd solved all her problems.
She'd start over. She'd build respect. Surely she hadn't
changed so much in a few weeks? She was still the same
person she was before her pa died. A couple of dresses
didn't change that, and a few lessons in deportment didn't
change who she was on the inside.

She'd wanted to earn respect. In the meeting yesterday
afternoon she'd had the attention of the business owners
of Cowboy Creek. Will hadn't interfered; he hadn't in-
fluenced the men. She'd earned their respect on her own
merit.

"When are you and the rest of the fellows leaving?"
she asked.

James wheeled his horse around. "Soon."

Normally the idea of a fresh crew left her chomping
at the bit. The familiar jolt of excitement never material-
ized. "How soon?"

"Day after tomorrow."

Her eyes widened. "That fast? Can you assemble the
crew that quickly?"

"I can. The boys are ready to light out of here. The sheriff is cracking down. There're rumors of closing up tent
city." He fixed her with a hard stare. Something in her expression must have given away her uncertainty. "Don't go
soft on me now, Tom. Are you staying or going? I can't
wait for an answer."

"I'm going."

The tension in his shoulders eased. "Good. We leave at
dawn the day after tomorrow."

This was exactly what she'd been hoping for all these weeks. Another job driving cattle. A crew she could trust. "Are you attending the opening of the opera house tomorrow night? Pippa Neely is putting on quite the show."

He shook his head. "No time. I've got some things to take care of before I leave."

She watched him gallop around the bend, her heart heavy.

She should have been happy. For the first time since her pa's death, she had a clear sense of her future.

As for Hannah's dress shop, there was no reason Tomasina couldn't gift her the money instead. It wasn't as though Tomasina's sewing skills were going to make the difference in the success of the shop. Her role had never extended beyond her investment.

All Hannah needed was enough money to set her on her feet. Cowboy Creek's newest seamstress would do just fine without Tomasina. Maybe even better.

Her vision blurred. Driving cattle wasn't so bad, but she wanted a job where she made a real difference in someone's life. A job she hadn't found yet.

The thought left her lonelier and more confused than she'd been before.

Chapter Nineteen

Friday evening the red-velvet curtain of the newly completed opera house rose to enthusiastic applause. Will glanced around the theater, pleased with the attendance.

Most of the town had turned out for the grand opening and inaugural performance. The red-velvet seats with carved mahogany backs were filled, and the balcony was standing room only. Pippa had insisted that Will, Daniel, Leah and Noah occupy the center seats of the front row.

Above them an elaborate chandelier cast flickering light over the proceedings. The raised velvet curtain revealed an empty stage save for a backdrop of a lush countryside. Two actors rambled into view from the wings. Judging only by their height and build, Will recognized Pippa and Tomasina. The two were all but unrecognizable. He'd heard rumors of Pippa's expertise with makeup and disguises, and he admired her skill firsthand. If he hadn't known the players already, he'd have had a tough time recognizing them.

The two women had dressed in voluminous dungarees and sported fake gray beards and shaggy gray hair. As round as they were tall, they must have stuffed a considerable number of pillows from the hotel into their costumes.

Pippa tugged down her beard. "Hey, Horace. What shall we do today?"

"I don't know, Gus," Tomasina answered in character. "The same as we did yesterday."

A bench slid out from the wings, and the fake Horace and Gus took their seats.

"Yep," the fake Gus spoke, patting his stomach.

"Yep," Horace replied, tugging on his beard.

"Did you see what I saw last night?"

"I don't know, Gus. What did you see last night?"

"I saw D.B. Burrows leaving work last evening. Late. Real late. Why do you suppose he was staying so late at the newspaper?"

"Now, Gus, you know I don't like to gossip."

The audience roared. The two men were famous for being busybodies.

Horace looked left and right. "Well, if you're not gossiping these days, what will we do instead?"

"We could play some horseshoes."

"That we could."

"Course we'd have to get up."

"That we would."

"What do you think Aunt Mae is serving up for lunch?"

"I guess we could find out."

When neither man moved, the delighted audience burst into applause.

The two women had captured the essence of Gus and Horace perfectly. Their impersonations were direct without being cruel.

"Say, Gus," Pippa said in character. "Did I ever tell you about the time a mountain lion chased my pa up a tree and got his teeth in Pa's boot?"

"You did not."

"He was pulling my leg. Just like I'm pulling yours."

The audience laughed on cue.

The two actors stood, took a bow and then exited the stage. The real Gus and Old Horace clapped the loudest. Gus even stuck two fingers in his mouth and blew out a whistle.

Between scenes, the band in the pit struck up a lively gig.

Aunt Mae came out next. Pippa followed close behind. She'd removed her makeup and donned a dress.

"Miss Mae is going to sing you a song," Pippa said. "There's nothing funny about this next act, so you all better behave yourselves."

"What happens if we don't?" someone shouted from the balcony.

Pippa waved her finger in the general direction of the heckler. "There'll be no fried chicken at the next county fair and no more pies at the Cowboy Café."

The audience booed.

"You've been warned." Pippa glared at the rowdy audience. "Settle down and listen."

After a slightly warbled start, Aunt Mae sang "True Lover's Farewell." A couple of the notes were a touch off pitch, but by the end she'd found her rhythm. The crowd grew hushed. When she finished, more than one person surreptitiously wiped a tear from their eye.

Aunt Mae bowed and left the stage, her exit followed by cheerful applause.

Pippa skipped onto the stage next. She wore a blond wig and carried a parasol. Her gown sat high on her waist, and her skirts were full to the point of exaggeration. A tall man Will recognized as Gideon, his blond hair covered by a dark wig, followed her out. The two reached the center of the stage and then faced one another.

"I love you, Leah," the man cooed.

"I love you, Daniel."

"I love you more, Leah."

"I love *you* more, Daniel."

Much to the delight of the audience, the two embraced. They separated and Daniel chased Leah around the stage, pinching his fingers while Leah giggled and evaded his seeking hands.

Will cast a sidelong glance at the real couple, who appeared to be taking the impersonation in stride. Daniel's face flushed, and Leah gently squeezed his arm. He grinned and rested his hand over her fingers. When Gideon and Pippa indicated them from the stage, the real Leah and Daniel stood and took a bow.

Fearing the worst, Will held his breath when the stage was set for the next skit. He recognized a fair replica of his rooms at the Cattleman Hotel.

Remmy Hagermann marched onto the stage carrying a cane similar to Will's. Amos Godwin, sporting a shaggy blond wig, clearly playing Noah, appeared from the opposite wing.

Remmy waved his walking stick, knocking over a lamp and a side table. "Rules. What this town needs is more rules."

"What this town needs is fewer people." Noah harrumphed. "A fellow can hardly swing a stick without hitting another person these days."

Will swung his cane and whacked the fake Noah in the leg. "I know what you mean."

Yelping, Noah hopped on one foot and held his ankle.

"You know what we need?" The fake Will spoke loudly. "A rule about swinging sticks. No swinging sticks in the town proper. We'll need a sign. I'll make one."

"You do that!" Noah announced. "I'll be putting some ice on this leg."

He limped off the stage. Will followed him off, muttering and swinging his walking stick.

The audience applauded, and Noah and Will dutifully stood and took their bow. More skits followed. Pippa Neely had outdone herself. The show was a mixture of singing and parodies, with most of the prominent residents lampooned in one way or another. The humor was always lighthearted and not mean-spirited. She paced the show well, never letting the audience's attention wander for too long.

During intermission, the patrons sat at tables arranged in the empty lot beside the opera house. Nels Patterson sold his famous chicken-salad sandwiches along with tart lemonade.

He handed Will a sandwich and a pickle wrapped in waxed paper. "This meal is on the house. I'm making a fortune on these sandwiches. That Miss Stone is smart as a whip."

"She sure is."

Instead of eating and mingling, Noah had used the intermission to check on his horse. Will caught sight of Dora seated with her parents. The banker, Mr. Wilson, who'd been her escort the night of the dance, was conspicuously seated at another table.

Leah and Daniel were seated side by side, their heads bent in conversation. The two might have been alone for all the attention they paid to the activity flurrying around them. Everyone was happy and occupied. He was welcome to join any of the conversations, but he held back.

Always a solitary man, for the first time in his life, he was lonely.

He welcomed Noah's return, though a stab of guilt dampened his enjoyment of the intermission. Constance, the bride they'd sent for on his behalf, was set to arrive soon, and he and Daniel had yet to speak with Noah. Somehow they hadn't found an opportunity. Each day that passed brought the time of reckoning closer.

Will took his seat for the second half, and the rest of the show proved just as entertaining as the first half. During the last break, he checked his program and discovered Texas Tom was the last act.

Pippa appeared on stage once more, her makeup removed, her hair glistening beneath the oil lamps. "We're closing out our show with a real first-class act. Texas Tom and her amazing roping skills."

She made a flourishing gesture with her hands and Tomasina took her place. As Texas Tom, she wore a fringed shirt and skirt with beading on the collar and hem. Twirling her lasso, she hopped in and out of the center. In a blur of skilled handling, she swung the rope left and right and over her head. Her movements were graceful and enchanting. The band struck up a tune, and the audience clapped in time. For the next fifteen minutes she delighted the crowd with her roping skills.

She brandished the rope over her head and took a bow.

Pippa joined her and the theater grew quiet.

"This night would not have been possible without the tireless efforts of one particular gentleman," Pippa said. "He believed in this theater. He believed in the people of Cowboy Creek."

Tomasina twirled the lasso above her head and swung the rope. The loop sailed over the audience and landed around Will.

A flush crept up his neck.

Pippa urged him to stand. "Let's have a round of applause for Mr. Will Canfield."

Grinning at his discomfort, Noah sank deeper into his chair. Will's guilt over the coming bride abated somewhat.

Tomasina struck a pose.

The audience applauded. All the townspeople who had taken part in the production filed onto the stage from both wings. When the stage was full to bursting, everyone took a bow and the crowd gave the talented players a standing ovation.

Will stared at the rope in his hands. He wasn't ready for her to leave. Not now. Maybe not ever.

He couldn't shake the feeling that Tomasina had just said goodbye.

Tomasina turned and discovered Will waiting in the wings.

He held out his hand. "I believe this is yours."

She accepted the coiled rope. "Pippa made me do it."

"Good. You were the best part of the show."

A blush stained her cheeks. "Pippa was the best part."

"Cowboy Creek is full of talented actors."

"You're a diplomat at heart, Mr. Canfield."

"Come back to the hotel," he said in a low, husky tone. "There's a party celebrating the successful launch of the Cowboy Creek Opera House."

Knowing her time was running short, Tomasina accepted the invitation. She'd enjoyed the show more than she'd expected. Her fellow performers had encouraged and supported each other throughout the many rehearsals. She'd enjoyed the sense of camaraderie and shared purpose. Still flushed from her performance, she wasn't ready to let the feeling go.

The mood was lively and patrons from the opera meandered down the boardwalk.

When they arrived at the hotel, the lobby was in chaos.

The staff crowded near the front desk, their voices raised in overlapping chatter.

Mr. Rumsford approached them, his face red. "We've been robbed."

Chapter Twenty

Ten minutes later, all the important guests from the front row of the opera house surveyed Will's suite. Simon, Mrs. Foster and Mr. Rumsford represented the hotel staff.

All of Will's rooms had been torn apart. Furniture was upturned, curtains ripped off the walls and cushions split. Stuffing and broken table legs littered the floor. Tomasina knelt and touched the pieces of a broken inkwell. She glanced at Will to gauge his reaction. He was shuttered off, and she couldn't read his expression. A sure sign he was upset. Will went ice-cold when angry.

"Who did this?" Leah lamented, clapping her hand over her mouth. "Why?"

Quincy Davis appeared in the doorway. "The money. After the council meeting, Will collected thousands of dollars of investments for Gideon Kendricks. Whoever ransacked the suite was after that money, mark my words."

Daniel set his mouth in a grim line. "Did they succeed?"

"No." Will shook his head. "The safe is located behind the desk in the lobby."

Mr. Rumsford straightened his collar. "The desk was manned the whole evening. No one touched anything."

A collective sigh of relief circled the room.

"How did the Murdochs get into the hotel without someone seeing them?"

"They didn't." Old Horace elbowed his way into the room. "I saw who done this. It was that drover. It was James Johnson."

Tomasina gasped. "No! James wouldn't do something like this. He's not a thief."

"I saw him with my own two eyes. He was walking out of the hotel not ten minutes before the alarm was sounded."

She liked Horace; there was no reason for him to lie. Yet she didn't trust his observation. The townspeople were always blaming the drovers. They'd become a convenient excuse whenever a crime was committed in town. The people of Cowboy Creek turned a blind eye to everyone else.

Quincy Jones replaced his hat. "I'll track him down."

Panic shot through Tomasina.

She grasped Will's sleeve. "You can't let them do this. James is putting together a crew. We're leaving for Colorado tomorrow. Why would he rob the hotel tonight?"

"Tomorrow?" Betrayal flickered in his dark eyes. "Did you plan on saying anything?"

"Yes. Tonight. I would have…" Her voice trailed off.

She'd been putting off the conversation. There was no use making excuses for herself.

"Round up James Johnson," Will ordered. "Since we have a witness, we have to question him."

The room cleared, leaving Noah, Will and Tomasina. Daniel had taken Leah home to rest, planning to return once they'd captured James.

Noah shook his head. "This is bad. People are furious with the Murdochs. They're tired of living in fear. If we're not careful, they'll lynch that drover."

Tomasina's hand flew to her throat. "They can't hang James."

"Quincy Davis won't let him hang." Will placed a hand on her shoulder. "We'll find out the truth."

"I know James. He didn't do this."

She'd never been more certain of anything in her life. James was many things, but he wasn't a thief. If a tiny thread of doubt lingered, she shoved those feelings aside. His insistence on leaving for Colorado immediately could be explained away for any number of reasons. Whatever James was running from, he wasn't running from this crime.

"I appreciate your faith in him, Tomasina," Will said, "but we have a witness. Sheriff Davis will investigate all the leads."

"You have someone who saw James leaving the hotel." She snorted. "That's not a crime. Every time something goes wrong around here, you folks are awful quick to blame the drovers. They're not all bad, you know."

"Sheriff Davis is following up on the information he's been given. Why was James here in the first place? Unless he was visiting you." Will searched her face. "If you were leaving together tomorrow, did he come to see you?"

"No." There was no use lying. The truth would come out sooner or later. "We spoke yesterday. He knew I'd be at the opera house." She snapped her fingers. "Unless he was leaving a message for me. He could have been, you know."

She clung to the glimmer of hope. With her rehearsals at the opera house, there'd been no time for planning.

"We'll ask him."

He clearly didn't believe her, and her heart sank. "What happens now?"

"The sheriff will bring him in for questioning. As long as he has a reasonable explanation for his whereabouts, we'll let him go."

"What if he doesn't?"

"Then James is in a lot of trouble." Will's tone was inflexible. "We need to know the truth."

Was a fair trial even possible? The drovers were easy scapegoats in the community. Not to mention she feared James had secrets. Secrets that might land him in even bigger trouble.

She reached the door, but Will caught her arm.

"Tomasina, trust me." His gaze flickered to where Noah stood, and he lowered his voice. "As long as James is innocent, he has nothing to fear."

"He's all I have left, don't you see?" Panic threatened to choke her. "He's all I have."

"You have me."

Her vision wavered. "I have to go."

He released her, and she dashed from the room. They were too different. He was a Northerner, she was a Southerner. He was bringing civilization West, and she was part of the old ways. He saw the drovers as a threat, she saw them as family.

She took the stairs two at a time and slammed into her room. At the sudden interruption, Hannah yelped.

Tomasina started. "I'm sorry. I didn't know you were here."

Hannah cradled Ava against her shoulder. "I was watching the baby. How was the show? What's wrong?"

Tomasina yanked at the pins holding her hat in place. She caught her reflection in the looking glass. Her costume was disheveled. She wasn't Texas Tom anymore.

"Someone robbed Will's suite. They were after the investment money Will collected for Gideon Kendricks."

The other girl's face paled. "When?"

"Just now." Tomasina paced the floor. "And that's not the worst of it. They think James Johnson was involved."

Hannah backed away. "I don't understand. Why do they think James is responsible?"

"Old Horace saw him leaving the hotel. The whole town is up in arms. There's been trouble before. Everyone is on edge. Unless James has a good reason for being here, he's in real hot water."

Tomasina rummaged through her wardrobe and then stood back. Did she wear her dress? Or did she wear her drover's clothing? If she wasn't Texas Tom any longer, then who was she?

She snatched the green calico. What did it matter what she wore? A man's life hung in the balance, and here she was fretting over her wardrobe.

Hannah set Ava in her bassinet. "I saw you packed. Are you leaving?"

"Yes. No. I think so." She tossed her discarded costume on the bed. "James found us a job in Colorado. He's put a crew together. We were supposed to leave tomorrow."

Wrapping her arms around her middle, Hannah stared out the window overlooking Eden Street. "When did you decide to leave?"

"Yesterday. Everything happened so fast. With the show at the opera house, I didn't have time to tell you." Tomasina tugged the dress over her head and shimmied the material into place. "James wanted to leave quickly. That's why I'm worried about him. I don't believe he's responsible for the robbery, but I think he's keeping secrets. If he isn't careful, his secrets will get him killed. These boys aren't fooling. They're out for blood."

Hannah pressed her fingers against the window. "What are you going to do?"

"Whatever I can. James is in trouble, and there's no one else who can help him."

"*Can* you help him?" Hannah asked without turning.

"I don't know."

To the law in this town, she was just another drover. Tomasina forced down her rising panic.

Her pa would expect her to stand by James. No matter what he'd done. No matter who he'd crossed. They were family.

She'd fight for James, even if that meant fighting Will Canfield.

Will watched the proceedings with a jaundiced eye. James had slouched in a chair set behind the table, one arm slung over the back, his expression insolent. The air in the room was charged. Too many weeks living beneath constant fear of the Murdochs had stretched the men taut. They wanted someone to blame, and James was sitting in front of them, refusing to defend himself.

The sheriff and his deputies had picked up the drover on the outskirts of town. He'd been packed and ready to flee. Thus far, he'd refused to answer their questions. His lack of cooperation only made him appear more culpable.

Daniel propped his hip on the table. "It's an easy question, James. All we want is the truth. Why were you visiting the Cattleman Hotel this evening?"

"I wasn't," he replied sullenly.

"More than one person saw you. Mr. Rumsford witnessed you crossing the lobby and taking the stairs. Horace saw you leaving the building. We know you were at the hotel this evening. All we want to know is why."

"You saw me in the hotel. That gives you the right to arrest me? You think I did something, prove it."

"You're not under arrest, James. Not yet. This is an informal questioning. Miss Stone has vouched for you, which is why we're at the hotel and not having this conversation in the jail. Is Miss Stone right in defending you?"

Tomasina scooted closer. "Just tell them the truth, James. Don't make this worse."

He looked away. "This has nothing to do with you, Tom."

The hurt flickering in Tomasina's eyes pained Will. She'd staked her reputation on her fellow drover, and he feared her loyalty was misplaced. James was guilty of something. Everyone in the room sensed his duplicity.

Tomasina faced the deputies. "James has a point. He visited the hotel, and he walked down the street. You can't convict someone for that."

"Then why won't he talk?" Deputy Watson demanded. "Why won't he tell us what he was doing?"

"Why must he prove he's innocent?" Tomasina half stood from her chair beside the prisoner. "If you can't prove he's guilty then let him go."

Sheriff Davis stepped forward. "If you're not going to talk, I'm taking you to jail."

James reared back. "You're not taking me to jail."

A flicker of apprehension snaked through Will. They were balanced on the edge of a precipice. Tensions ran high, and Quincy's control of the room could slip at any moment.

"You gotta understand, boy." The sheriff held out his hand. "It's for your own safety, son. There are folks in this town who are tired of being afraid. Unless you're willing to give us some answers, I have to take you in."

"Wait!" a voice called.

The room grew silent, and everyone turned toward the door.

Hannah appeared, Ava in her arms.

Will moved to block her entrance. "Hannah, you shouldn't be here."

"No. I have to be here." She straightened and threw back

her shoulders. "I'm the reason James was at the hotel. He was visiting me."

James lunged to his feet, and Quincy grabbed him, forcing the drover back into his seat.

"Don't say anything, Hannah!" James shouted. "Go back upstairs."

Tomasina glanced between the two, understanding flitting across her expressive face.

Ava fussed and cried.

"Don't excite yourself." Will put his hands gently on Hannah's shoulders. "Why don't you let me hold Ava?"

The poor girl was clearly hysterical, and he feared she'd hurt the baby.

She shook off his hold. "No! I have to say this. Ava is *mine*. She's my daughter."

Will dropped his arms and gaped. All of Hannah's odd behavior suddenly made perfect sense. Her atrocious clothing when she'd arrived on the bride train had been camouflage for her condition. The baby had arrived within weeks of her arrival. The girl's wan appearance and continued isolation had been due to Ava's arrival. Of course she'd been eager to assist Will with the baby.

A collective gasp went up from the onlookers before the room went eerily silent once more. Curious gazes flickered between James and Hannah. No one spoke, no one moved. It was as though everyone in the room had taken a collective breath.

James collapsed into his chair and rubbed his forehead. "Hannah, you don't have to do this. I can take care of myself."

"I know you can take care of yourself. You're selfish, and you don't deserve my help. But Ava is helpless. She's my baby. She's *our* baby." Her voice quivered with emotion. "If you don't tell the truth for once, someone else will raise her. I'm not letting that happen. I love you, but I'm through making excuses for you."

Spurred into action, Will led the overwrought young woman into a chair.

"Sit." He motioned for Simon. "Fetch Miss Taggart some tea."

His eyes wide, the boy nodded.

Sheriff Davis motioned to the rest of the men. The deputies and the others filed out of the room, their shocked gazes lingering over the couple.

Noah paused before Will. "Well that explains why James was at the hotel, all right. What now?"

"Fetch Reverend Taggart. Hannah shouldn't be alone with this."

Noah jerked his head in a nod.

Once the room had cleared, Will closed the double doors of the ballroom.

Tomasina had remained.

She stared at James in horror. "What have you done? When did this happen?"

James rolled his eyes. "Ten months ago, give or take."

Tomasina stood quickly, tipping her chair. "Save your jokes. You're a disgrace."

Will felt her pain and betrayal as though it was her own. Hannah had become her friend. She'd defended James. He was her escape from Cowboy Creek. Will knew that Tomasina valued loyalty above all other traits, and James had betrayed that loyalty.

With tears in her eyes Hannah rocked the baby in her arms. "We met in Harper, Kansas. I was on a mission trip. I'd never traveled alone before. James was handsome and charming. I'd never laid eyes on anyone like him before. He made me feel special. Worthy. We talked about the future. We had plans. I thought we were getting married.

I thought he loved me. Truly I did." Her watery gaze appealed to the small audience. "He left before I could tell him I was expecting."

Holding her hands over her mouth, Tomasina gasped. "James. How could you?"

"I didn't know," James cried, his voice strangled. "I didn't know about the baby until Cowboy Creek. I didn't even know Hannah would be here."

"She has a name." Hannah leaped from her chair and loomed over James, fiery color suffusing her pale face. "Her name is Ava. She's your daughter!"

Will wrapped one arm around the girl's trembling shoulders and led her back to her chair. "It's all right, Hannah."

Simon arrived with tea. He set the tray on the table and quietly backed out of the room. Agitated, the young woman clutched Ava against her chest.

Tomasina paced in front of James, her expression fierce. "Is this why you've been difficult since we left Harper? I'm not blind to who you are, but I expected better of you. Someone like Hannah deserved so much more. You should be ashamed of yourself. Be a man for once in your life. Take responsibility for your actions."

James clutched his head in his hands. "I'm a drover. How am I supposed to support a family?"

The door swung open once more, and Noah appeared with Reverend Taggart.

His expression bewildered, he approached Hannah.

Clearly panicked, the girl backed away from her father. "He doesn't know."

Noah rubbed the back of his neck at the point where his scars disappeared beneath his shirt collar. "Miss Taggart, your father is worried about you. Nothing more."

Tears streamed down her face. "I'm sorry. I'm so sorry. Ava is my baby. She's James's daughter."

The reverend collapsed onto a chair.

Hannah's father was silent and bewildered. His gaze shifted around the room, skittering over Ava, as though he didn't know where to look or what to say.

A rush of emotion flowed through Will. He recalled the first time he'd held little Ava. He knew what he needed to do.

He gently took the infant from Hannah. "Why don't you let the reverend hold the baby?"

She reluctantly handed over Ava. Will crossed the distance and presented the reverend with his grandchild. Reverend Taggart shook his head then leaned away.

Recalling how Leah had forced the issue on him weeks ago, Will pressed closer. "Meet your granddaughter, Reverend Taggart."

Ava's mouth worked, and her hands curled into fists atop the knitted blanket.

The reverend blinked back tears, and Will felt his own eyes burn.

James watched the meeting, his own expression unreadable.

Tomasina approached Will and Noah. "Someone should fetch Leah. This poor girl had a baby four weeks back, and she's had absolutely no care. No support. She's been hiding her condition from everyone for months."

Noah glanced at the new mother. "What about Doc Fletcher?"

"Let's let Leah decide," Tomasina said. "Hannah needs the support of another woman right now. Someone who understands what she's been through."

"Understood." Noah replaced his hat. "I'll fetch Leah, and if you don't need anything else, I'll be heading home after this."

"We need to talk," Will said. "This isn't the time or the place, but we need to talk. Soon."

A crease appeared between Noah's eyes. "About what?"

Will hesitated. "It's a long story. Daniel and I will come by your place the day after tomorrow."

"You aren't building another opera house, are you?"

Will's laugh was devoid of humor. "Nothing like that. The day after tomorrow. Before lunch."

"Sure."

"Good." Finally broaching the subject assuaged some of his guilt. "See you then."

Noah glanced at the reverend and the baby before leaving the room and closing the door behind him.

The reverend held out his index finger, and Ava wrapped her tiny fingers around his. He blinked rapidly. "She's beautiful. Absolutely beautiful."

Hannah sniffled. "She is."

Reverend Taggart leaned forward and wrapped one arm around his daughter's shoulder, pulling her into an awkward embrace over Ava. "You poor dear. You've been carrying this burden all alone."

Hannah leaned back and wiped at her eyes. "I'm fine. Truly. Telling people feels good. I'm so relieved, I feel a thousand pounds lighter." She turned to Will. "I'm sorry I came here under false pretenses. I know you were expecting a bride."

"None of that matters, Hannah. This is your home, and we're all here to help you."

The reverend had yet to look at James.

Will cleared his throat. Only one question troubled him. "Why did you leave her with me?"

"I didn't mean to." Hannah flashed an abashed smile. "James said he was staying at the hotel, in room 311."

James made a sound. "I was staying at a different hotel. The Drover's Place, room 113."

"I get my numbers mixed up."

Will recalled how Hannah tended to be early or late when caring for Ava. She obviously mixed up her numbers quite often. A soldier beneath his command had had a similar affliction.

"Once you realized your mistake," Will said, "you were stuck. So you offered to help."

"To be near Ava. I was hoping... I was hoping for time. To work out an arrangement with James. He didn't know about the baby right away. I wanted him with me because he loved me, not because of Ava. Not out of responsibility."

The drover had remained relatively silent since the arrival of the reverend. Will stepped toward him, and Tomasina blocked his path.

She punched a fist into her opposite hand. "I'll speak with James."

Aware of their audience, Will grasped her shoulders and pressed his forehead against hers. "Don't kill him."

"No promises."

He chuckled. "Never change, Tomasina Stone. Promise you'll never change."

Her hand fluttered against his chest. "That's the whole problem, though, isn't it?"

Before he could call her back, she'd approached James. Her melancholic expression had given him pause. Didn't she realize he loved her just the way she was?

He felt as though he'd been bushwhacked. His surroundings melted away, and an overwhelming sense of clarity overcame him.

He couldn't let her go, not now. Not ever.

He loved her.

Chapter Twenty-One

With Hannah and her father deep in conversation over the baby, Tomasina pulled James aside. "What are you going to do?"

"I don't know, Tom. I honestly don't know. Hannah deserves better."

"You're right...she does." Tomasina poked a finger in his chest. "If Hannah deserves someone better, then it's high time you became that man. You took advantage of an innocent girl. You're the father of her child."

"It wasn't like that. I loved her." He flushed. "I do love her. But I can't be the person she needs. I had to leave her. Don't you understand?"

"No. I don't."

"I can't change."

Her green eyes sparked with anger. "You're an idiot, James Johnson."

"Ah, c'mon, Tom," he scoffed. "We're two of a kind, you and me. We can't live in one place. That's a slow death for people like us. You know that better than anyone."

"You're a coward. For the first time in your life you were forced to take a good, hard look at yourself, and you didn't like what you saw. You've been lucky for a lot of years, but your luck ran out. You can't hide from this. Being the man Hannah needs won't be easy. Being the father Ava needs will be even harder."

"How do I start?" Raw anguish coated his plea.

"You have to face the reverend first."

"I can't."

"The boy who joined the Confederate Army at the age of fifteen was no coward. What happened to that boy?"

James looked away. "They kicked him out for being too young, remember?"

"I've said it all along, James. You're a man with something to prove and no way to prove it. Courage is courage. Whether you're facing a bullet or an angry father. You want to prove you're brave, now is the time."

"Courage. I never thought of it that way."

"I've known you for a lot of years, James. We've been through a lot together. You're a good man. You'll be a good father. You can even be a good husband." She chucked him on the shoulder. "Treat Hannah as good as you treat that ugly fringed vest and you'll be the happiest couple in Kansas."

He swallowed hard, working his jaw back and forth. "Do you really think so?"

"I know so."

"What about you, Tom?" he asked, his gaze searching hers. "We had plans. Will you be all right?"

Her throat tightened. "You're a better man already. Before today, you wouldn't have given a thought to my feelings."

"You didn't answer my question."

"I'll be fine. I was running, too. I have to find my courage, as well."

Lifting a brow, he gave her a curious look. "What were you running from?"

"Never mind me. You have other things to worry about." She grinned. "It's a sour pill to swallow, I'll tell you that, having to take my own advice."

"Thank you, Tom." He pulled her into a quick embrace. "I'm grateful to you. For everything."

"You're welcome."

He stood, and she saw the change in him immediately. Something in his heart had shifted. He pulled up to his full height, and she sensed in that moment he'd finally grown up. He'd finally become a man.

James faced her. "I want to apologize. You were right. I knew what happened between me and Hannah in Harper was wrong, and I hated myself for it. For the past year I thought I got away with something, but it was eating at me." His Adam's apple bobbed up and down, but he managed to go on. "When I saw Hannah in Cowboy Creek, I knew I had to make things right, but I couldn't. I thought Hannah was better off without me. I'd lost you. I'd lost your pa. I felt like I'd lost everything, and I was angrier than I'd ever been."

He rubbed his eyes with a thumb and forefinger. "At myself mostly. I took my anger out on you because I didn't know what else to do. Then, last night, Hannah told me about the baby. I think in my heart I always knew. Rumors about that abandoned baby have been floating around town for weeks. The timing was right... Hannah was here. I knew, but I didn't want to face the truth."

"I accept your apology." Tomasina pumped his hand in a firm shake. "We both had to grow up. You were right about me, you know. I can't be a drover any longer. The men don't respect me without Pa around."

Regret flitted across his expression. "You could earn their respect."

"That's the thing, James. I don't want their approval

anymore. I'd rather spend my talent on people who appreciate me."

"I'm real relieved to hear that." His shoulders sagged. "Because thinking about you with those drovers, all alone, terrifies me."

"You don't have to worry about me anymore. I'll find my way. Take care of your family. Take care of yourself."

He shucked his leather vest and slung the material over a chair. "If I'm going to ask for a lady's hand in marriage, I'd best look the part."

"I've always hated that awful fringed thing."

"I know."

She motioned Will over. "Cowboy Creek is about to throw another wedding."

Will hoisted an eyebrow. "I'll tell the reverend to put away his shotgun."

Running his hands through his hair, James stepped forward. "Do I look all right?"

Will shrugged out of his jacket. "Take my coat."

With murmured thanks, James slipped his arms through the sleeves.

Tugging her lower lip between her teeth, Tomasina studied the reverend's fierce expression. James was in for a tough time. The reverend wasn't going to let him off easy. She hesitated. Torn between wanting to help James and knowing he was better off standing on his own two feet.

Will made the decision for her.

He wrapped an arm around her waist and urged her toward the door. "He'll be fine."

They stepped into the lobby and discovered a crowd of people remained.

Simon scurried toward them. "What happened? Is it true about James? If he didn't rob your suite, then who did?"

Will held up his hands. "The show is over. We have proof that James is not responsible for the robberies."

Several of the men called out questions.

Quincy Davis pulled a bench from the wall and stood on top of the seat. "I know you all want answers. I propose a special meeting of the town council to address these issues. Tomorrow afternoon in the Cattleman Hotel ballroom. Bring your questions and your concerns."

Exhausted, Tomasina rubbed her eyes.

Will placed a hand in the small of her back. "It's been a long day. I'll have Simon bring you some warm milk."

She stifled a yawn behind her fist. "How do you always know the right thing to say and do?"

"I wish that were true." He took her hands in his. "Will you come to the meeting tomorrow?"

"Why?"

"I need you. The business leaders need your suggestions."

"I'll come, but I don't know if I can help."

"You're an asset to the town." He looked as though he was going to say something else then stopped himself. "You've made Cowboy Creek a better place, Tomasina. You're tired. I'll walk you to your room, and you can get some rest. I'll explain everything in the morning."

"I'll miss Ava," Tomasina said. "Even with all her fussing and all the uproar she caused."

"I'll miss her, as well. I'm grateful she's back where she belongs. Perhaps we can assume the role of her unofficial godparents."

"I don't think James or Hannah will mind. Having cared for Ava, I think we both realize they'll need plenty of help."

They paused on the landing. The lobby had emptied, and the hotel was quiet. Will leaned down and brushed his lips against hers. His fingers tangled in her hair. He pressed her close and deepened the kiss, pulling her nearer than she thought possible. Her heart thrummed in her chest. When she was shaken and breathless, he stepped back.

She staggered a bit and steadied herself with a hand against the wall. "What was that for?"

"You ask too many questions, Miss Stone." He wound a red curl around his index finger. "It doesn't matter if you're standing in the sunlight, moonlight or candlelight. Your delightful hair will always be my undoing."

With a sigh he released the curl against her cheek.

She absently touched the lock.

He descended the stairs once more and paused at the bottom. "I'll see you tomorrow. Sleep tight."

In an instant he was gone, leaving her shaken and confused. She turned slowly and made her way to her room, her feet dragging. Once inside she caught sight of her bedroll and tent bundled together in anticipation of leaving with James. How quickly her plans had changed.

When Simon brought her a tray, she handed him the bundle. "Can you chuck this in with the rubbish? I won't be needing it anymore."

She'd changed. For the better. For good. And she was ready to start her new life. She didn't need her drover's clothing anymore. She opened the wardrobe and touched the dress she'd donned as Texas Tom. She wanted to keep the memory of her performance at the opera house. The costume was a symbol of the friends she'd made in Cowboy Creek.

Tugging her lower lip between her teeth, she recalled Will's face when she'd lassoed him. He was a good sport.

He was also the only person who ever called her Tomasina. Not Tom or Texas Tom. She was Tomasina to him. She'd been searching for her true identity when he'd seen the truth all along. She didn't have to be the best drover, the best laundress, the best maid or even the best waitress for him. He'd supported all her efforts and comforted her when she'd failed. He admired her. They'd argued, they'd fought, they'd danced. They'd even kissed.

She wasn't Texas Tom any longer. She was Tomasina Stone.

She was also in love with Will Canfield, even with all his rules and regulations. Even though he was building the largest house in Cowboy Creek. Even though he was nothing like any of the men she'd known in her life.

No, that wasn't true. In a way, he was most like her pa. They were both honorable. They both looked out for their crew. They both knew what they wanted in life and how to get it.

Why couldn't she have fallen in love with a stinky old cowboy? Someone who wouldn't mind if she wore trousers and practiced her sharpshooting. Someone who ate peaches straight from the can in front of a campfire. Someone who didn't have his sights set on politics.

Except she hadn't fallen in love with a rough-edged drover. She'd fallen in love with Will.

The truth stole the breath from her lungs. She'd just spent the past hour lecturing James on courage and responsibility, and she'd only just faced the truth herself. She'd faced the truth, but she couldn't face Will. Not yet. The truth was too raw.

Bracing her forehead against the wardrobe, she groaned. Now what?

The meeting was in full swing when Tomasina arrived. She took a seat near the back and watched the proceedings in silence. As Will spoke about the robbery, her gaze was drawn to his lips. Just like everything else he did, he sure was a good kisser. He smiled a warm greeting, and her gaze skittered away.

At least the townsfolk had calmed somewhat since the incident with James. The tension remained, and they were all concerned about the Murdochs, but no one was calling out the drovers. There were several items on the agenda that afternoon.

Mr. Livingston announced that Noah Burgess had donated several acres of land west of town for the town cemetery. The plot was to be named Boot Hill in deference to the soldiers who had founded the town.

Quincy Davis proposed moving Zeb Murdoch to the larger jail in Morgan's Creek. The motion was approved, and Quincy and the deputies left to make the arrangements for the transfer.

Near the end of the meeting, Remmy Hagermann stood. "I'd like to propose a motion. The town council needs a spokesperson. We need someone dedicated to pursuing and developing business, as well as recruiting settlers to Cowboy Creek."

"That sounds awful fancy," Abram Booker said. "Why do we need someone to sell our businesses? Shouldn't we do our own advertising?"

"We create a stronger front if we're united," Remmy replied. "Last week Miss Stone recommended several ways for shops throughout town to exploit business from the drovers. A couple fellows and I got to talking and, if we all chip in, we can hire someone to come up with more ideas and coordinate the efforts among the owners. We also need a way to entice more settlers to our town."

"That seems like a big job," Mr. Booker called from the back of the room. "Who do you propose we get for that job?"

"Tomasina Stone."

Tomasina gasped and sat straighter.

Amos Godwin turned toward her. "I hope you don't mind, but I suggested your name."

"Of course not." She pressed her hands against her warm cheeks. "I don't know what to say. I'm not certain I'm qualified for the job."

"Please consider the idea," Amos said, his eyes kind. "We need someone who loves the town. Someone who can convince others of the benefits of living and working in Cowboy Creek."

"We need a girl, as well," Remmy chimed in. "The town needs more ladies."

At his blunt declaration, the men laughed.

Tomasina searched the room for Will. He'd insisted she attend the meeting. Had he known about the plan?

Despite her questioning stare, he said nothing. His expression gave her no clue if he was for or against the appointment. His gaze remained hooded, almost brooding. She had no idea what he thought of the announcement. Had he supported her name? Was he appalled? As one of the town founders, his opinion mattered.

"I'll consider the offer," Tomasina said. "Thank you."

His opinion mattered too much. His opinion mattered because she loved him. How could she see him every day, loving him, and never tell him the truth? Living in Cowboy Creek would become torture. Especially if he married one of the new brides. Even the thought of him courting someone else sent her stomach pitching.

He worked his way toward her, and she scooted aside. She couldn't face him. She was afraid of making herself more vulnerable. The feelings he evoked were powerful and frightening.

As soon as Remmy declared the meeting adjourned, Tomasina leaped from her seat and shot toward the door.

Will called out for her, and she pretended she hadn't heard. Sooner or later she'd have to look him in the eye, but not now.

She took the stairs two at time and reached the second floor in record time. Upon reaching her room, she shut the door and leaned back against the solid wood panels.

Hannah stared at her, her expression curious, Ava bundled and dozing in her arms. "How was the meeting? You left before I woke up this morning."

"Good." Tomasina shook the cobweb of thoughts from her head. "Has your father come around to the wedding?"

Hannah had returned late once again the previous evening. At least this time the reverend's daughter had been telling the truth—she'd been mending her relationship with her father. And though Tomasina had been awake at the time and curious when Hannah returned, she'd let the poor girl fall asleep immediately.

Hannah rolled her eyes. "The reverend has given the marriage his blessing. But not because of anything James or I said. Mr. Canfield spoke with him."

"He did?"

"James and I pleaded with him until we were blue in the face. I begged and James pleaded. The sun was rising, and we were all exhausted. Mr. Canfield checked on us and pulled my father aside. I don't know what he said, but James and I are getting married."

"That's wonderful."

"The marriage isn't the only thing. Leah came by, as well. She wants to throw an engagement party." Hannah peeled back the blanket and brushed her knuckles along Ava's cheeks. "I tried to refuse, really I did. But she was adamant. She said with all the talk in town, we might as well get everything out in the open." Sighing, she caught her lower lip between her teeth. "Since everyone knows about the baby, the rumor mill is running double speed. A party will give everyone a chance to gawk and get the gossip out of their systems. Then we'll just be another family settling in Cowboy Creek."

"Sounds like a good idea."

"You have to come. You're the only friend I have, and I want someone there if my courage falters. What if people aren't as welcoming as Leah says? What if no one comes at all? What then?"

"Oh, Hannah." Tomasina touched her shoulder. "I'll be there. I'll sock anyone who even looks at you wrong."

"I understand if, because of the circumstances, you'd rather not."

"Don't be a dolt. I know James, remember?" Tomasina grew somber. "Is marrying James what you want? Is this what will make you happy?"

"Yes." Hannah sighed, her eyes filled with love. "I know James has a lot of growing up to do, but he's a good man."

"He is. And he loves you."

A blush tinged Hannah's cheeks. "Do you think so?"

"I know so." Tomasina surveyed the room. "Let's get to the most important thing. What are you going to wear to the party?" They rummaged through the dresses and discovered one suitable for the engagement party.

Leah came by to check on Hannah once more. Despite her ordeal, Hannah was fit and healthy with no lingering effects from her pregnancy.

Leah examined the baby and declared Ava fit, as well. "Congratulations on your wedding. James is a fine young man. He approached Daniel this morning about renting a house."

Hannah beamed. "We're staying in Cowboy Creek. I want to be near my father, and James has a job at the stockyards. He might find something different, but this is a start."

Patting her stomach, Leah smiled. "Have you thought about the engagement party? I know you're worried, but I think you'll be pleasantly surprised at the welcome you'll receive. People come West for a fresh start...they understand that life isn't always easy."

"I am." Hannah gazed at Ava, her eyes brimming with love. "I'm not ashamed of Ava."

Leah touched her growing stomach. "Don't worry, I've invited everyone who's anyone to the party. With the support of Noah, Will and Daniel, no one will dare say a word against you. They know better."

Tomasina's chest lurched. She'd planned on avoiding Will until she'd sorted out her feelings for him. She'd hoped on taking weeks, possibly months. Maybe even a few years. Tomorrow was far too soon. She needed more time.

"I've already started planning a menu," Leah told them. "A garden party. We'll set up tents outside and serve sandwiches and salads and cakes."

Hannah brightened. "Are you certain?"

"I spoke with my helper, Miss Ewing, this morning. Aunt Mae is offering to make pies. Pippa has volunteered to decorate. We want this party to be special for you, Hannah. No matter what the circumstances, you're one of our brides, and you're getting married. That's cause for celebration."

The girl's eyes welled. "Thank you."

Leah squeezed her shoulders in a quick hug. "You're part of this community. We're happy to help."

After she left, Hannah stared at the door. "I can't believe how nice everyone is being. Considering what a mess I made of everything."

Tomasina perched on the bed across from her. "You're a good person, Hannah. Everyone makes mistakes."

"Even you?"

"Especially me."

She'd fallen in love with Will Canfield, hadn't she? How was she going to get through a whole party without blurting the truth? She'd become adept at hiding her emotions over the years, but she'd never felt like this before.

She'd never had to hide her love. Will had always admired her honesty. Did she admit her feelings or keep them hidden?

The answer remained just out of reach.

The day of the engagement party Will donned his best suit. Tomasina hadn't given the town council an answer. He didn't know if she was accepting the job or even if she was staying in Cowboy Creek.

Worse yet, she'd been avoiding him. He'd been trying to pin her down since yesterday. There was no way she was avoiding him today. She had to attend the party. No one refused Leah.

Simon held out his jacket, and he slipped his arms into the sleeves.

"Tomasina won't be able to take her eyes off you," Simon remarked.

Will sighed. "Am I that obvious?"

"Maybe not to everyone." The boy handed him a rose for his lapel. "I have a feeling Miss Stone returns the sentiment."

"I've never been less certain of anything in my life."

"Who could resist you?"

"Apparently quite a few people." Will followed him out the door. "Don't erect any monuments in my honor yet, I haven't even seen Tomasina since the town council meeting. She's avoiding me."

"You'll prevail."

Will admired the boy's confidence. If only he had some of his own.

Even with short notice, Leah had transformed her garden into a festive occasion. Tents were arranged in a neat row dissecting the garden path, with tables and chairs scattered around. The turnout was better than any of them had expected. Dressed in their Sunday best, folks milled around the tables, laughing and chatting.

In light of all the recent events, Will and Daniel had postponed visiting Noah another day. They still had time before the arrival of his bride. Not much time. But some.

James carried Ava and stayed close to Hannah's elbow. He doted on the two women in his life, hovering protectively when someone approached. When the party proved festive and singularly uneventful, James's shoulders relaxed, and he even laughed at something Remmy said.

Tomasina had donned the pear-green gown she'd worn to the dance. A coronet of flowers circled her brilliant red curls. She was enchanting. She was perfect. She was tying him in knots. He was a hopeless romantic, after all.

Following Daniel's toast to the new couple, Will approached Tomasina. She was tucked between the tent and the house, and there was no escape.

Her gaze darted around, and she looked like a rabbit trapped in a snare.

He blocked her exit. "You've been avoiding me again."

"Yes."

"Would you like to tell me why?"

"No."

He chuckled. She was nothing if not blunt. "There's something I'd like to show you."

"What?"

"It's a surprise," he said.

"I don't like surprises."

"Oh." His face tingled and his ears buzzed. "Um, well…"

"I'm only joking." She swatted his arm. "Are you all right? You look a little green. Has someone set the potato salad in the sun?"

"No. It's not the potato salad." This wasn't exactly an auspicious start to a romantic encounter. "I'm fine."

"All right." Her brilliant green eyes took on a misty look that confused him. "What did you want to show me?"

He stuck out his elbow. "Walk with me."

She glanced over her shoulder. "I promised Hannah I'd stay until she was settled."

"She's fine. Look at her."

Hannah was proudly showing off Ava to Pippa and Gideon.

"I suppose you're right," Tomasina murmured, a touch of wistfulness in her voice. "She's in capable hands."

"I'm right? Can I have that engraved on my plaque?"

"I thought you were embarrassed by the monument."

"I'd reconsider if you added that line."

"Get used to being embarrassed." She smiled. "I see right through you, Will Canfield. You're distracting me from my melancholy over Ava. I'll miss her, of course, but knowing she's in the loving care of her parents eases the pain."

How had he ever existed without her in his life? She delighted him and challenged him, and he reveled in their spirited exchanges.

Every minute of his life had led up to this point. He was both terrified and hopeful. She hadn't agreed to stay in Cowboy Creek, but she hadn't left, either. Together they walked to his house in companionable silence. The outside had been completed, and the finish work had started on the inside.

They stood across the street, and he sucked in a fortifying breath. "This house is what I wanted you to see."

She placed a hand over her chest. "Oh, my. That is a grand undertaking."

"This is my house."

Her gaze shifted away. "I don't know what to say."

"Then don't say anything."

He led her across the street, took the key from his pocket, opened the enormous front door and led her inside.

She tipped back her head and gaped at the elaborate crystal chandelier above her head. "You do everything on a grand scale, don't you, Will Canfield?"

"Yes." He chuckled. "While building this house, I employed over sixty laborers. Craftsman and workers who fell in love with the town and settled here. We're hoping Cowboy Creek becomes the county seat."

"And eventually you'd like to be governor?"

"Maybe. I don't know anymore."

She caught his sleeve. "You must. The country needs men like you."

"Do they?"

"Yes. They do."

"What do you need, Tomasina?"

Her smile was tinged with sorrow. "Do you know you're the only person who ever calls me by my full name? Everyone else calls me Tom."

"You haven't answered my questions. You were leaving with James. What will you do now?"

"I was never leaving with James," she said, meeting his wary gaze.

"You weren't?"

"Maybe for about ten minutes." She clasped her hands behind her back. "I considered leaving. But then I realized I couldn't."

"Why not?"

"Because I want to stay here. In Cowboy Creek."

Hope flared in his heart. "Can you be happy here?"

"I made the decision to live my life as a drover when I was just a kid following in my pa's footsteps. That used to be good enough for me. Not anymore. I want to do something on my own. I want to earn my own respect. I want to build something outside of what my pa created."

"Then you'd consider staying on in Cowboy Creek and helping with the businesses?"

"Yes." She grew somber. "I have only one problem with staying."

All his fears returned with the force of a rain-swollen river. He'd never been as defenseless as he was in that moment. The potent feelings she evoked had him terrified.

"What's that?" he asked, fearing the answer.

"I'm in love with you, Will Canfield."

His heart clattered discordantly. He reached for her and she braced her hands on his shoulders, keeping him at a distance.

"After seeing Hannah admit the truth about Ava, I knew I had to be brave. Just this once. I knew I couldn't stay in Cowboy Creek without telling you that I love you. But I don't want to hold you back. You have ambitions, and I'm not cut out to be a politician's wife."

"Who says?" He stared into her wide and wondering eyes. "You once told me the country needed men who understood the South to rebuild. What better person by my side than Texas Tom?"

"Are you certain you want to marry a former drover? Think of the scandal."

With slow deliberation, he slipped his hand against her neck and hauled her to him. "I want to marry you, Tomasina Stone, because I love you." Her eyes flared, and his heartbeat kicked up a notch. "If you want to drive cattle, I'll wait for you. If you hate this house, I'll sell it. If you loathe politics, I'll become a milliner and sell hats out of Hannah's store. All I want out of life is your love and the promise that you'll be my wife. Nothing else matters."

"Truly?"

"I survived a war. I know what's important." Leaning down, he pressed a soft kiss against her parted lips. "Truly."

"You better stick to being a politician."

"Are you certain?"

"The ladies of Cowboy Creek deserve beautiful hats."

"Then we'll hire a proper milliner."

Tomasina lifted a hand and tenderly cupped his jaw. "I don't deserve you."

"No. You deserve someone far better."

He silenced her objections with a kiss. She stood on her tiptoes and wound her arms around his neck, returning his ardent embrace with all the hunger and passion she possessed.

He'd lived in Cowboy Creek for years, and yet he'd only just come home.

Caught up in each other and the wonder of their newfound love, he ignored the commotion outside.

After a moment Tomasina pulled back. "What was that?"

Will glanced up. "Did you hear something?"

Her face paled. "That was gunshots."

Chapter Twenty-Two

Will clasped Tomasina's hand, and they dashed toward the center of town. Other townsfolk from the party joined them, and they followed the crowd. A gathering of people stood in front of the bank. The two deputies were there, but Sheriff Quincy was conspicuously absent.

"What happened?" Tomasina counted seven bullet holes riddling the bank façade. "Was anyone hurt?"

"It was the Murdochs," Deputy Watson said. "We were preparing to transfer Zeb up to Morgan's Creek. The Murdochs must have found out."

The second deputy, Buck Hanley, guffawed. "Probably because D.B. ran a story in the paper last night. He might as well have issued the Murdochs an invitation."

Will rubbed the back of his neck. D.B. had attended the meeting when they'd decided to transfer Zeb. He must have written the story immediately. The man was trouble through and through. Will scanned the crowd. D.B. was circulating among the onlookers, but he didn't show any signs of involving himself in the fray. Once the posse returned, there was going to be a reckoning.

Deputy Watson scowled. "The Murdochs split up and

came at us from both sides. Half of them swarmed the jail.
While we were distracted, they robbed the bank."

"What about injuries?" Will asked. "Did they get away
with anything?"

"A little money. Not much. But they took Zeb. Horace
was right—Zeb wasn't as sick as he led us to believe. He
knocked out one of the guards during the escape." The
deputy paused. "Sheriff Quincy was shot."

Will sucked in a breath. "How bad?"

"Don't know. He was gut shot."

Dread weakened his knees. Will had seen plenty of
wounds during the war, and a gut shot was the most uncertain. Sometimes the bullet missed vital organs, most times
it didn't. Though a shot like that was more often than not
mortal, there was still a chance Quincy might pull through.
A slim chance, but Will wasn't giving up on the man yet.

Unable to do more, Will uttered a silent prayer for the
man's recovery.

Daniel dashed toward them. "I heard the shots, and
Walter Fry filled me in on what happened. I've sent for
Noah. The rest of the fellows are putting together a posse."

Will took Tomasina's hand. "I have to go."

"I know," she said. "So do I."

The realization took a second to sink in.

His gaze dipped. "You can't go with me. It's too dangerous."

"I'm the best tracker you've got. I know the terrain better than anyone. I know where cattle hide and can sure find
where a man is hiding." She squeezed his hands. "This is
your first test, Will Canfield. If you want me as your wife,
you have to accept me for who I am."

"All right. You're coming." He cupped her cheeks and
pressed their foreheads together. "But you follow orders

just like everyone else. We stay safe. You and I have a lifetime together. Let's make it a long one."

"Yes, sir." She winked at him and saluted. "At your command, sir."

He pressed a quick, hard kiss against her lips.

"Everyone change clothes and fetch your guns," Will called. "I want the posse saddled and mustered at the livery in half an hour. If you're not there, we leave without you."

Spurred into action, the entire town went to work. Nels Patterson packed food for the posse while Leah and Pippa gathered supplies. Over at the livery, Walter Frye saddled the horses and added extra feedbags.

Mrs. Foster assisted Tomasina into a split skirt and she strapped on her gun belts.

"You be careful," the housekeeper ordered. "You promised to show me how to rope. A lady needs a few tricks up her sleeve if the guests get out of hand."

"Don't worry, I'll teach you to lasso with the best of them."

Moments later Tomasina was mounted on her horse outside the livery a full five minutes before the allotted time.

Will reined his horse beside her. Eight other men were saddled and ready for the search party. Noah joined them, his saddlebags packed and a bedroll tied behind his cantle.

Remmy caught sight of Tomasina and gaped. "Are you in the posse?"

"I'm the best tracker in Kansas," she said, lifting her chin. "Without me, you'll lose the trail before sundown."

"Then welcome aboard," Remmy replied. "I like to sleep in my own bed at night."

Daniel sidled his horse nearer. "With Sheriff Quincy laid up, who's leading the posse? We need a temporary sheriff."

"What about the deputies?" Will gestured toward the two men. "There's Buck Hanley and Timothy Watson."

"They're too young. Too green. We can't afford any mistakes," Daniel said. "We need someone who can pull the town together. A real leader."

"Then you."

"I can't." Daniel shook his head. "Not with Leah in her condition. Why not you? You were the captain."

Will met Tomasina's amused gaze. "My schedule is full."

Daniel shrugged. "Then it's you, Noah."

Noah jerked the reins, and his horse sidestepped. "Not happening."

"It's only temporary."

"What if Quincy dies?" Noah settled his jumpy horse. "What then? I don't have time to serve as sheriff."

"Let's not dig Quincy's grave just yet." Will rested his elbow on the saddle horn. "We don't know how bad he's shot."

A lengthy pause followed. Noah appeared to be grappling with some inner conflict. His two friends waited without comment.

Walter Fry trotted toward them. "Who's leading the posse?"

"I'll do it." Noah's tone was grudging. "But the job is only temporary. Once we catch the Murdochs, I'm done."

"Agreed."

Will and Daniel exchanged a triumphant glance.

Will placed one hand near his mouth and hollered, "All in favor of Noah Burgess as sheriff say 'aye.'"

A deafening chorus of "Ayes" erupted.

"All opposed."

No one dissented, not even Buck or Timothy, the two deputies.

Noah raised his fist. "Let's muster."

Aunt Bea marched from the boardinghouse and stood vigil in the center of the street, effectively halting the proceedings.

She paced in front of the assembled posse, her hands crossed over her chest. "No one is going anywhere. I'm looking out for the brides of Cowboy Creek, and I'm not letting this lady ride out with a bunch of men. Not after all the goings-on we've had with poor Miss Taggart."

She jerked her thumb toward the well-dressed guests from the engagement party. The reverend, Hannah and James, who held baby Ava, watched the proceedings from the boardwalk.

Tomasina glanced at Will. "Marry me."

"Now?"

"Now," she demanded.

"Right now?"

"Right now. The reverend is here. Let's get hitched and capture those Murdochs."

Will leaned over and kissed her full on the lips. "I will marry you, Tomasina Stone. Without delay."

Deputy Watson rolled his eyes. "Make it quick. We're burning daylight, and those Murdochs are putting ground between us."

Hannah rushed over and handed up a bouquet of wildflowers appropriated from one of Leah's centerpieces. "You sure had me fooled, Tom. I can't believe you're getting married before me."

"Me neither."

"I'm happy for you," she murmured. "We can exchange recipes, and I'll help you sew curtains for the new house."

"I'll, uh, I'll get back to you on that."

Tomasina didn't cook, and she sure didn't have any opinions on curtains and the like.

Hannah sketched a wave and joined James and her father once more.

Mr. Booker jogged up. He bent, clutched his side, heaved in a breath and then straightened.

"I brought this from my store," he said. "It's what they call a love knot. I thought it would suit you. It's like a rope."

The ring was a simple gold band with a loop in the center.

Tears pressed against the backs of her eyelids. "It's perfect. Thank you."

Mr. Booker handed up the ring.

Reverend Taggart took his place in front of them, his open Bible in his hands. The posse formed a horseshoe behind them, while practically the whole town of Cowboy Creek spilled from their homes and shops, lining the street.

Without dismounting, Tomasina took Will's hand.

Reverend Taggart cleared his throat. "We come together for the union of this man and this woman in holy matrimony. Marriage is a sacred undertaking and one which we do not enter into lightly."

Tomasina rolled her hand forward. "Speed it up, Reverend. I promise you can talk till you're blue in the face when we have a proper ceremony. Right now there're some nasty criminals on the loose."

"Point taken." The reverend balanced the Bible in one hand and dabbed at his brow with a handkerchief. "Do you, Will Canfield, take Tomasina Stone as your lawfully wedded wife? In sickness and in health, till death do you part?"

His expression somber, Will faced her. "I do. I love you, Tomasina. May your aim always be true and may your guns never be pointed at me."

The crowd chuckled.

Will tugged her closer and met her steady gaze. "I don't just love you because you're clever, beautiful and feisty, though you're all those things. I love you because there's no one else in the world quite like you and I can't imagine a future without you by my side. You are my partner, my soul mate, my wife. I love you with every beat of my heart."

The pressure behind her yes increased tenfold. "You *are* a romantic."

"You bring out the scoundrel and the romantic in me."

"A lethal pairing."

The reverend raised his arm. "All right, you two. Settle down. We're not done yet. Do you, Tomasina Stone, take William Canfield as your lawfully wedded husband? In sickness and in health, till death do you part?"

Tomasina had difficulty finding her voice. She'd never been a sentimental person, but she wanted to remember this moment forever.

"I do," she said, her voice husky. "My pa would have liked this wedding. He never was much for sitting indoors. He always said the gospel was in the trees and the grass and the flowers around us. He would have liked you, too, Will Canfield. He would have been proud to call you his son.

"When I came to Cowboy Creek I was trying to be what everyone else wanted me to be. Instead I found someone who loves me for who I am. I give thanks to God for sending me someone to love. For sending me you."

"I now pronounce you man and wife. You may kiss the bride!"

A loud cheer erupted from the onlookers.

Will cupped the back of her neck and pulled her into a deep kiss. He tipped back her hat and his fingers delved into her wild curls. The tears on his lashes dotted her cheeks.

"Let's roll out," Noah hollered.

Tomasina and Will reluctantly parted.

He caught her hand. "We'll finish that kiss later."

"Promise."

"Life with you will never be boring, will it?"

Her eyes sparkled. "Admit it, you love excitement."

"I love you, Tomasina."

"I love you, too, Will Canfield." She gathered her reins and dug her heels into the sides of her paint horse. "You have to catch me first."

She tossed her bouquet to Hannah, but the men had already kicked their horses into a trot. The bouquet landed square in Noah's chest.

Noah batted at the flowers as though someone had tossed a snake into his lap.

Will let out a whoop. The Murdochs were on the loose, he'd been married on horseback and his honeymoon was taking place in a posse.

Tomasina glanced over her shoulder with a mischievous grin. He'd catch her, all right. But she'd lead him on a merry chase for the rest of his life.

The crowd hollered and cheered as the riders passed.

Will kicked his horse into a gallop and gave chase.

He wouldn't have it any other way.

* * * * *

Dear Reader,

Thank you so much for taking the time to read Tomasina and Will's story. I was excited and honored when my editor invited me to contribute to the Cowboy Creek series. This was my first opportunity to participate in a continuity series, and the first time I've worked in the time period immediately following the Civil War.

I had a wonderful time collaborating with the other two authors involved in this project. Both Karen Kirst and Cheryl St. John are fabulous writers. They were incredibly generous with their time and knowledge. We enjoyed weaving together our story elements across the three books in the series.

I love connecting with readers and would enjoy hearing your thoughts on this story! If you're interested in learning more about this book or others I've written in the Prairie Courtships series, visit my website at SherriShackelford.com or reach me at sherrishackelford@gmail.com, facebook. com/SherriShackelfordAuthor, Twitter @smshackelford or regular old snail mail: P.O. Box 116, Elkhorn, NE 68022.

Thanks for reading!
Sherri Shackelford

COMING NEXT MONTH FROM
Love Inspired® Historical

Available June 7, 2016

PONY EXPRESS HERO
Saddles and Spurs
by Rhonda Gibson

Pony Express rider Jacob Young sets out to search for his birth mother, but instead he discovers his orphaned five-year-old half sister and her pretty guardian, Lilly Johnson. And when he figures out that someone's trying to hurt them, he vows to be their protector.

BRIDE BY ARRANGEMENT
Cowboy Creek
by Karen Kirst

On the run from a dangerous man, widow Grace Longstreet is determined to protect her twin daughters—even if it means pretending she's the mail-order bride Sheriff Noah Burgess's friends secretly arranged for him. But can their blossoming relationship survive her deception?

ONCE MORE A FAMILY
by Lily George

In order to bring his young daughter home, Texas rancher Jack Burnett needs a wife—but he won't marry for love again. And an arranged marriage to penniless socialite Ada Westmore will benefit them both...if she can survive life on the prairie.

A NANNY FOR KEEPS
Boardinghouse Betrothals
by Janet Lee Barton

After widowed Sir Tyler Walker's daughters run off their latest nanny, he hires the schoolteacher next door as a short-term replacement. But when Sir Tyler and his two little girls fall for Georgia Marshall, will the temporary arrangement become permanent?

LIHCNM0516

Reading Has Its Rewards

Earn **FREE BOOKS!**

Register at **Harlequin My Rewards** and submit your Harlequin purchases from wherever you shop to earn points for free books and other exclusive rewards.

Plus submit your purchases from now till May 30th for a chance to win a $500 Visa Card*.

-Visit **HarlequinMyRewards.com** today

MYR16R1